THE GUARDIANS

Four men assembled as an extraordinary team to protect the life of the President of the United States in the event of nuclear war. The One-Day War had come, and they had battled their way from a stricken Washington, D.C., to the safe haven of Heartland Complex, across an America in her death agonies, carrying with them Jeffrey MacGregor, newly sworn-in to the highest office in the land after the disappearance of President William Lowell's National Emergency Aerial Command Post. They had thought that meant their job was ended.

In fact it had only begun . . .

AMERICA'S FUTURE IS IN THEIR HANDS

*Also in THE GUARDIANS series
from Jove*

THE GUARDIANS
TRIAL BY FIRE

THE GUARDIANS

THUNDER OF HELL

RICHARD AUSTIN

A JOVE BOOK

THE GUARDIANS: THUNDER OF HELL

A Jove Book / published by arrangement with
the author

PRINTING HISTORY
Jove edition / August 1985

ISBN: 0-515-08327-5

Jove Books are published by The Berkley Publishing Group,
200 Madison Avenue, New York, N.Y. 10016.
The words "A JOVE BOOK" and the "J" with sunburst
are trademarks belonging to Jove Publications, Inc.

PRINTED IN THE UNITED STATES OF AMERICA

PROLOGUE ———————

It is now two months since the One-Day War drew the curtain on the modern world. The fallout's pretty much gone, but sundry plagues and pestilences have just gotten rolling. The death toll from famine has begun leveling off. The diminution curve of population has passed that of foodstocks in a lot of places, but, in the Northern Hemisphere at least, winter is on the way. A good many people who at the moment are pulling through will never see the spring.

Life, however, has a habit of going on. The hordes of refugees have begun to settle where they are, eking out lives as scavengers or squatters, picking through the rubble of cities or even trying their hands at farming—with indifferent success for the most part. For others, "pulling through" means preying on their fellow humans.

Often literally.

The old man sat and tended his fire as the sun fell toward the Pacific Ocean. He sat in lotus position on a rocky forehead of land that loomed several hundred meters above the choppy surface of the ocean and the two-month-old carcass of a small freighter decaying on the rocks below. Wind-carved granite boulders and scrub shielded sight of him and the little fire from the Pacific Coast Highway, which ran by a hundred meters or so to the east. Not that it was likely that anyone moved on the highway, now. It was tolerably full of cars, but they were all immobile, frozen as if in a photograph in some *National Geographic* pictorial on scenic California. Their owners had driven them away from the calamities that had befallen San Francisco and Los Angeles, driving until they ran out of fuel or overheated or simply became hopelessly mired in congestion, then abandoning them to go on afoot. Here, a few klicks north of Morro Bay, roughly midpoint between the two great metropolises, the cars pointing north and the cars point-ing south were about equally divided. Tens of thousands of refugees must have passed one another, fleeing in opposite directions. In the end it hadn't mattered much. One place was not so very much better than another here in California during the One-Day War and the dark days thereafter.

Had the old man stood up he would have been a centimeter or two above the average height. The loose folds of the volu-minous brown and black *aba*, the Arab robe he wore, con-cealed his form, but his hands and neck and sandaled feet were lean and sinewy, and no extra flesh cushioned the jut of his jawline. His head was narrow and angular; his forehead high; his eyebrows sharp ridges above pale amber eyes; his nose a blade; his cheekbones prominent over hollows. In fact, his visage was quite similar to this desolate thrust of land: hard, spare, weathered by sun and wind and rain. His hair, short wiry ginger fading to gray, was sparse on top, clustered in a comparatively neat goatee around his thin-lipped mouth, and bushed out extravagantly at the eyebrows in an effect reminis-cent of the scrub that crowned the rocky headland.

The wind sighed and whistled among the rocks and rustled in the brush. Overhead, sea gulls wheeled, a thousand burnished-copper figures in the dying sunlight. Their cries fell down about him like sleet. There were many sea gulls these days, more than ever before. Sea gulls were scavengers, and this was their time.

He leaned forward to stir at the little fire with a stick. Three stones had been pushed into a rough triangle around the fire. Resting on them was a brass grate rescued from a drain set in cement at a carwash. On top of the grate bubbled a can of Van Camp's pork and beans. The label was blackening at the bottom. He stirred the stuff briefly with the spoon attachment of a Swiss army knife, set the knife on a flat rock beside the fire, and straightened.

He could walk most men less than half his age into the ground, yet not even he could defy the laws of aging. He grew older. He was slowing down, and he had a lot of ground to cover.

How nice it would have been to salvage one of the thousands of wrecked autos lying dormant on the highway behind him. With patience he could have tapped sufficient fuel from the cars' tanks and gas lines to go quite a long way, and his mechanic's skill—just one of his many abilities—was such that he might not have had to search far before finding a vehicle he could get in working order, especially with so many spare parts to choose from.

But it was hopeless. The cars had lain two months under the torrential downpour that had followed the One-Day War. A decade before, a number of prominent scientists had declared that a nuclear exchange of any size would bring about the end of the world; that ash from burned cities would coat the atmosphere, reflecting back so much of the sun's light that the planet would enter a stage of darkness and cold from which it could never recover. It turned out they had vastly overestimated the amount of ash that would be thrown into the atmosphere by such a war. But the One-Day War had had its climatic effects, and one of them was a vast increase in the amount of rainfall, here at least. The myriad cars stranded on the Pacific Coast Highway were turning rapidly into lumps of rust. The old man had spent enough time investigating them to be certain he had no chance of resurrecting any of them.

He'd simply hope he would soon come upon a nest of survivors who had possession of a horse, or even a mule or a donkey. The idea of bouncing along on the back of an ass, like some early Spanish friar, brought a quick wry quirk to his lips. It was not an altogether inappropriate image, after all. He was himself a missionary of sorts, attempting to spread a certain message amongst the survivors of the calamity.

The scrape of loose gravel between a foot and the rock caught his attention. Outwardly, he gave no sign, but his already keen senses upped their degree of alertness. The world had entered that indeterminate time, that hanging fire between day and night when shapes and movement were indistinct and hard to perceive, before true dark settled down and eyes became accustomed to it. It was a time when an experienced foe might choose to strike—or an inexperienced one driven desperate by hunger or greed for whatever possessions were stuffed into the knapsack resting by the old man's side.

He decided it was most likely the latter. There were two of them, his ears told him, moving around to take him from two sides. From the speed and impatience of the movements he guessed they were both young. Undoubtedly, they were congratulating themselves on having found such a complacent old fart as their quarry, who simply sat there like a lump and let them sneak up on him.

In a short while the furtive scrabbling sounds ceased. The sun touched the red rim of the world. The old man half expected it to sizzle. Instead, it slid on down as it always did, disappearing with a silent scream of color, orange and red and tawny gold.

Only an incandescent fingernail of light remained when he heard the tentative step on his left. "Ah, hey mister?" a hesitant juvenile voice said.

A little surprised, he swiveled his head a few degrees to the left, cocking an eyebrow.

A boy stood there, blue work shirt hanging open over a torn and grimy T-shirt, cutoff jeans exposing painfully skinny legs that were scratched and sunburned, tennis shoes showing more bare skin than cloth or rubber. Unkempt, sun-bleached blond hair hung in his eyes and adolescent peach fuzz furred his narrow cheeks. "Um, mister? Could you, ah, like spare a little food?"

"Tell your friend to come out into the open and step around here where I can see him," the old man said curtly. His voice was dry and short, like the rapping of a stick on stone.

The boy blinked blue eyes and feigned surprise. "But I—but

I don't know what you mean. I'm here alone."

"Don't trifle with me. Tell your friend to show himself or go away."

The boy looked down at scraped knees. "I don't, ah—mister, you're, like, crazy. Nobody else around here."

With desperate speed the other youth launched himself from the scrub behind the old man's right shoulder, in the gangling leap of an adolescent panther. The old man never took his eyes from the blond boy. Instead, he simply wasn't there, had shifted up onto his left knee around a quarter turn. His assailant passed through the space he'd occupied and landed gracelessly in the dirt before the fire. He rolled heavily and sprang to his feet in a cloud of dust.

"You old motherfucker, you think you're so smart." He was short, stocky, dark-haired, in army jacket and jeans that were faded almost white. He brandished a knife in his right hand. "I'll show you. I'll cut you good with this—*take him, Terry.*"

The blond boy lunged. The old man sprang to his feet. With a bound, he was perched almost on the edge of the sheer cliff, his robe fluttering about him like the wings of a bird. Terry threw himself forward, fists flailing desperately. The old man caught one bony wrist in an *aikido* hold. Terry cartwheeled by and landed heavily on his back, yelping as the stone gouged his shoulder.

The boy with the knife moved then, fast—too fast for his own good. Before the old man had truly started Terry on his way, he was in action, his knife hand striking like a rattler. Badly crowded, the old man had no time to move with just the precision he desired. His own left hand snaked out, mongoose-quick. It snatched a sleeve, *pulled.*

The dark-haired boy screamed as he launched himself out over a thousand feet of emptiness. His arms and legs flapped frantically, as if trying to force evolution of the ability to fly in the last few seconds left to him. He brushed a knob of rock on the way down, rebounded, spun, fell down and down and down upon the rocks. Foaming white tongues of surf lapped at his blood, while from above the sea gulls echoed his scream at him, broken into a million pieces.

His hawk's face grave, the old man turned away from the

cliff. The blond boy sat up, rubbing his shoulder. His eyes
were blue and wide, his face the color of wood ash. Before the
old man could speak he had sprung to his feet and bounded
off into the scrub in a desperate run, one arm dislocated and
swinging helplessly at his side.

The old man stood a moment listening to his scrabbling
flight across the rocks. He would not be back. It was just as
well; the old man had no appetite for playing cat and mouse in
the darkness on these cliffs.

He turned to the fire. Miraculously, the can was still there,
bubbling cheerily on top of the salvaged grate. *Vicious young
animals*, he thought. *Willing to kill me for a can of pork and
beans.* Yet he felt a twinge at the way it had all gone. The one
youth had merited death, that was a fact. But it was also a fact
that the old man had not intended to kill him. Such impreci-
sion bothered him. Vicious animals they may have been, but
still he might have found a use for them.

If wishes were horses, I'd be riding north in high style. He
walked with crisp steps to the place he'd occupied by the fire.
As he seated himself a sound made him look up sharply.

The sky had shaded toward indigo, all except for a brilliant
red laser line of light marking the interface of sea and sky. The
stars shone out overhead, and from among them drifted a
thin, high whine. A mosquito amplified a thousandfold. The
old man's weathered brow creased in a frown. It was a sound
he hadn't heard in some time, the distinctive sound of a
propeller-driven airplane. It passed overhead and began to
fade to the south.

Ah, well. He'd have given much to know where the plane
had come from, where it was bound, who was privileged to
ride in such detachment above the shattered earth. He knew he
didn't possess anywhere near enough to buy those secrets.
Shrugging his shoulders inside his *aba*, he wrapped his hand
protectively in a fold of the robe, reached forward to retrieve
the can, picked up his spoon, and began to eat.

CHAPTER
ONE ————————————————

Moving as silently as any catamount, his face blackened with special nonreflecting paint, Tom Rogers slithered over the outcrop of volcanic rock. He couldn't see the cannibals' camp, except as a puff of yellow glare against the black of the night sky that lay ahead, but his ears and nose both told him that he was getting close to his objective. He was a professional at this work, trained to trip-wire tautness and thoroughly seasoned. Smell was just another sense to him.

He froze. A shift in the wind had brought a new aroma to his nostrils: the sweetish tang of dope being smoked. Cheap dope, he could tell. But then, he supposed that the cannibals were lucky to have any at all, eight weeks after the One-Day War had ended what most people had been accustomed to calling civilization. He waited patiently, his heartbeat slow, his breathing deliberate, almost silent. From somewhere across the badlands to the west began the song of a single coyote, thin and lonely. A moment later other voices joined in a yapping rising chorus.

From the camp a raucous voice shouted, "Shut the fuck

up!'' The coyotes complied. The cannibals laughed and cheered.

As the noise from the unseen camp quieted down to the level of conversation, Rogers heard the rasping hiss of someone sucking on a joint. Instantly he was in motion, moving up a man-high boulder of black volcanic rock as sharp and merciless as broken glass.

At the top he paused, suspended virtually in midair, peering carefully over the top of the lava rock. He made out the sentry, an emaciated, wild-haired form hunkered over its joint. It was difficult at first to distinguish him from the rocks that bulked about him like misshapen hunchbacked dwarves.

With exquisite care, Rogers began to move. Slowly he let himself down the side of the boulder to which he clung. He moved with an instinctive feel for the texture of the rock, carefully avoiding depressions where scraps of gravel and dirt—deposited by the slow erosion of wind and rain—had gathered to crunch beneath his boots. Moving from jut to jut of solid stone, he worked around behind the figure's bent back. The cannibal at least had the sense to cup his joint between his hands, but, as he moved, Rogers intermittently caught glimpses of the orange glow of the ember underlighting the man's face.

Then Rogers was in position. He gathered himself, sprang. His strong left arm snaked around the bearded man's head, muffling his startled cry. His right hand punched the point of a Mark Two combat knife through the right side of the man's throat and thrust outward. A gush of blood fountained, black against blackness.

In spite of what you have read in adventure books and seen in the movies, in spite even of what has made its way into various military combat manuals, you don't kill a man instantly with a knife. Any experienced E-room nurse could lay this myth to rest. She'd know all too well how many stab wounds were sported by the average bravo whose number had just been forcibly retired from the Saturday Night Knife and Gun Club. Nor will stabbing someone directly through the heart guarantee an instant kill, unless the weapon in question is a bowie knife as long as a big man's forearm and as broad as his hand. The heart is a large muscle, very powerful, and can frequently absorb more damage than the single thrust of a slender blade can deal it. Moreover, a man with his adrenaline up can sometimes keep his blood pumping by violent action—say, running as fast as he can, or even coughing at regular intervals.

Of course, someone injured in that way is not liable to survive long. Just long enough to blow his attacker away with a sidearm—or simply holler for help.

Tom Rogers knew this. He was professional to the core, experienced enough in the ways of the knife to carry two of them: one a solid Kabar of the sort originally issued to the Marines during World War II—for fighting purposes—and the other, the one he used now, a Gerber with a slender leaf-shaped blade. That knife had one purpose and one purpose only: the silent removal of a sentry.

So Rogers was shrewd enough to keep the man's mouth closed until his struggles subsided. Then he lowered the inert form to the sand blown into the slight declivity among the rocks. The body was oddly shrunken, seeming as light and tiny as a child's. Rogers felt no pangs. The sentry he'd just killed was no child—and even if he had been he would still have merited death by the hard code according to which Rogers lived. The testimony of the people back at the research station concerning the cannibals' depredations had been more than eloquent.

Softly Rogers moved forward. He peered down the slope. About forty meters away he saw the campfire. Dark forms sat or moved about it. He eased himself down into the concealment of rock and brush. For the first time he spoke. "Billy," he said. The word would have been inaudible a meter away; the mike taped to his larynx picked up subvocalizations as clearly as speech. "Rogers here. I took out a sentry."

"Roger that, Tom," McKay said. "I'm in position, too, in some kind of gully a little ways south of the camp. Casey'll let us know when he's ready."

His Heckler and Koch MP-5 submachine gun with integral silencer attached cradled like a toy in his big hands, McKay crouched in the arroyo. Whereas Tom Rogers was a square man of medium height, McKay was huge, six-three with a bull neck and shoulders, a powerlifter's massive chest. Yet for all his bulk, McKay moved with the same silent feline grace as the former Green Beret officer.

The cannibals' camp lay at the base of a looming volcanic butte, somewhere along the northern edge of Badlands National Park in South Dakota. There were perhaps a dozen of them gathered around the leaping yellow flames of a brushwood fire, men and women both. Their skinny, bony, filthy frames were bedecked with a bewildering assortment of garments; from the large white bath towel with blue sailboats printed on it, fastened as a sort of loincloth around the waist of a black-bearded man with a gleaming bald spot on the top of his head; to the tattered mink coat worn by a woman with a shock of sun-faded red hair, which hung open to reveal the naked body beneath, as wasted and hard-looking as the eerie wild land around. Mostly their garb was less baroque, consisting of cast-off army jackets, blue jeans, shorts, even blanket ponchos. Plenty of washboard ribs and prominent collarbones were in evidence.

The captives were in evidence, too. There were three of them: two women, and a man whom McKay took to be Dr. Mark Bollear, abducted early that morning from the Badlands Agricultural Research Station some kilometers to the northeast. The captives had been wound from shoulder to hip in stained nylon cord, the way Mickey Mouse and his cohorts used to be whenever they were captured by the Beagle Boys. They looked like rope coils with heads and legs. The bindings were dirt-smudged and clearly showed dark brownish stains. They had been used for this sort of work before.

Tom Rogers, former Green Beret, master of the tortuous ways of covert ops and assassinations; Sam Sloan, Annapolis man, hero of the Battle of Sidra Gulf; Casey Wilson, the top-scoring American fighter ace since the Korean War; Billy McKay, the leader, late of the Marine Force Recon and the dirty-tricks teams of the Studies and Observations Group, Southwest Asia Command. They were the Guardians. Four men assembled ostensibly as an extraordinary team to protect the life of the President of the United States in the event of nuclear war. The One-Day War had come, and they had battled their way from a stricken Washington, D.C., to the safe haven of Heartland Complex, across an America in her death agonies, carrying with them Jeffrey MacGregor, newly sworn-in to the highest office in the land after the disappearance of President William Lowell's National Emergency Aerial Command Post. They had thought that meant their job was ended.

In fact, it had only begun.

Several years before, a small cadre of concerned military and civilian leaders—including Major Crenna, the mystery man who had handpicked and trained the Guardians—began to assemble the resources required to reconstruct the United States in the event of some catastrophe such as nuclear war. A compendium of the latest technology, the highest-powered experts: scientists, engineers, theoreticians in half a hundred arcane fields. The greatest assembly of technology in human history—the Blueprint for Renewal.

Should the Blueprint fall into the wrong hands, the potential for mischief was almost infinite. So it was broken down into components, human and hardware, which were stashed away in secret locations across the country. The master key to the whole thing was carried along with the President at all times. In the event of war, the key was to be transmitted to the computer banks buried in Heartland, deep below the rolling farmlands of Iowa. Using that master list, the Guardians were to reassemble the scattered components into one potent whole.

Except the key never got transmitted. When President Lowell vanished, the master list to the Blueprint vanished with him.

Computer technicians at Heartland had produced a list of four names of experts projected to have a greater than 90 percent chance of being part of the Blueprint. The Guardians' best efforts had only gotten one of those named back to Heartland. Now the Heartland team was reduced to throwing out much lower-probability names, in a desperate race against time.

First of those names was that of Dr. Mark Bollear, a research ecologist now studying the ecosystems of the badlands of South Dakota. . . .

The Guardians had arrived about noon that day at an agricultural research station plunked down in the middle of a dusty tromped-down land beneath the lowering leaden sky on the edge of the badlands. They had found a small clump of prefab structures in an advanced state of disrepair. The cannibals had attacked before dawn, with clubs, knives, and a few firearms. Dr. Bollear and a couple of assistants had been carried off. The remainder, mostly clerical types and research personnel, were skittish and fearful, obviously unsure of what to do. Their position was precarious. They had supplies for a few months—one of the few fringe benefits of their isolation was that it had made stockpiling a necessity. But when those provisions were gone, none of them knew what they would do to survive. In any event, none of them was of a particularly warlike disposition. There had been much discussion of sending an armed party in pursuit of the cannibals, but the fact was there weren't more than two firearms to be had in the small research station, and no one expert enough in their use to think about going after human game.

The Guardians had been both well equipped and perfectly willing to undertake such a hunt. Following the cannibals to their lair in the badlands was no great chore. Both Rogers and Sloan had a hunter's eye, and with the two of them riding on the angular snout of Mobile One, the Guardians' ultramodern Cadillac Gage V-450 armored car, they were able to follow the tracks left by the retreating marauders across the dusty landscape as the flatlands gave way to fantastically eroded shapes of red sandstone.

Periodically they stopped so that Casey could climb to the top of a butte to scope out the terrain farther along the cannibals' line of march. Eventually he'd spotted them leading their captives here, to the foot of this promontory. In the slanting rays of the setting sun, his keen eye caught the burnished-copper sheen of daylight on water. There appeared to be a small pond or stock tank beside which the cannibals had made their camp. Apparently a spring rose nearby.

They left the vehicle concealed in a steep-sided draw and moved off on foot around the prominence, which resembled a beached whale. As full dark came down Casey took up position on its very crest, looking down on the camp from forty meters, the bull barrel of his M-40 sniper's rifle propped on a beanbag he carried with him. The other three made their way down the face of the ridge.

An arroyo ran down from the top of the butte and passed within perhaps twenty meters of the southern side of the cannibal camp; this was the gulch McKay was lurking in. Rogers was stealing down to take up a position roughly across the leap of the cannibals' campfire from McKay, though far enough up so that when they made their move they wouldn't catch one another in the crossfire. Finally, between them, Sam Sloan had already acknowledged that he had taken up position in the rocks just thirty meters above the cannibals' camp. The three men's faces were blacked, and all were armed with silenced .45-caliber submachine guns and concussion grenades. It was just like one of the hostage rescue drills the one-eyed Major Crenna had run them through back at the Project Guardian training camp in Arizona.

Right now it looked as if the cannibals were torturing a chicken for their amusement and the edification of their captives. They chivied the animal this way and that with sticks and lighted brands. It ran frantically from one side to another of the grinning, laughing circle, flapping its wings frenziedly and emitting panicky coughing cries. At last the apparent leader of the cannibals—a tall, lanky man with curly blond hair and beard and eyes that seemed to be outlined in kohl, wearing a leather vest, khaki shorts, and tennis shoes—gave a final caw of laughter and swooped like a hawk. One bony hand caught the animal up by the neck. He held the struggling bird in front of the captives and with a single wrench of his hands twisted off its head.

He brandished the jerking creature, spraying the captives with its blood. The cannibals applauded enthusiastically. They reminded McKay of something out of a Tobe Hooper horror flick. He wouldn't be sorry to put the wood to this gang of scumbags.

"Billy." It was Rogers. "I'm in position now."

"Great, let's hit 'em. Sam?"

"Right here."

"You got your flash bomb ready?"

"Affirmative," Sloan said.

"All right, count three and let 'em have it."

McKay waited, like a tiger poised above a staked lamb. His breathing sounded harsh and megaphone-loud. He knew that was an illusion. Through the bone conduction phone taped to the mastoid bone behind the ear, he heard Sloan's down-home Missouri drawl: "One, two, *three*."

Something landed in the campfire, knocking a burning chunk of driftwood spinning up into the night. The cannibals gasped and jumped back, looking wildly in all directions. A hemisphere of white light, like the miniature fireball of a nuclear explosion, covered the camp for the blink of a scorched eyeball.

The concussion grenade had been developed by the West Germans for the use of their elite GSG-9 anti-terrorist squads. It combined a nominal noisemaking charge of dynamite with a quick-acting magnesium flare, the purpose being to dazzle and deafen any bad guys who happened to be in the same area with it. It worked like a goddamn charm.

McKay swept his MP-5 from left to right across the camp, squeezing off short bursts at about chest level. The gangly blond leader was fast. He spun, holding the decapitated chicken in his left hand, while his right dropped to the walnut grips of the big single-action revolver strapped around his bony hips. McKay's slugs caught him in the chest and shoulder and flung him flopping to the ground.

The cannibals reacted with a beautiful panic—just the way things were supposed to work in all the counter-terrorist manuals, yet somehow never did in real life. Some of them leapt to their feet to be cut down by Sloan and McKay, who were scything bullets back and forth above the heads of the three captives. Others sat where they were, frozen in the blank, wide-eyed terror of a jacklighted deer. These Tom Rogers picked off one by one, punching single shots through their skulls with the precision of a drill press. It was a massacre, and mercifully brief.

All but two of the cannibals were down when McKay's MP-5 ran dry. Sloan chopped one of them down with a quick burst. The other, a short man with bushy black hair, took off into the desert, his arms pumping madly. He'd gotten perhaps fifteen meters when a shot from Casey struck between his shoulder blades, knocked a quick puff of dust from his army jacket, and flung him face-forward onto the hardpan. Grimly satisfied, McKay slid the empty magazine out of his weapon and began to remove a new one from the Rhodesian ammo pouch slung across his broad chest.

—and a weight came down on his shoulders like a leaden blanket, entangling his arms. Something struck the back of his close-cropped head, sending bright red lines like laser beams lancing through his brain. He staggered.

Not again, goddamnit! McKay thought. He was a genuine iron man, certified death with nothing but his bare hands, an expert killer with virtually every weapon known to man. And yet since the very outbreak of the One-Day War, the opposition had consistently been catching him at a disadvantage.

A thick choking stink, compounded of blood, sweat, and rancid human grease, clogged McKay's nostrils. He stumbled forward a couple of steps, letting his MP-5 fall to the Israeli-style sling hung around his thick neck. His hands clawed for his unseen assailant even as the attacker brought a chunk of lava rock slamming down on his skull a second time.

If this is the way my goddamned luck is gonna run, McKay thought wildly, *I swear to Christ I'm not gonna take a dump ever again while I'm out in the field.* He'd just learn to keep his asshole tight for as long as it took. The way things were going, it was only a matter of time before some hunger-crazed Girl Scout caught him squatting behind a bush with his trousers down around his ankles and garroted him with her neckerchief.

His left hand intercepted a bony arm descending to brain him with the rock again. This was getting old. He was barely recovered from being hit on the head with the ax handles of Reverend Josiah Coffin's inaptly named Brothers of Mercy back at the Denver Federal Center some weeks before. If people kept doing this to him, his brains were going to turn to mush and run out his frigging ears.

Getting a grip on the arm with both hands, he jackknifed abruptly forward, heaving with all his strength. The cannibal rocketed over his head, thudding down on the hard ground. Instantly it started to spring up. McKay took a quick step forward, launching a savage front kick with his right boot. It caught the cannibal in the chin. The head snapped back. There was a loud crack, as of kindling being broken over someone's knee. The figure spasmed briefly on the unyielding earth, then lay still.

McKay crouched, quickly slamming another magazine into his MP-5. It didn't look as if any others were sneaking up on him from behind. "Billy," Sam said, "are you all right?"

"I guess so. Move on into the camp. I'll join you in a sec. Tom, Casey, keep us covered."

Hunched over, McKay stepped forward to where his attacker now lay inert. The half-open eyes gleamed like Jell-O in the starlight.

"Jesus," McKay said aloud. It was a woman who lay there gazing sightlessly at the sky, a woman who'd almost canceled his check for him. "Shit. I must be gettin' old."

Sam Sloan scuttled forward. The cannibals' camp was a blood-soaked shambles. There were bodies everywhere, some still stirring feebly, most not. He paused briefly to boot one still form out of the fringes of the campfire. No sentimentality moved him to do it, simply the fact that his nose couldn't take the stink of burning flesh and hair any longer. That done, he moved to the prisoners. Instinctively gallant, his first impulse was to go to the bound women. Then he *was* shocked, noticing that both of them were naked from the waist down, the insides of their thighs streaked with dust-caked dried blood. One was a middle-aged woman, plump and curly-haired, the other young, blond, straight-haired, slender. Had her face not been so puffy from beatings and hopeless crying, she probably would have been quite pretty. He sawed their ropes loose with his Kabar.

Both women watched in silence as he worked to free them. He made small meaningless sounds of reassurance, saying anything that came into his head. They failed to respond at all.

Billy McKay lumbered out of the darkness as Sloan moved to Bollear. The ecologist was a stocky man of average height, with a square red-cheeked face, thinning hair of a color Sloan couldn't make out in the orange firelight, and the squint of an eyeglass-wearer whose spectacles have gone the way of the buffalo. As Sloan knelt by his side, cutting at his bonds with the knife, the young blond woman rose and picked up a head-sized chunk of lava. She walked over to stand above the blond-bearded cannibal leader. He lay looking up at her from half-closed eyes. His skinny chest rose and fell feebly. Blood trickled from the corner of his mouth into the foul tangle of his beard.

Without a word she dropped to her knees and began methodically to bash his head into pulp. "Jesus *Christ!*" Sloan yelled. "Billy! Shouldn't we put a stop to that?"

McKay looked from the woman to Sloan. "Can't think of a single reason why."

His stomach doing flip-flops inside him, Sloan looked at the woman. For a moment the Missouri farm boy he'd been born and bred warred with the urban sophisticate he'd tried so hard to become over the years. The farm boy won. "No," he said. "Reckon I can't either."

Bollear was free. He stood up, massaging his arms, blinking at the two Guardians as if they'd just appeared out of a flying saucer. Sloan realized his rescue might seem as abrupt—and unlikely—as a UFO landing.

McKay wandered over and fixed Bollear with a firm blue gaze. "Doctor," he said, using the code greeting, "We've come for the blueprints."

Bollear looked at him, and his watery eyes blinked so rapidly they seemed in imminent danger of capsizing. "Say what?" he asked.

CHAPTER
TWO _____

"Take a ride, ride, ride, ride, ride," sang Casey Wilson's tape player, *"on heavy metal/It's the only way that you can travel down that road—"*

Outside the glass-and-plastic-laminate vision ports of the Cadillac Gage Super Commando V-450 armored car, the dreary, tawny desolation of the Mojave Desert rolled by, kilometer after repetitive kilometer. To Billy McKay's eyes it looked like a backlot of hell. Then again, Billy McKay was an Easterner and a city boy used to prowling the narrow byways of the asphalt jungle. From occasional visits to the farm in western Pennsylvania owned by some rednecked Polack cousins of his mother's, he knew what countryside was supposed to look like: green and lush and rolling. To him *desert* would never qualify as *country*—and even his long years of service with the Marines and SOG-SWAC in North Africa and the Mideast had done nothing to change that opinion.

From the dreamy expression on his thin, boyish face, Casey Wilson didn't feel the same way. He was craning his neck this way and that as he steered the ten-ton armored car along the superhighway, as if thirsty to drink in this desperate vista through the yellow lenses of his Zeiss shooting glasses.

Ignoring the determined ugliness of the Mojave Desert sliding by on one side, and to distract himself from wishing that
the car's air-conditioning worked well enough that his buddies
would let him light a cigar, McKay savored a certain unfamiliar optimism. It seemed that despite the embarrassing mistake
made with Dr. Bollear, their luck had turned. Now they were
bound for the magic land of California with not one, but two
leads to follow—one rock solid, the other much less so.

The Guardians had returned a bemused Bollear and the two
depressed and disheveled women captives to the Badlands
Research Station. Over the Guardians' radio Major Crenna
suggested they go ahead and bring Bollear in if he was willing
to come. He was, after all, quite a knowledgeable man in a
field that could prove useful to the work of the Blueprint for
Renewal. Bollear, perhaps not too sanguine about the prospect of being stuck out there in all that desolation with steadily
dwindling supplies of food and water—to say nothing of
the ever-present prospect of raids by more marauders out of
the badlands—had consented to return to Heartland with the
Guardians.

Since they were, after all, not a very great distance from the
complex in central Iowa that was the current seat of the government of the United States of America, such as it was, the
Guardians found themselves driving into the huge concealed
cement doors of the underground facility before sundown the
following day. When they deassed—short for deaccessed,
military slang for *leaving*—the V-450, Major Crenna himself
met them in the echoing emptiness of the underground garage.
The intact half of his mouth was twisted into something which
might have been a smile. "Welcome to Heartland, Dr. Bollear," he rasped in that gravelly ruined voice of his. He turned
to the Guardians, who filed out of the big vehicle. "Well,
McKay, I understand you got it in the head again."

Technicians in fluorescent-looking jumpsuits had oozed out
of the coarse pores of the concrete walls and begun swarming
over the big armored car, which was shedding the heat of the
Midwestern summer sun in a series of pings and creaks.

McKay felt a hot flush creeping up his cheeks. "Yes sir, that's just what happened, sir."

Crenna barked a short laugh. "Happens. See that it doesn't happen too damned often. If nothing else, the rescue went as smoothly as things like that ever do. Chalk it up to experience and forget the hell about it." He turned away, started to walk off toward the stairway; stopped, turned back. "You guys knock off and get a good night's sleep. In the morning you're heading out again. For California."

Casey Wilson's ears perked up. "California?" he asked brightly.

Crenna nodded. "Looks as if your little trip to Kansas City last month wasn't quite so much of a dry run as we thought," he said. "Any of you guys happen to remember what Dr. Okeda's dying words were?"

Sam Sloan's weatherbeaten James Garner face creased in a look of concentration. "As near as I can remember, it was something about the Taj Mahal."

Crenna shook his head. "No. What he said was 'Mahal, Mahal.' "

"Well yes, that's what I said," Sam Sloan said defensively.

"No, you said *Taj Mahal*. Okeda didn't. He was trying to get out a word and not quite succeeding. Or a name, rather. Our computer boys were able to dope it out. He was trying to send you to Dr. Georges Mahalaby. According to our files he was an old friend of Okeda's. They worked together at Stanford at one time."

The Guardians traded startled glances. They had all taken Okeda's last words as the aimless maunderings of a mind shocked by irreparable, fatal damage. McKay felt fresh respect growing for the stoic little *nisei* scientist. *He hung in there until the last,* McKay thought approvingly. *Pretty hardcore.*

"Mahalaby?" he said. "Sounds like a Lebanese name to me."

Crenna nodded. "It is. He's a Lebanese Christian. Immigrated to the States in the mid-seventies to escape the civil war over there. He's an agronomist. Some kind of miracle agriculture expert. From what our files have been able to bring up, the work he's doing out there at his New Eden laboratory will knock the old Green Revolution into a cocked hat. He's the Einstein of genetic engineering. If he's still alive, he could be one of the most vital of all Blueprint personnel.''

McKay frowned. "I thought the Blueprint was more involved with restoring America's industrial capacity," he said.

Sam Sloan looked at him with pity on his homely country-boy face. "Anybody could tell you're a city boy, McKay. All over the country, food stocks are running low—"

"Not exactly," Crenna interjected dryly. "Our projections indicate that the population has been dropping faster than the food supplies, like Malthus in reverse—plague and famine at work. But drive on, Sloan, I think you're on the right track."

Sloan nodded thoughtfully. "Well, maybe people are dying off faster than they can eat up the food supplies right now —but winter's on the way. Anybody who manages to make it through the cold months is going to need all the help he can get, come spring. If this Dr. Mahalaby has cooked up, say, some increased-yield or high-speed growth strains of common cereal grains, he just might make the difference between life and death for a whole lot of people."

"He's got those and more," Crenna said. "Matter of fact, we're looking at being able to get some crops into the ground —and *harvested*—before the end of the growing season. Maybe enough to make a difference. We don't have the production or distribution facilities to ship food on any kind of large scale, but Heartland could just possibly serve as a distribution center for some of these miracle seeds Mahalaby's supposedly developing. So bring him back alive, boys. The country needs him."

The Guardians nodded. The techs were busy checking the vehicle's engine, steering, suspension, electronics, and sundry other systems, working in a kind of tightly controlled frenzy to get the armored car turned around and ready to roll out the next morning. Even as the five men stood here talking, armorers were carrying belts of linked .50-caliber and M-19 40mm grenade ammunition into the vehicle to replace that devoured by its ever-hungry turret guns.

McKay wondered how the technicians were being paid. He didn't think blue-backed Federal Reserve notes, much inflated even before the war, would be too easy to pass these days. He thought of Ben Turpin, the wiry former Treasury agent transferred to the Secret Service's elite Presidential detail who'd made the breakout with the Guardians from a stricken Washington, D.C. He'd always been smartassing around about his old job protecting the nation's number one counterfeiter from unlicensed competition. Now he was dead, greased in an ambush in Indiana. The brief reminiscence was like a cool dank gust across the thick nape of his neck.

"One more thing," Crenna said. "McKay, you better take it easy on that beer you brought back from Colorado. You got a long drive ahead of you in the morning."

Next morning, the four Guardians presented themselves bright and early at the briefing theater on Lambda Level. At least, they guessed it was bright. Since they were several hundred meters beneath the surface, Iowa could have been buried under the biggest blizzard in a hundred and fifty years for all they knew. One thing was certain, it was too damned early.

A little resentful of his utter lack of a hangover, McKay settled into one of the little seats. He'd allowed himself to consume two whole cans of his beloved Coors the night before, by way of celebrating what success they'd had on the Bollear grab mission. It hadn't been much, but then that was just about his assessment of the recent mission. The seats were no help either. They reminded him of the little writing desks he'd been forced to cram his already large adolescent frame into in high school.

Crenna faced them from the lecture desk, as dapper and trim as if he'd been dressed by some kind of machine, or maybe an undertaker. McKay knew that he'd worked most, if not all, of the night shepherding the computer technicians struggling to piece together the vast puzzle of the Blueprint for Renewal. McKay was a pretty hard dude. The Marines were not precisely a wuss outfit, and he'd served with the toughest of the tough: first the Marines' Force Recon, and later a covert-ops team of the euphemistically named Studies and Observations Group of the Southwest Asia Command. In his day he'd had to do a lot of hard humping on very little sleep. Yet sometimes he wondered just how Crenna managed to appear so fresh under the killing burden he must be hauling around on his thin shoulders.

"Good morning, gentlemen," Crenna said, speaking out of the right side of his mouth. It wasn't sarcasm that inspired him to do this; he simply didn't have a left side to his mouth, or not much of a functional one. The left half of his face was a mask of scar tissue, hideously twisted and grooved by some sort of ghastly accident. Scuttlebutt had it that a defective Claymore mine had gone off from a ground static discharge while being implaced back in the old days of the Vietnam War, tearing off the side of Green Beret officer Crenna's face, yet by some miracle not killing him. McKay didn't know the truth or falsity of that rumor, but whatever had happened had left half of Crenna's face looking like the badlands the Guardians had so recently visited.

"There's more to this mission than simply going off to find Mahalaby. That should be the easy part, providing he's still alive. The hard part is, we're sending you to look for someone whose name we don't know, whose description we lack, and whose location we can't pin down any much more exactly than to say we believe he's somewhere in the state of California."

Heartland's climate control system hummed faintly to itself in the abrupt silence. The Guardians were decked out for the road, wearing desert cammie fatigues in various tones of tan and khaki. Their outfits contrasted oddly with the carpeting in the briefing theater, which was a peculiar pattern of lavender on mauve. It was pretty hideous, but, all things considered, McKay at least liked it better than the scientifically soothing faded green that most of the briefing theaters sported. He hated feeling like a rat in a goddamned Skinner box.

"No problem," Sam Sloan said lightly. "We'll have it all wrapped up next week, and then we can get on to squaring the circle, discovering the philosopher's stone, and making the Augean stables good and shipshape."

"I don't blame you for feeling that way," Crenna said. "But this is the way it is: our computer-analysis staff has inferred—and I concur—that somewhere there should be a man, or woman perhaps, carrying around a sizeable chunk of the Blueprint in his or her head. It won't be all of it—only President Lowell had that, and he's dead now." His mouth quirked in a right-handed grimace of a smile. "For that matter, I have a sizable chunk of it in my head, and it hasn't done us much damned good. Most of the people whose names I knew didn't survive the blast. The analysis boys have every scrap of information I possess. I even let them pump me for it under hypnosis."

McKay raised an eyebrow. He didn't know much for sure about the enigmatic Major, but he did know that Crenna was an intensely private man, and he assumed, on the basis of his own vast experience in the shadow world, that Crenna's head was as crammed full of top-secret information as any man's could possibly be. That Crenna had let them pick his brain apart under hypnosis indicated just how much concern he felt.

"Project Blueprint was put together on the strict need-to-know principle—probably the strictest since the Manhattan Project. But it stands to reason that some might have had reason to know a great deal more than their fellow participants. There are the specialists who put the concept together in the first place. Also, somebody had to be prepared to oversee the damned project once we got it together. Our magical computers think that one of these people may be running around loose in California.

"So this isn't just a snipe hunt I'm sending you boys on, much as it may seem like one. We've got to get the Blueprint together and we've got to do it fast. The Federated States of Europe are breathing down our necks. They may be as badly off as we are, if not much worse, but we can't just make that assumption. They've got a lot of what political power is left in the world in their claws. And, even if terrorists did take out the ruling council, they left the big man intact, the man who was the brains of the FSE and of the Internationalist Council before that. You're familiar with the name by now—Yevgeny Maximov."

"*Maximov*," McKay said, eyes narrowed to ice-blue slits. Too bloody right the Guardians knew that name, as the SAS Troopers McKay had trained with at one point would have said. Sloan and McKay had a particular reason to know that name—and hate it. They'd first heard it from the thin, bloodless, aristocratic lips of W. Soames Summerill—conservative gadfly, internationally successful novelist, and secret master of the Central Intelligence Agency. At the time, he'd been an apparent convert to the bizarre Church of the New Dispensation, preached by the late Reverend Josiah Coffin. But when he'd had Sloan and McKay under interrogation in the machine shop in the bowels of the Denver Federal Center, that mask had come off pretty quick.

He was the head of the faction that had seized control of the Central Intelligence Agency after the One-Day War, and he regarded the mad prophet Coffin as the potential key to control of the entire United States of America—thus his apparent conversion. He'd insinuated himself into the great man's graces and become a trusted lieutenant, commander-in-chief of Coffin's own devil's militia, the Brothers of Mercy. It was he who had engineered the trap into which McKay and Sloan had walked on that fateful day in Denver, some weeks before.

But Summerill wasn't his own man, powerful as he was. He had revealed to his captives that he was working on behalf of none other than Yevgeny Maximov, strongman of the remnants of Europe. He was going to own the whole world, Summerill told them, and they had the choice of signing on with the winning team or dying in an extremely unpleasant manner.

For the two Guardians there wasn't any choice at all. And if overzealous Church of the New Dispensation troopies hadn't prematurely reported the demise of Mobile One in the wreckage of the Denver suburb of Lakewood, McKay and Sloan would probably still be tied to poles set inside the lip of the crater left by the twenty-five-megaton warhead the Soviets had plopped down on top of Cheyenne Mountain near Colorado Springs, dead in horrible agony, their bodies too heavily irradiated even to rot.

"If things go well—and they probably won't, but just for the moment let's pretend—you'll probably be able to use Mahalaby's New Eden as a base. Conduct your search any damned way you please. If we think of anything shrewd to tell you, we'll be letting you know. We may even be able to give you some support on this one. We've got a few VSTOL packet jets for shipping back Mahalaby's seeds, or maybe bringing our mystery man home, if and when you find him; and if Mahalaby really can deliver the goods, it's probable we can spare a Hercules transport plane for heavy hauling.

"Otherwise, you boys are on your own. You're trained to play it by ear. I've got every faith in you, so good luck, and good hunting."

The Guardians stood up and filed out one by one. "McKay."

McKay stopped at the door of the briefing theater and glanced back at Crenna, who'd stepped down off the low platform. Was that the trace of a dark smudge beneath the remaining steel gray eye?

"Listen," Crenna rasped. "About last night. I shouldn't have taken that cheap shot at you. Not at all, especially not in front of the other Guardians. I'm sorry. Now get the hell out of here."

McKay looked at him for a moment. He was struck utterly speechless. *Crenna apologizing*? McKay thought. *Jesus. We are* really *in the shit.*

McKay's moodiness dissolved on the way south from Heartland. The huge experimental farm known as New Eden nestled along the western flank of the Sierra Nevada range, about midway up the state, somewhere northeast of Fresno. The most direct route would have taken the Guardians along Highway 80 from a ways just west of the pocking of huge craters where Omaha had been, through Salt Lake City, across the Sierra Nevada near Reno and then down into the San Joaquin Valley at Sacramento. The Guardians had been advised that route was not a very wise choice. McKay gathered it had something to do with the Mormons around Salt Lake City. They were among the best set-up of America's survivors, since part of their doctrine called for each member to keep a year's supply of food on hand. While Salt Lake City itself had been hit hard, and Provo had collected a warhead of its own, there was still a knot of fairly well to do survivors clustered right along the Guardians' projected route. According to Crenna's intelligence, they were in a hostile, paranoid mood; attempts at proselytization by Coffin's faithful, followed up by a few raids from road gypsy gangs who had been converted to the New Dispensation, had turned the Mormons flat sour on outsiders.

Instead, the Guardians would veer west-southwest in

western Nebraska, just shy of the Colorado line, head down Interstate 76, carefully skirting Denver, and proceed on through Colorado, southern Utah, and the very southern tip of Nevada. From there they'd proceed down through Barstow and then west through the tail end of the mountains, giving a wide berth to the slaughterhouse that had been the Los Angeles area and the well-nuked Edwards Air Force Base. Skirting Bakersfield, they'd head north to their destination.

To McKay's surprise it was working out just that way.

They'd had one or two scrapes along the way, but that was to be expected. The trickiest had come when they'd rounded a bend in the road in the mountains near Grand Junction, Colorado. Some enterprising would-be hijackers had pushed a pickup nose to nose with a sizable flatbed truck across the road. Making a split-second decision, Casey had put the pedal to the metal and smashed right between the two vehicles in a classic roadblock-bursting maneuver, while Sam Sloan and the turret had played rock and roll with the M-2 and the grenade launcher. Those ambushers who made it to the safety of the pine woods on either side of the road were just as glad to see the last of Mobile One.

They had spent the night near a cache at the tag end of Nevada and rolled across the border into California at around 1000 hours. A hundred or so klicks later they'd rolled over. McKay got the worry seat, the Electronic Systems Operator's chair up front. Sloan moved into the driver's seat next to him while Casey climbed up into the turret to take his place behind the guns. Rogers was off. He laid himself down on an air mattress behind the turret root, and with the ability shared by cats and soldiers to doze off any place at any time, went comfortably and quietly to sleep.

Now McKay was listening to an old Don Felter tape of Casey's and watching the Mojave go by with a certain horrid fascination. One of the fringe benefits of being a Guardian was that they got to ride around in a state-of-the-art armored car, a contrivance privately developed by the Cadillac Gage Company, so new and excruciatingly high-tech that the military hadn't even gotten around to testing it for official adoption. Project Blueprint wasn't restricted by standard purchase and requisition requirements. Crenna'd had a secret off-budget treasure chest to fund his project. He hadn't skimped where his men were concerned. One of the many beauties of the V-450 called Mobile One—and also *home,* when they were on the road—was that it had a climate-conditioning system that actually worked. Outside, the heat was throbbing off the rolling vistas of sand and sagebrush. The heat on the tacky asphalt was so hot it shimmered in the middle distance, looking like huge puddles of water to McKay's eyes. Mirage. It was well over a hundred degrees out—McKay had never accustomed himself to the centigrade temperature system —and so dry that you could feel your nose hairs crisping if you were foolish enough to stick your head outside. When they had all clambered out to stretch their limbs and take a leak at the rollover, the breeze on McKay's face hadn't been cooling at all. It felt like a dragon's breath.

The long gullet of Highway 15 was choked with cars strung out like a dull glittering necklace, rising and falling with monotonous sameness and straightness. There'd been a lot of goddamn cars in the L.A. basin, and it looked as if every last one of them had come running this way when the balloon went up, driving until they ran out of gas or overheated or just plain got caught in the Great Terminal Traffic Jam of the Twentieth Century. Along with the skeletons of cars were no few skeletons of drivers and passengers. Even in the short time since the war the alternation of fierce, unnatural winds spawned by the shitstorm and the baking desert sun had stripped and scoured them to white bones festooned with a few brown shards of dried flesh and a few garish wisps of cloth fluttering in the hellish breeze. Hundreds, maybe thousands of people had left their cars and simply wandered off into the desert to die. There wasn't anything else to do.

McKay watched it all go by with a kind of numbness inside. He was an old soldier, an old campaigner. He'd seen horror before, in Beirut, in Tripoli, in Damascus after the Israelis had flattened the Syrian capital in a protracted one-week's bombing, but he'd never seen anything on this scale. The death tolls in the old days had run into the thousands, yeah, even the tens of thousands. Here it was the millions.

And here it was home. It was the desert, it was the other goddamn end of the continent from the vicinity he knew, but it was home.

They passed a lot of small towns along the way. Cheapjack motels and trailer parks, curio shops, lots with fading used cars sitting in neat rows. Ghost towns, all dead as last week. Now and then they saw movement: blowing paper; a rolling, bouncing ball of dried dead weed tracery—a tumbleweed, like something out of a Western movie. Once in a while there was a flash of clear, purposeful motion. Dogs flitted in and out of the wreckage like gaunt, hungry specters. Once a four-footed gray-and-tawny something stood in the shade of a burned-out gas station and watched them pass. It seemed that all the gas stations they passed were burned out. Apparently the people had fought over the precious fuel they contained until a stray bullet or a Molotov or who knows what made the issue academic. Sam Sloan chuckled to himself. "See that, McKay?" he asked.

"Yeah. What about it?"

"Coyote," Sloan said. "Never expected to see the bastards so bold that they just stand there in broad daylight and watch a car roll past. People around here would have shot one on sight for trying that, a couple of months ago." The grin slipped off one side of his face. "Guess maybe they might just end up inheriting this real estate."

"And fucking welcome to it," McKay said sourly.

A couple of hours of this brought them to Barstow, where they veered a few points—Sloan was driving, after all, and he was an old Navy man. About five hours later, well into a parched evening, they reached the outskirts of Bakersfield. Bakersfield had never been a particularly charming city, and it hadn't been much improved by the one-megaton warhead that had detonated above it. It had had no conceivable military significance. On the other hand, McKay had visited Bakersfield a couple of times on leave, once during an unpleasant period when he was training at the Twenty-nine Palms Marine Base southeast of Barstow; and from that experience, he reckoned it had been targeted by some Russian strategic officer who had visited Bakersfield too, and felt inclined to do the world a favor.

They worked their way overland, to avoid the rubble and congestion of the stricken city. Billy McKay had the wheel as they went bumping off through fields grown weed-rank and dry through neglect and lack of irrigation. Sloan identified them as being mostly planted in barley and beans. "Think of the people who could be fed if this produce had only been harvested," he remarked sadly from the turret. Actually, California agriculture had been in trouble for some years before the war. Federal and state policies had for years kept the price of water artificially low, thereby subsidizing overly lavish irrigation on a grand scale. The water supply throughout the West had begun to run low as early as the 1980s. In the early 1990s a drought had wiped out over a quarter of the crops in Southern California. This had prompted a flurry of new regulations and a lot of rhetoric about people saving their bath water and not watering their lawns, and had been a major contributing factor in passage of the Emergency Farmland Reclamation Act. The sensible thing to do, of course, would have been gradually to let the price of water rise to its market level, thereby nudging farmers in the direction of more efficient water conservation techniques. Naturally, no one thought of that.

McKay was cruising along a weed-filled ditch, too narrow for Mobile One to traverse—a perfect tank trap —when he heard the whine of the servomotors that traversed the one-man turret. "McKay," Sloan's voice said over the intercom. "Something moving. About two o'clock, range 800 meters."

Wildly, McKay started looking around for cover. The weed-strangled bean plants didn't come up any higher than the hubcaps of the big armored car. That was one of the disadvantages of riding around in this beast, and as an old-style infantryman McKay felt it keenly at moments such as these. The thick foamed-alloy armor of the V-450 was perfect for keeping off rain, small-arms rounds, and the occasional chunk of shrapnel, and a true delight when it came to taking the sting out of penetrating gamma radiation. The car was even well proofed against chemical and biological weapons, as the Guardians knew firsthand from the awful day near the headwaters of the Rio Grande, when the Church of the New Dispensation had used aerosol nerve gas to defeat the forces of

the Northern Rio Grande Valley Federation. But the goddamn
thing was a positive magnet for antitank weapons, from brief-
case-carried laser-guided missiles to simple bottles filled with
gasoline. A lucky hit —or an unlucky one, depending on your
point of view —could incinerate all four of them before they
had a chance to bail out. McKay had seen the remains of too
many tank battles in the Near East, knew too well how easy it
was to turn into a shrunken, black mummy, with hideously
leering white teeth—teeth never seemed to be hurt much by
fire—surrounded by blackened seaweed streamers of heat-
warped, plastic-sheathed wire. He had no desire to end up like
that.

"I've got a fix on it now, McKay," Sloan said. "A couple
of kids running through the fields toward a house."

McKay squinted around to the right. He could see them
now. Small figures bounding like frightened deer through light
that had just begun to mellow toward dusk. They were making
for a low ranch house, which even at this distance had the
hollowed out, dead-eyed look of a derelict building. They were
the first living human beings the Guardians had seen since
entering California.

"Think we should go take a look at them?" Sloan asked.

"I think they're just squatters come down out of the hills,"
Rogers remarked from the ESO seat. "Trying to scratch a living."

"More power to them," McKay said. "Negative to scoping
them out, Sloan. They don't have anything to tell us and we'd
probably just scare them shitless."

A little farther along they came to a packed-dirt-and-plank
bridge run across the ditch. Like much such rough-and-ready
rustic engineering, it was overbuilt, stout enough to accom-
modate the crushing weight of the V-450. McKay frowned as
he guided the vehicle gingerly across it. Maybe these poor,
squatting farmers *did* have something to tell the Guardians.
They were supposed to be finding the mystery participant of
Project Blueprint. Just where the hell did they start with that?
He shook his head slowly and steered along a dusty road
across a fallow field of rust-colored earth.

Ten minutes later, Tom Rogers said, "Billy, Heartland for
you."

Through the miracle of modern satellite communications—the Soviets had tried detonating nuclear devices outside the atmosphere to knock out the communications-satellite net that served America and the NATO countries, but the sky was just so cluttered with the damned things that they hadn't been able to make much headway—a tight-beamed signal was cast upwards from Heartland and reflected down into the central valley of California without having to trouble with the intervening spine of the Rockies. Rogers's finger flipped a toggle on his console and a familiar voice grated in McKay's earphone.

"McKay, Crenna. We've intercepted a communication from Europe that might just interest you boys."

"I'm all ears, Major."

"Maximov's people were acknowledging a communication received from Alaska—in a Russian code we broke two years ago. It was a confirmation that an agent has passed through Alaska on his way south to the States. The Soviet commander seemed under the impression Maximov's boys were some kind of KGB headquarters. They seem to think they're the last outpost of empire up there." A dry chuckle like a handful of ball-bearings dropped into a mess tin. "In kind of a pathetic way they're right."

"Any mention of where he'd be dropped off?" McKay asked.

"None that we got. It's luck that we managed to catch the message at all. It was sent via satellite on a tight beam, too, but the high-atmosphere effects of the war are still causing all kinds of weird scatter and reflection of signals."

"Great," McKay said, "all we need is people listening in on us."

"Good reason to cut short the chatter. I know I don't need to tell you this, McKay, but I'll tell you anyway: keep your damned eyes open. Crenna out."

"McKay, over and out." McKay squinted savagely ahead into the rays of the lowering sun. "Shit." The idea of Soviet forces on American soil really rankled his ass.

"Listen up, you guys. Got some news for you."

CHAPTER
THREE —————————————————

They were in trouble the minute they touched down.

"See. I told you you had nothing to worry about." The grizzled bush pilot chuckled as he swung the little, incredibly ancient high-wing Piper seaplane to a stop. Its port wingtip seemed almost to brush the cliffs that walled the tiny inlet on three sides. "I told you I could bring us down safe and sound in this here bay."

Colonel Ivan Vissarionovich Vesensky, late of the KGB, allowed himself to release a breath he didn't realize he'd been holding. He had more than common reserves of courage, but being landed in the narrow end of twilight in a bay seemingly no larger than an American football field by a drunken madman from Alaska had come close to depleting his supply. He forced himself to grin. "Sure, Frank. I never doubted you for a moment." When they'd set out from Alaska several days before, he'd spoken English with a muted Oxford accent. Now his words had the slightly tight-throated lilt of the native-born Californian. The pilot nodded and scratched thinning hair under the souvenir baseball cap that had come from somewhere in a Juneau that with any luck had been vaporized in the

One-Day War. "Well, I tell you, Mr. Victor—"

Out of the corner of his eye, Vesensky caught a quick flickering of orange light from the near shore through the windscreen. Sounds like hammerfalls hit his eardrums three times in succession: *thud, thud, thud.* Frank Lawson, the pilot, frowned. "Say, that my engine acting up—?"

A longer burst starred the windscreen with bullet holes.

In a world shattered by the most cataclysmic single event since the beginning of human history, only a phenomenal concentration of resources could have brought Ivan Vesensky from the huge chalet in the Bernese highlands of Switzerland to the rocky California coast near San Luis Obispo in less than a week's time. In all the ruined world, one man alone possessed such resources: Yevgeny Maximov. Ukrainian emigré, man of mystery, billionaire financier who had made himself the master of a stricken Europe. He was Ivan Vesensky's master as well, and Vesensky was his most perfect servant.

But even Maximov could mount such a convulsive heave of effort only once. For though Maximov had raw political power at his disposal, the survivors of the armies of NATO and the Warsaw Pact and the police forces of a dozen nations —secret and otherwise—his huge domain possessed little in the way of surviving industrial capacity. He could produce little food, little shelter, and none of the amenities of life for the millions who had survived the war. Unless something could be done, not even his well-armed minions could keep control of his empire.

What was needed was leverage—high-tech leverage, state-of-the-art know-how in production, reindustrialization, and the growing of food. A compendium of minds, experience, and material. Before the war, he knew, the American government had assembled just such a compendium under the title of *The Blueprint for Renewal.* But in the tumult of the war they'd lost it.

Maximov wanted it.

His first attempt to get it, using what in the vernacular of the spy trade was called an *in-country asset,* had proved unsuccessful. Now Maximov was sending in his first team, the man who for years had been his virtual right hand.

The world knew him as Ian Victor, a British playboy transplanted to the Continent: lady-killer, lover of fast cars, near-Olympic-caliber skier. The KGB knew him as its own Colonel Vesensky, a spy-master who'd run invaluable rings in Europe and the United States—and as an expert assassin. The most valuable Soviet covert operative of the 1990s.

As it happened, both were wrong.

The Soviets were closer. He was, in fact, Ivan Vesensky. He was, in fact, a colonel of the KGB. He was also a traitor.

Maximov, whose only loyalty was to himself, had turned him years before. For a man of Maximov's skills and insights into human character it had been a piece of cake. For one thing, he had possessed a piece of information about Vesensky that, if revealed, would have quite comprehensively dislodged Vesensky from grace with the humorless septuagenarians who ran the KGB. In the event, it was a lever Maximov scarcely had to use. Disenchanted with both the KGB and the ponderous, inept government it served, Vesensky was already tipped, poised, desiring nothing more than to be given the final push into treason.

It had been a surreal journey from Europe. After a briefing in Maximov's mountain fastness, he'd been helicoptered into Berne, where he'd been placed aboard a sleek Fokker Aurora Borealis, a luxury ultraprop aircraft for wealthy executives. It had been a straight shot, more or less, over the North Pole to Alaska, where the town of Nome was being occupied by the only alien force to have successfully invaded the United States of America since the War of 1812. It had been a peculiar, if not unpleasant, experience, flying alone in the well-appointed splendor of the luxury craft, fussed over by no fewer than two gorgeous stewardesss—who were ever so well-bred at hiding their disappointment that this tall, well-dressed man with wheat-blond hair, eyes of sea-green, and trim whipcord body showed utterly no interest in availing himself of the huge satin-sheeted bed in the rear compartment of the cabin, and one or both of their tender young bodies.

The Soviet brigade that had landed in Alaska in the darkness just hours before the missiles of the One-Day War began to fall possessed a more or less intact airfield near the conquered city of Nome. That was as far as the Borealis would take him. It was a purebred, long-legged as a greyhound, but also as neurotic and delicate of constitution. In an out-of-the-way field such as Nome, it would take several days to properly maintenance and get ready to take to the air again. In the meantime, Vesensky had to be on his way.

Impressions of Alaska lingered in his mind during the endless hedge-hopping trip down to California: a surly, half-subdued populace, watched warily by a special picked brigade of Siberians, both ethnic Russians and Asiatics of one sort or another. The Caucasians were a hardy breed, sons of the Czars' involuntary pioneers—and not only the Czars'. They had the almost unbelievable fortitude of the Russian peasant, an increasingly rare commodity in an increasingly urbanized Russia, but they lacked the Russian peasants' traditional stolidity. They had boldness and initiative, and no small amount of bravado. If any unit could have handled the tough task of being the spearhead of a proposed Soviet invasion of the United States of America, it was the 2301st Special Air-Landing Brigade.

But the invasion had never followed. The question now was whether the exiled sons and grandsons, the Kurds and Tartars and Mongols and Siberyaks, gave a good God-damn for the glory of a Mother Russia who had despised them and had, in any event, died and left them here on their own, strangers in a stranger land.

There had already been trouble. They'd made the leap across the Bering Strait and been offloaded from their landing craft in the Bering Land Bridge National Preserve, a hundred seventy-five klicks north of Nome, under the command of an ethnic-Russian brigadier, a bullet-headed Red Army Regular type from Smolensk. He'd been killed by a stray bullet at dusk that same day while observing a skirmish between one of his motorized rifle battalions and an American patrol helicoptered up from Fort Davis near Nome. How a bullet had strayed into the General's broad back when his front was toward the battle was a question no one had managed to answer. As of now, command of the brigade was shared between a gaunt-eyed colonel from Yakutsk—a Siberian of European descent, like the balance of his men—and a stocky political officer out of Leningrad who thought he was the reincarnation of Marshal Zhukov.

It hadn't been a happy prospect. Vesensky had been all too pleased to leave Nome behind, even if it meant heading south in this tiny, wretched airplane, his fate held in the shaky hands of an alcoholic madman who was himself a traitor. The forty-three-hundred-kilometer journey from Nome to this stretch of California coastline near the small town of San Luis Obispo had taken three days in an airplane loaded with extra fuel tanks, jerky, beans, some freeze-dried meals of dubious provenance, and several cases of Old Crow whiskey, which Frank Lawson, the pilot, had accepted as part payment in lieu of the customary thirty pieces of silver.

At landing places near Anchorage, a thousand klicks to the southeast, and a thousand klicks farther southeast in the Alexander archipelago, Lawson had managed to promote refuelings on his own, telling his bush-pilot cronies that Mr. Victor was an important playboy who'd been hunting in the Brooks Range and was offering him a shitload of real gold to carry him down to the lower forty-eight. Three more refuelings along the coast of British Columbia, near the Oregon-Washington border, and again somewhere south of Crescent City in Northern California, had been arranged through the magic of Maximov's net. How Maximov had worked it at such great distance, in a continent wracked by such disorder and so starved for fuel, not even Vesensky knew. He guessed Maximov had employed some of his hired hands within the Central Intelligence Agency. However he'd done it, it had taken a prodigious effort, and served to confirm what Vesensky already knew: his master desperately needed the Blueprint for Renewal.

It gave him a warm feeling inside that Maximov had chosen him to undertake this vital and demanding task. But then again, Maximov had never really had a choice.

Vesensky had the side door of the aircraft open and was sailing out over the pontoon in a long flat dive while Lawson was still gaping at his punctured windshield. The icy embrace of the water made his muscles clench, driving the air from his lungs. He managed to keep back a half breath, and swam underwater for a long ways with firm sure strokes while his chest burned.

He surfaced a good forty meters from the aircraft, shook

his head, and paused a moment, treading water and listening. Several automatic weapons were yammering from scrub along the shoreline. Their slow cadence confirmed what Vesensky had already guessed. The ambushers, whoever they were, were using Soviet-made weapons. Kalashnikovs, in the old style, firing the short 7.62 cartridge, AKMs or maybe even venerable AK47s. Even under fire and freezing his butt off in the cold bay, Vesensky had to smile ironically. The odds were quite good he himself had provided his unseen assailants with these weapons.

Has the mission been compromised? He doubted it. He knew perfectly well just what kind of lunatics were liable to be running around the California coast in the aftermath of the Third World War, firing at total strangers with Russian-made automatic weapons. He had helped bring a lot of them together in armed revolutionary bands. They may have been thinking of seizing the aircraft for their own. They may have been firing it up out of paranoia, or even sheer envy. There were groups that were that crazy. Odd as it seemed, they made the most malleable tools—if you possessed Vesensky's virtuoso skill in molding such men and women to your ends.

Frank Lawson was returning fire now with the quicker, higher-pitched chattering of a 5.45 mm AKS-74. Vesensky had gone out the passenger door, which faced to seaward. Even as he watched the seaplane being lit from inside by jitterings of orange muzzle flash, he heard across the water a soft grunt or exclamation of pain that somehow carried through the sounds of battle. The muzzle flashes inside the aircraft ceased. A moment later there came a small splash, not as if a body had fallen into the water, but perhaps as if an assault rifle had.

A half-dozen flame flowers blossomed spastically from the shore. The sound of bullets striking the aircraft's fuselage was distinct. "Fools," Vesensky said out loud. With any luck it would be half an hour before they noticed that no one was firing back at them anymore.

He took a deep breath and let his head slip beneath the icy water.

There were three vehicles parked at the bottom of an uncertain dirt track that ran down the slope from the heights above, probably beaten by kids who liked to drive down here, build fires on the beach, screw in the sand, and get stoned. A Jeep CJ, a late-model four-wheel-drive Toyota pickup truck, and some kind of mongrel dune buggy. The sole sentry was a lanky black man in an army jacket and cammie pants, with a cammie-patterned handkerchief tied around his head as a headband. He had a Kalashnikov slung across his narrow back. He had his butt propped against the Toyota and was rocking his torso back and forth. "Man, oh man," he was crooning to himself, "give it to those motherfuckers, just give it to them." He seemed oblivious to the way he was clanking the receiver of the assault rifle against the metal cab of the truck.

The muttering and clanking made it painfully easy for a dripping-wet Vesensky to come up from the scrub to the tailgate of the truck. He crouched for a moment, then lunged, striking at the sentry's temple with the butt of his heavy H&K VP70 pistol. The side of the man's head gave way with a sickening crunch and his legs folded up beneath him.

Vesensky caught him halfway down and eased him to the ground. Working quietly and confidently in the darkness, the Russian first relieved the man of his automatic rifle, then searched his pockets. The search revealed a dollar or two in change, a ring full of keys, a couple of little cards from some sort of supermarket contest, the remnants of an ounce of marijuana, a depleted packet of Zig-Zag rolling papers, and a faded, dog-eared card identifying the bearer as a member of a group called the Avengers of Cinque. Vesensky's thin lips twisted in a quick, dry grimace. This was indeed one of the groups he'd had contact with in his earlier sojourn in the States.

Have I been set up for ambush? Unlikely. Knowing better than most just how lethal the factionalism that plagued revolutionary leftist groups could be, Vesensky had not sent word of his coming ahead, even though he had used surviving fragments of his network, Soviet contacts, and Maximov's system, to give himself a good idea of where the man he sought could be found.

More than likely, the Avengers had simply happened to be camped by this little inlet and responded to the sudden apparition of the tiny seaplane with their usual response to a stress situation, i.e., by opening fire with everything they had. They'd always been a peculiarly trigger-happy lot.

The walls of the little cove echoed with the stuttering clamor of gunfire. Trying to sort out the progress of a firefight by sound isn't usually a productive pastime, but Vesensky had the distinct impression that the fire was coming from several widely spaced locations. The grimace became a grin. Almost certainly, the Avengers had spread out along the rocky shoreline in order to get more advantageous points of fire. In the confusion and excitement and darkness, they'd begun shooting at one another. With any luck the idiots would be at it for another hour or so, provided their ammunition held out.

What the keys taken from the dead or unconscious guard were for, Vesensky never found out. There was a set of keys in the Toyota. The engine turned over at once, faltered, caught, and began to purr quietly. The blasts of gunfire continued, ragged but unabated.

Leaving the truck engine running, Vesensky slipped out—fortunately there were no interior utility lights. Like the truck, the other two vehicles were recent models, but not so recent Vesensky wasn't basically familiar with them. Working by feel, he quickly entered the two unlocked vehicles and pulled out the fuses from the electrical systems. He returned to his appropriated vehicle, and humming a French rock tune that had been popular just before the war—Maximov abhorred rock music, and wouldn't permit it to be played on the few government radio stations he allowed to operate—Vesensky began to pick his way up the scree slope to the clifftops looming in the darkness overhead.

He didn't even flinch when, halfway up the grade, the interior of the truck was lit from behind by a sudden garish flare of yellow light. The Avengers of Cinque had finally succeeded in setting off the seaplane's gas tanks.

The little Toyota truck rolled up over the top and was gone.

CHAPTER
FOUR ───────────────────

Sitting *za-zen* on the front deck of Mobile One, Casey Wilson stiffened, hand going to the pistol grip of his Ingram M-10, which rested by his right thigh. Something was moving, his keen ears told him, stirring inside the trashed-out store.

The Guardians had taken shelter for the night in the receiving bay of a warehouse food mart that rejoiced in the name of *Baggit*. It was partly burned and mostly picked bare; inside the store proper were charred, tumbled shelves, checkout counters with cash registers busted to shit and gone by looters, an incredible profusion of paper trash. The broad sliding door of the bay still worked when Rogers tried it, so they raised it, cruised inside, and slid it shut behind them. Nobody in his right mind would take on an armored car as potent as the big Cadillac Gage—but as the Guardians knew too well, there were lots of crazies running around loose these days. They all figured it was better just not to call attention to themselves.

The night air was dry and hot. Inside the loading bay it tasted of tired cardboard and some former vegetables that had long since decomposed past the point of stinking, and instead lent the place a dull humus smell. Casey heard it again, the furtive *rustle-rustle-rustle* of debris, echoing slightly inside the vast hangar of the store.

The V-450 was blacked out, the other Guardians asleep within. Briefly, Casey considered waking them, then thought better of it. He was acutely conscious that, for all his record as the top-scoring American air ace since Korea, old-time squaddies McKay and Tom Rogers considered him a rank amateur on the ground. He'd handle this himself. With luck, the others would never even know of the intrusion. That would suit him fine.

He unfolded, reflexively checking that the foot-long suppressor was screwed firmly on the Ingram's snub barrel. He slipped to the floor, the rubber soles of his combat boots making no sound on the stained cement. Noiselessly he slipped toward the sprung double doors that led into the store.

A faint puddle of moonlight shone in the broken wall-sized windows at the front of the store. A feeble glow, but enough for the ex–fighter pilot to make out a black shape huddled in the doorway. He brought up the Ingram, hissed, "Hold it!"— and the black shape rushed him.

Unconsciously he expected it to unfold upwards and at him, like the crouched human he'd taken it to be. Instead it went for his throat like a spear shot from a diver's gun. Not even Casey's almost inhuman reflexes were enough to crowd a shot into the microsecond before the hurtling figure hit him, smashed him back, with agony stabbing his kidneys, into the front fender of the armored car, then bore him down onto the cool cement. The best he could do was jam his piece sideways up under the thing's pointed muzzle and deflect flashing fangs from his throat.

Reeking carnivore breath flooded his nostrils and made his stomach roll. He had an impression of massiveness and strength, of rank matted hair like black wool, of starlight glinting off furious eyes. *What the hell is it?* he wondered, as close to panic as he'd ever been in his life.

Then with a many-voiced snarling the rest of the dog pack lunged into the warehouse. Trying to push his attacker off with the machine pistol, Casey kicked wildly as one grabbed his ankle in its mouth. His free foot swept around, connected with a thud. The dog let go of his ankle and rolled away, squealing like locked brakes.

The Ingram was an ideal weapon for close combat, but not hand-to-hand. It wasn't built for clubbing or muzzle-thrusting. The best Casey could do was try to shove it between the powerful jaws snapping to tear off his face, and hope for the best. His wiry body bucked off the cement, trying to pitch the black monster off. He couldn't dislodge it—the damned thing seemed to weigh as much as a small man. And maybe it wasn't such a good idea, because the rest of the pack was circling with savage barks, apparently unwilling to horn in on their leader.

Then Casey heard the most beautiful sound he'd ever heard in his life: the rutting-bull-elk bellow of Billy McKay. "What the fuck's going on here? Tom, hit the lights!"

McKay had come awake when Casey's challenge to the intruder whispered in his bone-conduction speaker. He was up at once, .45 in hand, moving sock-footed for the side hatch. By the time he popped it, all hell had broken loose outside.

He yelled, stepping forward, and something lunged at him out of the blackness. He fired from the hip. A yellow German shepherd folded in midleap with a scream and rolled under the 450, dragging a rear leg that had been torn almost free at the hip. Another was in the air right behind it; McKay caught it in the gut with a forward snap-kick, triggered the big combat-modified Colt less than a hand's breadth from one madly rolling eye, and blew the animal's head apart in a black cloud of blood and brains. The bay was full of flitting, howling ghost shapes. He fired at one, heard a whine and a loud impact as the copper-jacketed round ricocheted against the steel-titanium alloy skin of Mobile One. By the wind of passage he'd felt it hadn't missed him by half a meter, and he remembered belatedly that the bay had concrete walls. He half-turned in time to see Sam Sloan poking the barrel of his Galil–M-203 combo out the open hatch. "Jesus, don't fire that thing in here!" he roared. Sam jerked the rifle up, surprised, and a machine-shop vise closed on Billy McKay's right forearm.

The loading bay exploded in white light as Rogers hit the turret spot. Several dogs yelped shrilly, blinded. McKay jammed his eyes shut, reopened them to see a Doberman, black and tan and barracuda lean, hanging from his arm and bearing down with the force of a trained attack dog. He couldn't bring his sidearm to bear on the beast. Kicking at the other rangy dogs snapping at his shins, he drew his heavy-bladed Kabar knife from its sheath left-handed, and plunged it into the narrow gut behind the sharp vee of the sternum. The dog kicked and bore down harder; red sparks flashed at the backs of his eyes as he felt the bones of his arm grind together. He twisted the blade as blood jetted over his wrist, inside the sleeve of his cammie blouse. The dog released his arm and dropped to the cement, snapping at the ropes of intestines spilling out of its torn body. McKay kicked it, staving in the flat skull and snapping its neck.

He shoved the .45 back in its holster and turned to Sloan, who was standing frozen in the hatch. "Gimme that." He tore the Galil from Sloan's hands and spun, holding the weapon by the barrel like a club.

A *pop!* bounced off his eardrums. Instantly the bay filled with thick pepper-flavored smoke, tightening like a noose around McKay's throat and blinding him with tears. He heard Sam yell in outrage. Rogers had popped a CS grenade without warning his buddies to mask up.

It was a good move. There hadn't been a spare half second, and the dogs' eyes and ultrasensitive noses were a lot more susceptible to the stinging tear gas than humans'—especially the Guardians', each of whom had had to field-strip and reassemble his main weapon in a room filled with the stuff, without a mask. Yelping frantically, the dogs poured out of the bay as McKay sheathed his knife and pulled out his mask. He blew into it to clear the goggles of the white CS powder and pulled it on.

McKay still heard snarling. He ran around the front of the car to see the biggest fucking dog he'd ever seen standing on Casey, ripping at his upflung arms with his teeth. Something odd about the creature's appearance tugged at the back of his awareness. Disregarding it, he swung up the Galil, stepped forward, and brought the weapon's butt slamming down on the small of the dog's back.

The animal's spine broke with a gunshot crack. Still it

slavered and snapped at Casey. McKay's next blow caved in the ribs on its left side and rolled it off onto the pavement. Panting, bloody tongue lolling out over black lips, it struggled to rise. Casey stuck the front of the suppressor into its mouth and blew its brains out with a single shot.

Mckay helped Casey to his feet. The young man's face was white under a gleaming mask of sweat and saliva. "Jeez, what *was* that thing?" Wilson panted. He wasn't even noticing the tear gas; he was too wrung out.

"Most dangerous predator on the North American continent," Rogers commented from the open turret. "Pack o' dogs. Ord'nary household pets."

"But what was that?"

Hanging onto McKay's biceps for support, Casey gestured at his antagonist with the Ingram. McKay and Sloan studied it, and then the ex-Marine broke out laughing.

"That's a lick on you, Case!" he roared. "Don't you know what that was?"

Sloan was shaking his head and clucking into his mask. "I've never seen one before. An Imperial—they really are the size of Irish wolfhounds."

Casey stared at them through red-rimmed eyes. "Like, what are you guys *talking* about?" he demanded, exasperated for the first time anybody could remember.

"Only you," said McKay, clapping him on the shoulder, "could almost get your ass taken out by a fucking poodle."

In the morning the sky was a shield of crudely beaten lead with clouds hanging low and heavy, seemingly just above the top of the turret. Below, the day was parched. The heat baked in waves off the flat bottomland as a very quiet Casey Wilson and the other three Guardians drove north past Delano and Tulare, the grape-farming towns of the lower San Joaquin Valley. The few kids they'd seen the night before racing over the abandoned fields toward what they gathered was their home remained the only human life they saw.

Of death there was plenty of evidence. Sun-bleached skeletons or, occasionally, huddled mummies, lying by the roadside, sprawled amid broken buildings. Once they came upon a pack of wild dogs harrying the fresh-seeming corpse of a half-

clad young woman. On duty in the turret, Sam Sloan scattered
them with a blast of .50 caliber that rolled the dogs along the
pavement like tumbleweeds before the wind. McKay chewed
his ass briefly for wasting ammunition and calling attention to
them, but his heart wasn't in it.

Like Bakersfield, Fresno had been the recipient of a Soviet
warhead. The Guardians were frankly puzzled. Neither town
had any particular or imaginable military significance. Was it
sheer vindictiveness on the part of the Soviets, an attempt to
deny the Americans use of the resources of the richest state in
the union? Or had they been following some kind of bizarre
crackpot theory of their own, trying to jolt the famed San An-
dreas and related faults into a cataclysmic series of earth-
quakes? Even a mild earthquake released more energy than a
megaton-range blast, and a real grand slam like the L.A.
quake of '68—to say nothing of the 1906 earthquake in San
Francisco—released more energy than both the Soviets and
the Americans together had possessed in their pre-war nuclear
arsenals. On the other hand, McKay knew perfectly well that
no idea was too goony or totally, ludicrously impractical to
escape the serious attention of the swivel chair cavalry in any
nation's high command.

North of Fresno they turned right, climbing quickly into the
abrupt blue jut of the Sierra Nevada range. Maps stored in
Mobile One's capacious computer memory led them to the
turnoff of an unimproved county road, next to yet another
burned-out gas station and country store combo. Shortly it
evolved into a narrow dirt track twisting back and forth across
the face of the mountains, crowded close on both sides by
looming, elegant pine and fir trees. New Eden lay in a valley
high up the side of 3,200-meter Maldita Peak. The high mountain watershed provided adequate water, and, since achieve-
ment of self-sufficiency was one of New Eden's goals, the
isolation of the farm was not considered a drawback.

In the event, its survival—if indeed it had survived—could
probably be attributed to its very isolation.

They popped the hatches and rode with their heads poked
out into the pine-tangy mountain breeze. The leaden ceiling of
clouds overhead had begun to break up a little bit. Sunlight
spilled down from above, dappling the roadway and the iron

flanks of Mobile One. The road was a rich reddish color, deeply furrowed by tires and natural erosion. Taking his turn in the turret, McKay began to admit to himself that Casey might just have something about California after all. This was pretty country. On the other hand, Wilson was still welcome to the Mojave and draggle-assed dusty *Grapes of Wrath* valley below.

They came around a wooded shank of a ridge and found themselves face-to-face with a sight McKay had never seen before, except in picture books: an ancient single-arch steel truss bridge of the type once popular for highway and railroad bridges and now almost as rare as the covered bridges of the Northeast. It put McKay in mind of box kites and erector sets.

A pair of streams flowed down Maldita Peak and joined, to emerge from the narrow single entrance to the valley as Maldita Creek. Unusually heavy rainfall in the Sierra Nevada—probably an aftereffect of the war—had turned the generally unassuming creek into a torrent, frothing its way down toward the Sacramento River in the San Joaquin Valley below. It had jumped its banks, turning the whole mouth of the valley to marsh. Fortunately the road into the valley had been built on a causeway, so it remained passable. The V-450 was a rugged vehicle with excellent amphibious capabilities, but McKay wasn't too happy at the prospect of ordering Tom Rogers to slog the thing through mud. Too damn easy to bog down, amphibian or not.

The far end of the funny little bridge was blocked by an old flatbed truck. The bed had been piled high with huge boulders. Through the vision blocks of the one-man machine-gun turret, McKay could see several men crouching behind the truck, pointing at the V-450 in apparent dismay.

Rogers rolled boldly up to the south end of the bridge and stopped. "Will that damned thing bear our weight?" McKay asked over the intercom.

"Oh, sure." Casey said cheerfully.

Suspecting Casey of California partisanship, McKay said, "Tom, what do you think?"

"Reckon he's right. They built these things pretty sturdy."

"He's right, McKay," said Sam Sloan, who had roused himself from the air mattress when they started up the valley.

"They still had a few of these things in the Ozark country I come from when I was a boy."

"Question is," Rogers said, "whether those fellas on the other side are gonna let us by without an argument."

"Casey, put me over the loudspeaker," McKay said. He settled himself back behind the twin heavy weapons. In a moment the young ex-fighter-jock gave him the go-ahead. "Listen up, people. This is an official U.S. Government team on a mission from the President himself. We're on our way to New Eden. We're asking you to let us pass."

The half dozen or so men crouched behind the old flatbed truck conferred in consternation. One of them poked his head around the side of a granite slab and cupped his hands over his mouth. "You clear out, now, y'hear? We don't want no trouble."

"I repeat, we're on official United States Government business. It's imperative that we be permitted to pass." With difficulty, McKay controlled his temper. He could understand that the huge drab-gray armored car wasn't a particularly reassuring sight. On the other hand, didn't these assholes know that if they'd meant them ill they'd have announced their presence with a burst of heavy-caliber machine-gun fire?

The men behind the truck conferred some more. "We just can't let you by on our own hook. We'll have to ask the General."

"Shit," McKay said. "Tom, how about it, could we bulldoze that fucking truck out of the way?"

"Billy!" Tom and Casey said at once.

"This ain't a bulldozer, Billy," Tom Rogers said. "We could push our way through a lot of obstacles, but Mobile One was never meant to push past something that heavy."

Mckay tapped thick fingers impatiently on the feedbox for the M-19. He was getting tired of dicking around with these fools. He could see the muzzles of long arms poking out here and there from behind the truck and the boulders. It didn't look like any of them had any tank-busting weapons, and he was a long way from convinced that any of these stalwarts had either the balls or the brains to make good use of them. Of course in this day and age—and especially in California, terrorist capital of North America—anything was possible. But

Mobile One had to get to New Eden, and trying to sneak a ten-ton, diesel-engine armored car into a small and peaceful mountain valley in the dead of night didn't seem a very promising pastime.

"All right, Tommy," he said. "Take us for a swim."

He held on as Rogers twisted the wheel left and goosed the heavy vehicle off down the low embankment and into the swamp along the western edge of the road. Here the channel of the river ran along the far side of the causeway. They churned forward through the mud, sloshing heavily like a giant wading in galoshes. Green reeds slapped the metal flanks of the vehicle.

Then they were sloshing into the channel, the swollen creek itself. The heavy armored car rocked slightly as it bucked the current, swimming parallel to the bridge and about forty meters upstream from it. Sliding aside the interior armor shutter and peering out his side vision block, McKay could see the men on the bridge gesticulating excitedly. He hadn't condescended to traverse the turret to keep the car's weapons bearing on them, and he halfway hoped one of the fools would take a shot at him. None of them did. Unmolested, Mobile One forded the creek with the lumbering grace of a hippo and clambered out into the weeds on the other side with brown water cascading off its deck, sending a flight of ducks flapping and squalling up into the blue sky. Several of the men on watch were running for horses waiting under saddle in the cover of the flatbed truck as Mobile One trundled back up onto the causeway and off along the road.

They crossed the cement culvert where Elk Creek met the Maldita, then turned off up a dirt track that followed what their maps called Good Morning Creek, up a flat-bottomed three-hundred-meter-wide valley between two wooded spurs of ridgeline. Up at the head of the valley something glinted in the sun like large sheets of glass. It seemed to be at the wrong angle to be reflection off standing water.

As Mobile One rumbled up the freshly graded track, McKay heard Sloan mutter in surprise, "This looks like the Midwest in miniature. Or seen from the air, maybe."

Puzzled, McKay looked around. City-born and -bred, it took him a moment to make sense of what Sloan was saying.

Then his infantryman's eye snapped back into focus.

The valley around them was a checkerboard, as farmland generally was—but in most cases the checks consisted of plots greater than fifty meters on a side. Here, towering green cornstalks crowded together against one another like commuters on a Nip subway. There, some kind of low lettuce-looking plant formed a knee-high green mattress that looked solid enough to lie on. Here right beside the track was a tiny plot of some sort of gold-tuffed cereal grain. The plants crowded so tightly together that it looked as if all you'd need to do is string some number sixteen wire around them to make one big bale out of the lot. "Jeez," Casey said disbelievingly. "How do they grow all this stuff, packed so close like this?"

People worked in some of the plots, men and women in coveralls, most with heads shaded by wide-brimmed straw hats against the intense mountain sun. They straightened to watch the car as it passed, curiously, but showed no signs of apprehension. One plot over from the road, two men and a woman stopped shoveling some sort of brown material out of the back of a mule-driven cart to watch Mobile One as it passed. "High-tech, huh?" McKay said derisively. "This is the bright new hope of America?"

"If they get results like this on this small a stretch of land," Sloan said seriously, "I don't think it matters how they do it."

"Maybe they sacrifice lambs to the Earth Mother," Casey suggested cheerfully.

McKay snorted. "Just so they don't want to burn me in some fucking wicker cage," he said, recalling a horror movie he'd seen as a kid, oh, fifteen years before.

As they drew close to the head of the valley, they saw that the reflections they'd observed from the lower end were caused by the sun glancing off the plastic sheeting of huge greenhouses, which covered a hectare or more. Above the greenhouses lay several long, low, prefabricated-looking buildings, which McKay guessed contained storage areas and probably laboratories. Farther along, an expanse of lengthy picture windows interspersed with doorways seemed to be set into the earth itself on the northern slope of the valley. McKay recognized the Trombe walls of substantial semisubterranean living quarters, set to catch the warming rays of the sun in wintertime. They were reminiscent of the prevalent style of dwellings of the Freehold community in Colorado's San Luis Valley, where the Guardians had made their first—and to date only—successful pickup of a Project Blueprint person. Except, whereas the slightly crazy individualists of Freehold had insisted on single-family dwellings, these seemed to be something like passive solar dormitories instead.

The track expanded into a sort of graded plaza. It was thronged with busy people in coveralls, working at rabbit hutches, digging some sort of drainage ditch, and, somewhat to McKay's relief, repairing an old yellow John Deere tractor with a parasol over the driver's seat. "Hold it right about here, Tom," McKay said. He popped the overhead hatch as Rogers slowed the bulky vehicle to a stop and boosted himself out, so that his head and massive shoulders showed.

A door opened in the immense greenhouse about twenty meters away, and a man walked out. McKay assumed he was a man, on the basis of his cream-colored, well broken-in coveralls, and the sunbright discs of round spectacles in the area of the face. What he mostly looked like was a somewhat grizzled bear. He must have stood close to two meters tall, much taller than Billy McKay, with a build to match. Big shoulders, big chest, a promontory of a belly, short sturdy legs somewhat bowed, scuffed but sturdy work boots. Black hair shot with gray hung down to sloping shoulders, and most of his face that wasn't covered with the glasses or didn't consist of a round nose was covered by a thick salt-and-pepper growth of beard.

"Morning," McKay said to the bearlike man. He dominated the little plaza, and not just on the basis of size alone. Everyone who had stopped work to stare at the V-450 now turned their heads to gaze reverently at him. "My name's Billy McKay. We're a U.S. Government team on a special mission for the President himself. We're looking for a Dr. Georges Mahalaby." Having spent considerable time in Lebanon and other former French colonial holdings, he didn't have a hard time with the French first name.

A huge smile so white it could have been used to peddle toothpaste split the beard. "But I am Dr. Mahalaby!" the giant exclaimed, holding wide his arms. "You are welcome to

New Eden, Billy McKay. You and your friends, whoever they may be." He spoke perfect English in a booming, basso roar, with only a touch of accent that sounded more French than Middle Eastern.

"Pleased to meet you, too, Doctor. We've come for the blueprints."

On the front deck of Mobile One Tom and Casey had both popped their top hatches and poked their own heads out into the fresh air. "Welcome, gentlemen, welcome," Mahalaby boomed, striding forward. He slapped the angular snout of the armored car with a huge, work-hardened hand, as familiarly and affectionately as if it had been the haunch of a favorite mule. Behind him several other people, also dressed in coveralls of muted earth tones, had begun to emerge from the vast greenhouse. "We'd begun to fear you would never come, that we would have to commence the work of the Blueprint on our own."

Well, McKay thought, *so much for security.*

CHAPTER
FIVE ————————————————

"I cannot tell you how pleased I am to see you, gentlemen," boomed Dr. Georges Mahalaby. The deep reverberations of his voice filled the spacious commissary on the ground floor of the two-story semisubterranean residence of New Eden called the "Main Habitat." "We believed we would hear from the Project much sooner than this. We'd begun to fear we would be on our own."

Trying not to grimace, McKay took a sip of the steaming tea the willowy woman with the waist-length, white-blond hair had served from an earthenware tray a few moments before. It was some sort of herbal concoction. To McKay it tasted like boiled paper. It couldn't even be relied upon to give him a lift; Mahalaby had informed them in grave, round tones that the stuff was totally lacking in caffeine, which from his manner he thought to be a very good thing indeed. McKay wondered if it would be in poor taste to ask if they had some good organic whiskey on hand to jazz the stuff up a bit.

"The truth is, things have gone a little bit awry with the Project," Sam Sloan said. He knocked back a hearty slug of the insipid tea. McKay watched without knowing whether to admire or pity him. "If it hadn't been for Dr. Okeda, we might never have learned of your existence here."

Mahalaby's eyebrows crawled up his sunbrowned forehead like furry black-and-white caterpillars, "Jim? And how is he?"

McKay and Sloan exchanged hesitant glances. Grateful not for the first time that Sloan was the glib member of the team, McKay let his glance wander to the big southern-exposed windows. Outside, the denizens of New Eden, men and women invariably looking young and enthusiastic in their earth-tone coveralls, went about their business. Beyond them the slope rose gently. Cloaked by a dense cover of sunbrowned grass, the yellow pine-clad spur separated them from the valley to the south. The weather was volatile, as it seemed to have been since the One-Day War. The grim overcast of that morning had broken up into cottony puffs of white cloud rolling breezily across the blue sky.

When it became painfully apparent that McKay wasn't going to say anything, Sam Sloan said, "I'm sorry, Dr. Mahalaby. Dr. Okeda is dead. He was killed by anti-tech demonstrators at the Oppenheimer Particle Accelerator Facility in Kansas City."

Mahalaby's eyes filled with tears. Embarrassed, he blinked rapidly and stared down the slope of his chest and belly. After a few moments, he rumbled, "Jim. A tragedy—he had so much to live for, so much work to accomplish; and the neo-Luddites, the poor benighted fools, they killed him."

Curious, McKay cocked an eyebrow at him. His blond eyebrows had faded in the sun almost to the point of invisibility against his tanned and weather-beaten face, but he cocked one nonetheless. "Don't want to seem disrespectful, Doc. But I sort of had the impression you people out here were back-to-the-earth types yourself."

Mahalaby's huge head snapped up. He glowered at McKay. "How dare you say that? I should think that a man who had—had been in the world as much as yourself should know better than to make such facile assumptions!"

McKay held up a callused palm. "Say Doc, ease off," he said hastily. "I didn't mean any offense."

"Lieutenant McKay wasn't being deliberately offensive,"

Sam Sloan put in hastily, letting just a touch more than usual of down-home Missouri creep into his voice, the way he did when he was playing the peacemaker. "He just wondered—as did I—how you felt about the type of research Dr. Okeda was engaged in. I mean your orientation here is uh, uh—" He began tripping over himself as he realized there wasn't any very diplomatic way that he could think of to say what he was trying to say.

But when Mahalaby turned his head to look at Sloan, the storm had already passed. "I understand. Here at New Eden we try to live in harmony with the good mother Earth. And you are misled by this—for so many of those who believe in coexisting with nature, rather than struggling against her, hate and fear man's technology. Yet I ask you, are the artifices of man any less a part of nature than the nest of a wasp, or a beaver dam?"

He rose from the table, dashed back his steaming tea with a flick of his thick wrist, plunked the pewter mug down on the tabletop. "Come," he said. "See what it is we do here in New Eden. My friend Jim—Dr. Okeda—himself played a pivotal role in the work we are accomplishing here. See for yourselves that he has been martyred in the service of all humanity."

"Just as people have their likes and dislikes, and flourish in some company, while they wither in others," Dr. Mahalaby said, "so also do plants. Plants have their favorite companions, whose nearness encourages them to grow and produce. So in this patch here, corn grows side by side with bush beans and beets. And in this patch here"—a wave of one dark-furred paw— "wheat and barley thrive in proximity with soya beans."

The doctor was leading McKay and Sloan along the network of low ridges that separated the tiny, incredibly crowded garden patches of New Eden. All around them the energetic young people of the commune/research lab worked the patches, weeding, turning the soil with spades and forks, planting seeds with infinite care as to placement and depth. To McKay's surprise, he noted that several of the people engaged in planting referred frequently to the flat LCD screens of notebook computers. *Guess I'm starting to see what Doc*

Mahalaby means when he talks about using technology in con-cert with nature, he thought.

It was fortunate that he was getting the drift of at least some of this. He was tagging along behind the bearish scientist, squinting his eyes against a wind strong enough even to fray the edges of Mahalaby's booming voice, and not understand-ing more than one word in three. Sloan, on the other hand, strolled along with his hands thrust deep in the pockets of his gun-metal fatigues, nodding his head and going, "Uh-huh, uh-huh," for all the world like some hayseed farmer with his hands stuck into his bib overalls, talking crop rotations with the good ole boy from down the road.

"I gather you use a combination of the biodynamic and French-intensive styles of gardening," Sam Sloan remarked.

Mahalaby beamed and bobbed his huge head as McKay blinked in incomprehension. "Just so. But we have done more than merely imitate the methods of Rudolf Steiner and Alan Chadwick." He squatted down, endangering the seams of his coveralls at belly and rump, and plucked a bright red tomato from a squat wide-leafed plant beside the raised pathway. Weeding on her hands and knees beside the plant, a young Oriental woman with gleaming black hair caught up in a bun and covered with an orange bandana looked at Mahalaby and smiled worshipfully. *These people treat Mahalaby like he was a combination of Albert Einstein, Saint Francis of Assisi, and Santa Claus,* McKay thought, admiring the way the rust-colored fabric of the gardener's coveralls molded itself to the curve of her buttocks.

She turned to him and smiled again, in a way very much dif-ferent from the way she'd smiled at Mahalaby. *Hmm,* he thought.

Mahalaby straightened and, cradling it in the palm of his hand, thrust the fat tomato at Sloan with the air of a man proffering the Star of India. "Taste." Sloan hesitated. "Don't be afraid. No insecticides are allowed to sully our lovely produce. By judicious planting of selected herbs, and meticulous and scientific care of the soil, we keep our gardens free of pests." His teeth gleamed through the thicket of his beard in a secret smile.

Shrugging, Sam Sloan took the tomato, raised it to his lips, and bit. He chewed a moment and then his eyebrows went up. "Say, this is pretty darned good." He poked it under McKay's nose. "Here. Try it."

McKay eyed the fruit dubiously. He didn't personally see much use in a tomato, unless it was sliced and resting safely between a sesame-seed bun and a slab of hamburger in the company of pickles and plenty of mustard. Nonetheless, winning the hearts and minds of Project Blueprint participants was definitely part of his mission briefing. It would be rude to refuse to taste the thing, so he picked it up gingerly with his fingertips, turned it around so that he could take a bite from the other side than Sloan had bitten into, and tasted it. "Hmm," he said, "not bad." And in truth it wasn't. On the other hand, he still sort of wished he had the rest of the burger to go with it.

"The succulent treasure that you have tasted is not merely a product of our gardening techniques, nor even of the loving care which we lavish upon our plants." Mahalaby positively glowed with pride. "It's also a product of genetic engineering. It's vastly more insect resistant than a normal tomato, takes a third as long to grow, and can survive a much greater range of temperatures and climatic conditions. All of our crops consist of specially mutated stocks. And Dr. Okeda, poor dead Jim, was instrumental in developing them."

Sloan and McKay looked at one another with a new appreciation of the quiet little *nisei* whom they'd busted through a mob in a suburb of Kansas City, Kansas, to rescue, only to see him shot down by a sniper as they tried to bundle him into Mobile One. "I think I get it," McKay said. "You've stored up a lot of food that you can distribute to people who need it."

"That's not all, McKay," Sam Sloan said. "This high up, winter cuts the growing season short, but down in the valley they grow crops all year round. Think what a few truckloads of *seeds* hauled to the survivors down below could accomplish. . . ."

Mahalaby was nodding his head enthusiastically. "You have grasped it, gentlemen. We've begun preparation to distribute both stored foods and, more importantly, seeds, and booklets of instruction to explain how best to grow them, for distribution throughout the state. And as the stocks of seeds we shipped to Project Blueprint are distributed, even as late as it is in the year to commence growing, thousands—maybe even millions—may be saved from hunger.''

Once again Sloan and McKay looked at one another. ''Er—ah—'' Sam Sloan said, and McKay went, ''Uh—yes, well—shit.''

The doctor's shaggy eyebrows knit together. ''But what is wrong?''

McKay took a deep breath. ''Uh, Doc, do you happen to know where those seeds *went?*''

''Why, no. We sent them by truck down to Fresno, where I gather they were loaded on trains and shipped to some storage facility. Isn't that where you came from?''

''Well, no,'' Sam Sloan said, gazing off at the ridgetop.

''But I thought you came from the Project Blueprint?''

''We do, Doc,'' McKay said. ''The problem is, we sort of, uh, lost the master key to the Blueprint. We don't know where any of these stockpiles are.''

Mahalaby squeezed his eyes shut, and murmured something that sounded to McKay like Arabic. ''Dear merciful God. This is not the way it was to go at all—''

A shout floated down the wind. The three men's heads turned. A skinny young man with long kinky black hair was running up the dirt road from the foot of the valley. He was waving his hand and calling for their attention.

''Why, Louis, whatever has you so excited?'' Mahalaby asked, as the young man pelted up.

The young man pointed his skinny arm off down toward the valley. ''It's men from General Edward's ranch, Doctor,'' he said excitedly. His cheeks were flushed with color. ''They say they've come to commandeer the armored car that drove in here this morning—in the name of the United States of America!''

Ivan Vesensky hadn't had to drive the Toyota more than twenty or thirty klicks from the cove where the seaplane had been ambushed to the brushy draw off Highway 101 where it now lay hidden. All the same he'd been glad for the transportation.

Physically, Vesensky was a very tough specimen, very fit. As a member of the despised Georgian national minority of the Soviet Union, he had been no child of privilege. His national service had been spent in the *Raydovikii*—the Soviet Army's paratroops—where he'd won noncommissioned rank the hard way. He'd passed the grueling training for the elite *Spetnatz* sabotage teams with which the Soviets had hoped to paralyze NATO command and communications centers in the event of war. Subsequently, he had undergone the toughest training the KGB had to offer, including the special commando and clandestine-warfare programs that would-be revolutionaries and guerrillas from all over the world paid high tuitions to undergo. And, finally, he'd completed the arduous and demanding training necessary to become a member in good standing of the sinister Executive Department of the First Directorate of the KGB. His usual cover, which he'd kept intact over almost a decade of operations all over the world, was the persona of a wealthy continental playboy and international ski-bum, and in fact Vesensky was both a downhill and cross-country skier of near-Olympic quality. All that aside, he was no fool, and saw no reason to walk when he could ride.

He had, however, turned his stolen truck off into the hills that ran along the inland side of the highway here, before coming in sight of the turnoff leading to the headquarters of the man he had come across half the world to contact. Last night Vesensky had seen ample evidence of the stability of the men his contact might be expected to set to guard his privacy, and besides, Vesensky had no inclination to waste time bickering with some flunky of a gate sentry. So he'd driven the Toyota into a defile well up out of sight of the main highway, concealed it with brush, and, ignoring the discomfort of his still damp clothing, settled into the driver's seat for a short nap.

When the sun pushed itself up above the rocky Santa Lucia Range, which paralleled the highway, he had awakened. He'd breakfasted on a packet of granola, which he mixed himself, sealed into plastic bags, and carried with him at all times against just such emergencies as this. Now he was making his way inland over a tangle of ridges and hills, on a heading that should take him to the twisty two-lane blacktop road leading to his contact's stronghold. Though not yet very high in the sky, the sun was hot, and Vesensky's damp clothes had dried out. Shortly he worked his way up to the top of a hill, and saw the dull, slate gray serpentine of the road undulating beneath him.

Quickly he descended, and started off up the road at a brisk walk. Though he'd taken off his hiking boots and spread his socks on the seat beside him when he settled in for his sleep, they still squelched slightly as he walked. He ignored the discomfort, keeping his senses alert for the sound of an approaching motor vehicle. He doubted that there was much chance of encountering a patrol on foot, and if by some mischance he did, it was likely they'd be making enough noise chattering among themselves to be heard half a kilometer away.

Twice before he reached his destination he had to dive off to the side of the road. The first time he went into the scrub it was to evade a shiny silver Mazda fourwheel-drive truck filled with armed men in faded army jackets. The second was more intriguing. The road had begun to mount upward into hills covered with trees—not just the scrubby live oaks that grew naturally hereabouts but real honest to God *trees,* oak trees, fruit trees, cedars, gingkos, in bewildering profusion. The shade they daubed onto the narrow road was quite welcome. While at one time they had been manicured and pampered with the utmost care, their bases now were surrounded by a respectable growth of underbrush. Into this Vesensky threw himself at the sound of a large engine laboring up the grade beside him. From concealment he watched a big Peterbilt diesel tractor pulling a tanker trailer, with GASOLINE painted in big red letters on the side. He chewed the lining of his mouth reflectively as he watched it pass.

Another couple of twists and turns up the road and he came within sight of the castle itself. Or rather four castles, in a mixture of Spanish and Italian styles, dominated by a huge baroque structure sporting twin cupolaed towers. A flock of lesser buildings clustered around like courtiers dancing attendance on a quartet of ancient dowagers. As Vesensky leaned for a moment against the straight, rough, red bole of a spruce tree, he could see through the greenery to his left a section of

Roman colonnade, the marble gleaming like bleached bone in the sun.

San Simeon Castle: William Randolph Hearst's monument to himself, if not precisely to good taste. For centuries this stretch of coastline had been notable only for its rugged desolation and frequented only by the poorest sorts of Indians. Then, along about 1919, workmen had planed the top off an unloved and unlovable lump known as Camp Hill, which its new owner had named, somewhat optimistically, *La Cuesta Encantada*: the Enchanted Hill. From then until the time of Hearst's death, workmen toiled to make the isolated prominence live up to its name. The big baroque castle was built as Hearst's residence, and the other three palaces put up by way of guest accommodations. The whole Hearst had filled with exotic bric-a-brac from all over—paintings, sculptures, columns, the odd sarcophagus, up to and including whole rooms from various epochs of European architecture. As an appropriate setting to this peculiar architectural gem, Hearst had the environs planted with a vast forest of trees from all over the world. At one time the sprawling estate had even included a wellstocked zoo.

It was the sort of thing that communists pointed to when they wanted to abuse the capitalists.

It was also the headquarters of Geoffrey van Damm, former Lieutenant Governor of the State of California, now the great white hope of many radical Americans.

As Vesensky stood there, he could see men through the trees, moving around and in and out of the four great structures and their attendant buildings. Most of them carried automatic weapons. *And now,* Vesensky said to himself, *we face the problem of getting in to see the good Lieutenant Governor without being shot by an overzealous guard.*

CHAPTER
SIX ——————————————

The Honorable Geoff van Damm, ex-Lieutenant Governor of the State of California, rose from behind the sixteenth-century Dutch moneychanger's table he was using for a desk, a look of utter astonishment on his theatrically handsome features. "Ian!" he exclaimed. "Damned good to see you."

Behind van Damm, between a sixteenth-century Venetian miniature landscape on one hand and a thirteenth-century Persian tapestry of mounted lancers hunting gazelles on the other, stood a man Vesensky recognized as van Damm's personal bodyguard, Marlon. A bit over medium height, with close-cropped hair of an indeterminate pale color, a boyish Charlie Brown piepan of a face, and round rimless glasses, Marlon had the well-stuffed, taut-skinned appearance of a recent graduate of one of the armed services' boot camps, where virtual force-feeding of protein and carbohydrates was the order of the day. Forearms crossed over the Greenpeace logo of his T-shirt were thick with bulky muscle. He gave the impression of being of roughly uniform width from armpits to hips.

Under his left armpit a Smith & Wesson .41 Magnum revolver nestled in a shoulder holster. The well-worn walnut grips were outsized custom models by Guy Hogue. Since a major part of politician van Damm's platform was across-the-board gun control, when the former Lieutenant Governor made public appearances, the ever-present Marlon always had on at least a light windbreaker—and no matter if the appearance was taking place in Death Valley in mid-July.

Vesensky gave Marlon a quick grin, which the bodyguard acknowledged with a slight nod.

The two army-jacketed types who'd prodded a spruce-looking Vesensky into the august presence at the point of their AKs exchanged puzzled glances. "We caught this motherfucker skulking around outside, down by the road." It was the man behind Vesensky's left shoulder, a gangly bearded young man with curly blond hair and an apparently unnecessary red headband. "Said he knew you. Thought you might want to talk to him for a bit before we shot him."

Van Damm stared at the two in horror. "Say what? This man's an old friend of mine. An old"—he grinned, suddenly boyish—"*comrade* of mine. I've been expecting him, but I didn't expect to see him so soon."

He stood up off the stool and came around the darkly gleaming wooden table. Geoff van Damm was a compact man in his late thirties, a blond and sunbrowned man whose resemblance to actor Robert Redford had often been remarked upon, not to say actively traded upon. He wore a red plaid Pendleton shirt, Levi's, good quality hiking boots. All in all, he looked as if he should have been sitting on a rock beside a high mountain stream somewhere, with a copy of the shooting script in one hand and a cup of coffee in the other, chewing the fat with the key grips in between scenes.

As a matter of fact you might have been able to see van Damm in just such surroundings a year or two before, during his unsuccessful run for the Senate in the last elections. Public disenchantment with ever-increasing taxes had lowered what his public relations analysts had termed the market viability of his economic redistribution schemes, so he'd been pitching heavily for the environmental vote instead. And in fact, he had spent some time chatting with the key grips—though he hadn't much enjoyed the experience; they were all so limited in their outlook, and politically uneducated.

He put an arm around Vesensky's shoulders and gave him a brotherly hug. Also like Robert Redford, van Damm was not exactly on the tall side, so he had to reach up a ways to do it. "Great to see you, Ian, I just can't tell you how glad I am. You're needed here. This is really the golden opportunity for the revolution."

The two guards were gaping in openmouthed astonishment, the muzzle brakes of their AKs wandering in all directions and endangering several zillion dollars' worth of arcane knick-knacks. Van Damm noticed them out of the corner of his eye and rounded on them. "I told you he's with me, damn it. Now get the fuck out of here!"

They fled. Van Damm steered Vesensky to an ornate Louis Quatorze chair embroidered with real silver thread. "Sit yourself down, make yourself at home. Can I get you something to drink?"

Vesensky's stomach muttered judiciously. "I think I'd rather have something to eat, if you could spare it." The Soviet agent's chameleon English had changed colors again, to a muted British accent that was part of his Ian Victor persona.

Van Damm sat down behind his moneychanger's table. "Food? Sure." He reached out a hand, which Vesensky noted was still immaculately manicured and picked up the handset of an antique phone on the desk. Vesensky felt a thrill of *déjà vu*. The telephone was gold-plated, identical to the one that commonly sat on one corner of Yevgeny Maximov's vast desk in the Bernese uplands of Switzerland. Van Damm propped the handset between shoulder and ear and twitched the dial a couple of times. He raised his eyebrows at Vesensky. "Still a vegetarian?" Vesensky nodded.

After a brief consultation with whoever was at the other end of the telephone, van Damm ordered up an assortment of stir-fried vegetables and a pot of herbal tea for his visitor. He replaced the ornate receiver in its golden cradle and sat back, shaking a shock of blond hair from his eyes and grinning. "The ultimate monument to capitalist decadence," he said, waving a hand at the gaudy opulence surrounding them. "What a magnificent irony, eh? To orchestrate the rooting-out of the last vestiges of capitalist corruption from right here in the belly of the beast. The poetic justice of it all aside, this is an ideal headquarters. It's got the facilities to house an army. Our technicians are already upgrading the communications system the State Parks people had set up here before we booted them out. And we've got truckloads of expropriated supplies—food, fuel, medicine, ammunition—coming in here every day. Where you're standing now is going to be the nerve center of the new California." Van Damm laced his fingers behind his head and showed flawless teeth in a grin. "And of the new America, if I've got anything to say about it."

Vesensky made a thoughtful mouth and nodded. "Very impressive."

"That's just the beginning," van Damm said. "We've got this place set up as a clearinghouse for liberation organizations from all over this state. We've got the Joaquin Murieta Brigade, the San Fernando Liberation Front, the Avengers of Cinque and the Sons of Hayduke, and several formations of the People's Liberation Army of California. We've got some representatives from the People's Republic of the Bear that's been set up down south around L.A.—I'm afraid we're going to have to purge them; they're riddled with revisionist elements. As an extra added bonus, we've even got a baker's dozen from the Japanese Red Army. They were on their way to blow up the Indonesian Embassy in Ottawa. We had them stashed in safe houses when the balloon went up."

Van Damm looked to Vesensky like a young boy looking for paternal approval. Vesensky let himself smile and nod approvingly, but he raised an eyebrow at the mention of the latter group. The Japanese Red Army was crazy. Its members combined *samurai* ferocity with a blazing revolutionary fervor. In 1972, during the cataclysmic climax of *Rengo Sekigun*'s first heyday, a group of JRA stalwarts, forted up under police siege in a resort, had put half of their own number to death for various heresies. Now, more than twenty years later, the Japanese Red Army still survived. It had gone through several generations of devotees, each more rabid than the last. The current crop was single-mindedly homicidal and genuinely whacky. But, like mercury, they could be surpassing useful if handled with the proper care.

"Yeah," van Damm said, "it's going to be one hell of a job

keeping all of these elements in line. And you're just the man to do it."

"Thanks," Vesensky returned with a sardonic smile. The task he was being offered—the task, in fact, that Maximov had sent him here to take on—was like a combination of slaying the Hydra and teaching the snakes on Medusa's head to sing in harmony. Vesensky felt a warm thrill of anticipation begin to burn within his belly. He was a man who only felt alive when confronted by a genuine challenge.

Van Damm regarded the new arrival fondly. "Ian Victor, my man." He smiled the smile of those who are in on a secret. He knew full well that Ian Victor was the cover name for a Soviet espionage agent. He did not, however, appreciate the full extent of the joke: Department V—for Victor—was the other name for the Executive Action Department of the KGB's First Chief Directorate. This was the outfit devoted to "wet affairs" such as kidnapping, sabotage, and assassination, in which Vesensky had been the rising young star before the One-Day War. "So tell me, my man, what have you been up to since I saw you?"

Vesensky settled in to tell him the story. His high-priority flight from Europe, his meeting with the Air-Landing Brigade in Alaska, his subsequent puddle-jumping journey down the West Coast of Canada and America in the little seaplane. One thing that Vesensky most carefully did *not* tell van Damm was that he no longer served the interests of the Union of Soviet Socialist Republics. Because, in his own way, and according to his own lights, the former Lieutenant Governor was a True Believer.

As a student at the University of California, Berkeley, Geoffrey van Damm had been a lone voice of late sixties-style radicalism crying in the wilderness seventies of student apathy. Like many of the New Left's leaders, van Damm came from old money: in the late 1890s Great-Great-Grandfather van Damm bought several thousand acres in the desert in the southern half of the state. Much of it was later known as L.A.

As befitted a young man of his aristocratic background, van Damm did not deign to follow the tramplings of the herd, even within the Movement itself. Like Tom Hayden before him, van Damm had dared to espouse a doctrine unpopular even on the Left: an old-fashioned, dyed-in-the-wool, GPU Stalinism. The very boldness of the approach had won young van Damm a good portion of recognition from the media, if not among his fellow students. And like Hayden before him, van Damm had acquired more polish, more sophistication as the years had gone by. Maturity had softened the rough edges of his rhetoric; he had also learned that he would win a far greater hearing among those who might actually offer sympathy to his cause if he wore a three-piece suit than a torn sweatshirt, dungarees, and tennis shoes.

In time, the talk of Stalin and armed propaganda had ceased. Geoff van Damm had flowed with surprising celerity into the Hollywood pool-party and Democratic hundred-dollar-a-plate dinner circuit. Now he preached a blend of economic redistribution, mistrust of corporations, and blow-up-the-oil-wells bullshit that was practically middle of the road by California standards. And as more and more Americans began to tire of their government's almost reflexive involvement in any military confrontation anywhere in the world, a lot of the old New Left's strayed sheep had begun coming back to the fold, joined by increasing numbers of young people who weren't particularly happy about being drafted to have their asses shot off to preserve another dictatorship. The self-appointed shepherd of this flock was Geoff van Damm. He'd won enough influence to have become lieutenant governor as a participant in a Democratic coalition deal a few years before and while his last run at the Senate had been unsuccessful, the pundits gave him a better than fifty-fifty chance at taking the prize the next time.

Vesensky wound up his tale. Van Damm was just laughing his robust laugh at Vesensky's discomfiture of the men who had ambushed the seaplane when the telephone rang. Still chuckling and red-faced under his tan, van Damm picked it up, stuck it to his ear, and said, "The Chairman here."

His expression rapidly set into brow-furrowing disapproval. "He's *what?*" He demanded. "Hang onto the stupid fucker. I'll be right there."

He jumped to his feet. His whole wiry body trembled like an agitated fox terrier. "Come with me," he snapped. "There's trouble in the poolroom." He led the way along corridors that appeared to have been decorated by painters on acid, with Marlon trotting silently at his heels, and Vesensky bringing up the rear.

Van Damm led them down to the ground floor of the main house, Hearst's *Casa Grande*. Vesensky heard angry voices ahead and then they burst out into the poolroom. One of William Randolph Hearst's most celebrated excesses, and a great favorite of the tourists who had flocked to San Simeon castle since it had been made into a state park, the indoor pool was a nine-and-a-half-by-almost-twenty-five-meter extravaganza of Venetian tile and carved marble ladders. Roman marble statues, some suffering in stoic silence the loss of a limb or two, kept watch over a vast room with gold-worked blue walls, illuminated both by sunlight streaming through tall arched windows and a number of globed electric lights perched on pedestals. Vesensky noted with interest that van Damm thought it worthwhile to run the generator, among other things, to keep this area lit. The whole montage looked like something a Renaissance Prince might have fabricated to wash his whores in.

A number of freedom fighters, male and female alike, swam naked in the pool. Vesensky had no time to admire the male swimmers' trim young bodies, however; a few meters from the entrance several fully dressed young men were wrestling with another, a stocky, bearded, and bleary-eyed Chicano in a black beret. "Shit," Vesensky heard van Damm mutter. "Those fucking Murieta Brigadiers again. We get nothing but trouble from them."

A skinny, clean-shaven young black man in black pullover and black jeans approached van Damm. "The dude's gone stone crazy," he said aggrievedly. "Fucker says he's going to pee in the pool."

"It's a political statement!" the bearded man shouted, struggling to free himself from the men who held his arms. "I want to show my contempt for this decadent palace the Anglos built on the land they stole from my forefathers."

"But we're *swimming* in it," protested a young Hispanic woman with her elbows propped on the pool's tile side, her long, wet, black hair hanging lankly down her bare back and billowing out like a cloud of squid's ink in the water behind her.

"Manuel," van Damm said with unnatural deliberation. "You know the standing orders. This facility is dedicated to brave fighters in the struggle for liberation as a recreation and relaxation area."

"But it's all imperialist *waste*, man. I gotta do something, you know, strike a blow for the oppressed—"

Van Damm scowled dangerously. "So you feel you have a statement to make *in spite* of orders, Manuel?"

The Murieta Brigadier nodded enthusiastically. "It's what the revolution's all about, man. The freedom to express, you know, spontaneous outbursts of revolutionary sentiment." His dark eyes flashed in transports of self-dramatization.

Tan fingers stroking his chin, van Damm nodded. "Very well, then. You can do whatever you feel moved to do by your, ah, revolutionary conscience." He looked to the men restraining Manuel. "Let him go."

Manuel got his penis out of his cammie pants. As he steaded it with one hand, van Damm looked sideways and caught Marlon's eye. Standing at his master's side at the entrance to the poolroom, the bodyguard nodded once.

He slid his booted feet apart, flexed the knees slightly. His right hand moved like a striking rattler, snatching the .41 from its holster and snapping it into a police-academy isosceles firing stance. From the corner of one eye, Manuel caught the flicker of movement. He glanced around and up, and his eyes grew very wide.

Pumpkin-sized balloons of orange flame flashed twice from the stubby muzzle of the revolver. The poolroom filled with shattering noise. Arms flailing helplessly, Manuel was flung back against a statue of Venus.

From the shelter of the goddess's marble arms, Manuel stared in horror at Marlon. His pecker ejaculated joylessly down the front of his green and tan cammie pants in the body-wrenching spasm of a clean heart shot. A whimper, thin and childish, escaped his throat. Manuel slid down to the floor and died, leaving a shocking scarlet smear down the immaculately white breasts and belly and thighs of the Goddess of Love.

"The first requisite of an army of liberation is discipline," van Damm announced, as the last echoes of the gunshot reverberated through the cavernous room. Ears ringing, faces blank, his soldiers, male and female, stared at him without speaking.

He threw one arm around Vesensky's shoulder again. "Enough of this. It's been a long time since there was anything in the wine cellars here, but we expropriated some good stuff from some rich pigs' down in San Luis Obispo." He grinned and bobbed his head at his boon companion Ian Victor. "Let's go and raise a few toasts to the new day dawning in California."

He steered Vesensky from the room, while Marlon, his pistol back in its holster, padded quietly behind. Behind them, blood congealed slowly on cool marble.

CHAPTER
SEVEN ─────────────

"So what can you tell us about these bozos of General Edwards's?" Billy McKay asked. Dr. Mahalaby and the four Guardians had gathered in his crowded, cluttered office. Given New Eden's emphasis on high technology, McKay had expected the doctor's office to be impressive. Instead it consisted of an ancient, green-painted metal desk buried under sheaves of paper, seed and seedling specimens in plastic bags, soil sample kits, and bound notebooks. Inevitably, half-covered in the clutter sat a compact desktop model computer, with an old-fashioned CRT screen, and a detached keyboard sitting negligently atop it.

Also crammed into the room with Mahalaby and the four Guardians were a compact young man with curly dark hair and blue eyes seeming to glow from his deeply tanned face, and the willowy blond woman. Because of the way she had waited on them earlier in the commissary, McKay and Sloan were startled to discover that she was Mahalaby's personal aide and *de facto* second in command of New Eden. For Sloan, that had come as something of a jolt, until he realized that *everybody* deferred to the doctor, fussed over him, waited on him; Susan Spinelli's behavior toward Mahalaby did not reflect any degraded condition of women in the commune, but instead the near-adoration with which its inhabitants regarded their leader. More old-fashioned, McKay thought the arrangement perfectly natural from the very outset, and didn't bother himself about it.

McKay crossed his arms across his chest and frowned. "Now let me get this straight," he said. "These fools claim they're acting in the name of the United States Government. That's nice. Only trouble is, *we're* representatives of the government. Haven't these ass—ah, clowns been listening to the radio the last few months?"

Once securely ensconced in the Heartland complex in Iowa, President Jeffrey MacGregor had made a number of broadcasts to the country at large, assuring citizens that their government was still intact, and reminding them of their common duty to work together for a rapid recovery of America. As far as McKay could see, it had not made one damned bit of difference; he couldn't remember having talked with anyone who'd actually listened to the broadcasts. But he was just a grunt. When he was ordered to saddle up and go, he saddled up and went, and that was all there was to it.

The sturdy, tan young man, who wore blue jeans and a black-and-red striped soccer shirt instead of the coveralls that were New Eden's normal costume, grinned. "I don't know if they recognize the authority of this President MacGregor," he said. Middle Eastern hand McKay's sharp ears detected a trace of the soft roundness of an Israeli accent. "General Edwards is an important figure in the California Free Militia."

"What the hell is that?" McKay demanded.

Casey Wilson was shaking his head. "Bummer," he said.

"I understand they're some kind of right-wing paramilitary organization." Sam Sloan turned his head and arched an eyebrow at the young man. "Somehow I didn't think you folks here at New Eden paid so much attention to mundane political affairs."

The young man's grin widened, white against the darkness of his face. "I don't know if I would call General Edwards's activities *mundane.*"

Mahalaby threw up his hands. "But it is impossible *not* to

be aware of the General's activities. He himself is—how you say?—indisposed, an invalid. But his people are always over here pestering us with talk of the communist menace." McKay noted how, in times of excitement, Dr. Mahalaby's speech took on the accents and intonations of an educated Lebanese who had absorbed both English and French as second languages. He wondered idly how such an obvious *Sabra* as the young man, who'd been introduced as Ari Lavotsky, had wound up not only associated with but subordinate to a Lebanese. Most of the Lebanese he'd encountered who had any use for the Israelis at all were of the same stripe as he took this General Edwards to be. And he'd met few if any Israelis who'd take kindly to the notion of taking orders from an Arab.

"The arrogance of those men." Susan Spinelli's voice was a husky contralto. "To think they can march in here with their guns and order us around."

Mahalaby shrugged like a mountain interested in losing a few alpinists. "But what is to be done? We are peaceful here."

Privately, McKay thought it was something more than arrogance that impelled a couple of the General's boys, assault rifles slung across their backs—and since the ownership of even semiautomatic assault-style weapons had been outlawed a couple of years ago, he bet they had the capacity for full auto fire—to march in here and boldly assert ownership over a stray armored fighting vehicle. Sheer stupidity was more like it.

Unless . . . He gave Tom Rogers a quick glance. The ex-Green Beret's steel gray eyes met his, and Rogers frowned briefly. McKay guessed he was thinking the same thing he was. For a couple of yahoos armed with .223-caliber small arms to go poking at an armored monster that, in the normal course of events, could turn their valley into a smoking ruin, and its defenders into dog meat, was extreme even by the exacting standards of California nuttiness. Unless they knew their General possessed the means of cancelling the advantages the V-450's firepower and armored hide gave it. Anti-tank weapons were even more illegal than auto-weapons, but McKay somehow doubted this General Edwards would lose much sleep over that.

He also doubted the boys on watch at the bridge would be quite so easy to buffalo next time.

"So what do we do about it, McKay?" Sloan asked. McKay guessed the former Naval officer had missed the implications of General Edwards's boldness. "Just send them on their way, and ignore the whole thing?"

"Like, if this General Edwards is really a wheel with the Militia, he might come down pretty hard on these people here if we pissed him off," Casey Wilson said.

"Then we'll clean their goddam clocks for them." Taking the offensive with AT weapons was a *lot* harder than defending with them. And McKay was sure his Guardians could deal with any raggedy-assed self-appointed commandos General Edwards had managed to scrape together.

Tom Rogers frowned again, more deeply this time. "We won't always be here, Billy," he said, in his gentle, vaguely Southern-inflected voice.

That brought McKay up short. Rogers was as much a past master of the arts of combat as he was. He didn't speak very often, but when he did, it made sense. McKay slouched lower in the gray auditorium chair and glowered at Mahalaby's desk. "Yeah, you're right. We're gonna have to do something about this general, and just cruising on in there in Mobile One is really going to leave our asses flapping in the breeze if they've got any LAW's. Hell, who knows what kind of ordnance those nuts may have stashed away?"

Mahalaby was gazing down at his desk like a doleful circus bear. "We have no wish for disputes with our neighbors. But more than this, we cannot afford them."

"Yeah, don't worry, Doc. We'll settle this," McKay said, with a self-confidence he didn't exactly feel. He turned to Lavotsky. From the way the young man moved, the way he held himself, McKay guessed he'd had military training—and if he'd grown to adulthood in Israel, that was a foregone conclusion anyway. He gathered the young man was New Eden's equivalent of a security officer. And for all the New Edenites' prostestations of non-violence, and the community's seeming lack of firearms, McKay had a feeling Lavotsky's role wasn't just nominal.

"So what sort of security arrangements does this general have?" he asked.

"Elk Creek valley is enclosed by chain-link fences topped with barbed wire. The gate where it opens into Maldita Valley is a normal steel one, not reinforced."

"Yeah, we noticed that driving in." Sam Sloan's face was creased in puzzlement. "When we went by, it looked as if there was just one guy guarding it." He shook his head. "Doesn't seem like they could withstand much of an assault."

"They don't have to," Ari Lavotsky said. "They're meant to handle individual stragglers. They don't like to show off the real strength of their defenses, possibly for our benefit. But if any large group manages to push its way into the valley—and a number did, back in the days just after the war—the guards alert the General's ranch by walkie-talkie, and they mobilize a fairly heavily armed force in response."

"Murderers." Spinelli's lips were a thin line of disapproval. "They turn the needy away, or gun them down like dogs if they push their way past the bullies at the bridge. Most of them are refugees, just desperate people searching for shelter and food."

Mahalaby reached out a hairy hand to where his aide stood beside his desk and gripped one of her white clenched fists. "Their methods are too abrupt, too brutal," he said. "But much as we hate to we must admit the bitter truth. The General's people do us a service. If all those poor, starving refugees were permitted in, they would swamp us. In attempting to ease their need, we would have no time for our greater task of attempting to help those masses who are not within convenient walking distance of our little valley." His voice was thick with sadness.

"So what about these stragglers?" McKay asked.

Lavotsky smiled thinly. "Sometimes, one or two slip by, usually at night. The man on duty at the gate questions them. Occasionally, if they have some contact with the people the General has gathered around him, they are permitted inside. More usually they're turned away."

"What happens if they don't want to be sent away?" Sam Sloan asked.

Lavotsky shrugged. "There is a single gunshot. And the unfortunate would-be entrant does in fact gain entry—feet first."

While he was speaking, Casey Wilson, as usual slouched at random in a chair by the wall beneath a sepia-tone poster depicting the life cycle of a tree, suddenly became tense, watchful. Looking narrowly at Lavotsky, he said, "Sam, you're a science fiction reader too. Is this, like, starting to sound, you know, familiar?"

Sloan rubbed his jaw. "Wait a minute. You're right. I remember something a lot like this. Let's see—"

"*Lucifer's Hammer.*"

Sloan snapped his fingers. "That's it!" Suddenly he smiled, very, very broadly. Looking at him, McKay was reminded of the comic books he'd read as a kid, where if a character had a bright idea a light bulb would appear over his head.

"Billy," Sloan said, "I think I've got an idea. . . ."

Ignoring the lopsided little kiosk with the corrugated tin roof, which General Edwards had reluctantly ordered built to offer the gate guards a modicum of protection from the torrential rains that had followed the One-Day War, Monitor Lewis strutted back and forth across the dirt road that led into the valley, just inside the steel gate. He moved with a curious swagger, legs somewhat bowed, hips swinging, chest thrust out like a pouter pigeon's. An observer might have concluded that either he was pretending he was a cowboy or he had an itchy rectum, and didn't want to go grabbing at his ass out here in front of God and everybody.

In fact, he was rehearsing for greatness.

General Edwards had laid it all out for them. After he had consolidated his control on the broad shallow valley that stuck out like the limb of a Y from Maldita Creek, General Edwards had called his soldiers together, and told them that they would provide the core of a new America, one which trusted in God and force of arms. It was his destiny to restore America to greatness. Even the least of his loyal followers would know wealth and a greatness beyond imagining.

Monitor Lewis, in fact, came close to being the very least of General Edwards's faithful. At a casual glance he appeared to be a fat boy. Yet the body encased by his faded yellow-tan twill shirt with the military-looking shoulder tabs, dusty olive drab corduroy jeans, and Army surplus combat boots, was as hard and spare as a true Californian addiction to jogging and aerobic exercise could make it. No, it was only Monitor Lewis's *face* that was fat. He had plump cheeks, squinty water-blue eyes, thin washed-out brown hair swept back on his head, and funny prominent lips, like the ones on those kissing fish.

Before the One-Day War, Lewis had been a mathematics and physical education instructor at a private school in Sacramento, with a degree in accounting from USC and no time, somehow, for going out with women. Not that there was anything, well, *peculiar* about him. Not him. Monitor Lewis thought that gays should be rounded up and shot—preferably after torture. It was just that, somehow, he never saw much need for women.

He thought of his earlier days as a prep school instructor as his "civilian" life. In fact his only approach to "military" experience—and the predominance of his social life, in the days before the War—had been his participation in General Manton V. Edwards's California Free Militia. His zeal in physical fitness had enabled him to rise to the exalted position of section leader. His administrative skill, meantime, had caused Edwards to tap him to be the organization's secretary.

Unfortunately, even his new title of Provost Marshal for the Valley did not exempt him from having to take a go as gate guard. Sometimes, at the back of his mind, he wondered if the others of Edwards's inner circle—Waller and Halpern and the rest—actually took him seriously. None of *them* had to pull sentry duty.

Still, duty as gate guard wasn't real onerous. You were, after all, mainly there for show. You had a walkie-talkie at your belt to refer back to the Big House in case anyone tried to get in. And if someone pressed the issue . . . About a hundred and fifty meters away, in a dugout concealed in brush on the military crest of the ridgeline that separated Edwards's Valley from the degenerate freaks of New Eden, there was a marksman-rated sharpshooter armed with a flat-shooting, hard-hitting bolt-action .243 built around a Sako action and equipped with a six-power Zeiss scope, that could just about dot the *i* on the NO TRESPASSING sign tacked up next to the gate.

Anybody trying to force his way into General Edwards's private paradise would never hear the shot that killed him.

So basically all Lewis had to do was to keep an eye out for unknown parties approaching the gate. Since there wasn't much good cover between the tall grass along the Maldita down below and the pines that covered the ridges, that wasn't a particularly difficult task. It left Lewis with lots of time and energy for rehearsal.

"I'll show you bastards some discipline," he muttered under his breath. "When I get finished with you, you won't know whether to puke or go blind!" He spoke in a curious manner, jaw clenched, words jetting out through his teeth like squirts of venom from a spitting cobra. It wasn't his normal mode of talking. As a very young boy, his daddy had taken him to see the movie *Patton*, starring George C. Scott. It had left its mark. Now, whenever he envisioned himself addressing his troops as a *gauleiter* in Edwards's New America, he saw himself as George C. Scott, resplendent in mirror-polished helmet, medal-bedizened green jacket, jodhpurs, and riding boots. What he actually looked like was the evil Nazi from *Raiders of the Lost Ark*. But you couldn't tell him that.

Movement tickled his peripheral vision. He stopped in mid-strut, his head snapping around. Rounding the end of the ridge between the Valley and New Eden were three riders on horseback.

Fingers trembling in excitement, he fumbled the microphone for his walkie-talkie away from its clip on the main unit's holster. "Argus to Zeus," he said, whispering as if the riders were already looming over him. "Three riders approaching from Tartarus." His heart fluttered in the base of his throat. It had been weeks since any outsiders had come to the gate while he was on watch. Perhaps—perhaps he would get to raise his left hand, palm out, to his left ear: the sentence of death.

Who the hell could be coming to visit us from that nest of perverts? he wondered. Squinting into the hot late-afternoon sunlight, he made out two tall male forms, one bulky, one slimmer. They didn't belong to anybody he recognized. The same couldn't be said for the third rider. The slim, willowy form, the long blond hair, almost white in the sunlight, blowing free in the stiff breeze—that could only belong to Susan Spinelli, Mahalaby's "personal secretary." Lewis's gut tightened. He wasn't fooled for a moment, and the thought of that slim, pale body clasped against the obscene hairy bulk of that Wog doctor always made his blood boil.

They drew closer, and he stiffened. With the light at their backs, he'd been unable at first to tell how the two male riders were dressed. Now he saw that both of them wore some kind of steel gray fatigue uniforms, totally unfamiliar to him, but obviously military in cut. Neither uniform displayed badges of rank or unit insignia. Each man had on a beret of a gray so dark as to be almost black, with a unit flash displayed on it. Both men wore web gear belts, and both carried sidearms—the lean one with the dark hair spilling out from under his cloth cap a chromed Colt Python .357 Magnum in a shoulder rig, the man with the cigar, the linebacker's build, and the blond hair cropped almost to white sidewalls, a Colt Government .45 in an open holster at his right hip. *I hope George's alert up in his little nest,* he thought. Though none of the riders was making any kind of threatening display, nor doing anything but riding up to the gate at a brisk walk, he acutely felt the lack of any kind of weapon of his own.

"Afternoon," sang out the dark-haired man, as they came within about fifteen meters of the gate. "My name's Sam Sloan, and this is Billy McKay. Ms. Spinelli you know." He nodded at the blond woman with a smile, which was returned in a way that made Lewis feel queasy inside. "McKay and I are with a special team on a mission from the President himself. We drove in with that armored car earlier in the afternoon."

He leaned forward, crossing his forearms over the wide flat horn of the Mexican-style saddle and grinned engagingly. "Now, as I understand it, a couple of your boys wandered into New Eden this afternoon, claiming they were commandeering our vehicle in the name of the United States Government. Isn't that the strangest thing?" He nodded to his partner. "Our boss, here, thought we'd mosey on over and ask General Edwards about it."

Lewis opened his mouth, shut it again with an audible click. His Adam's apple rose up and dropped quickly away in a nervous swallow. "Ah, I'll have to, ah, call in about that—"

"Take your time," Sam Sloan said. "Just don't take too much. Billy McKay's not what you'd call a patient sort of guy." The man with McKay stenciled over his left breast pocket glowered at Lewis from beneath almost invisibly pale eyebrows.

Hurriedly, Lewis muttered into his mike. "They say I can take you up, but you'll have to be disarmed first." Actually, what the General himself, summoned to the radio for this development, had said was that the outsiders should be brought up to the big house under guard. Lewis was to get them to disarm, and then a squad would come down in a car to take them prisoner.

"Fuck that," McKay growled around the stub of his cigar. "And if your frigging General has any bright ideas about sending a bunch of squaddies down to take us, tell him to think the hell again."

Monitor Lewis flushed deeply. "I won't listen to you accuse the General of bad faith—"

McKay looked to Sloan. "That's what I thought. They're trying to screw us." McKay swung his heavy head back toward Lewis. "Call off the goons."

"Things will go so much more smoothly," Sam Sloan said, "if we don't have to do this with a pistol barrel stuck in your ear."

Blinking rapidly, Lewis said, "Ms. Spinelli, you're a neighbor! You can't let them talk to me like this."

"I'm a nonviolent person," Susan Spinelli said in her throaty contralto. "But it is kind of pleasing to see you get a dose of the medicine you people are so liberal about doling out."

This was clearly getting out of hand. It was time to let the unseen George thin the opposition by one. Then the survivor would be in the proper frame of mind to talk to Mick Waller and his bravos. Deliberately, so as not to alarm his intended victims, Monitor Lewis raised his left hand to his left ear.

Deafening silence ensued.

After a moment, Lewis became aware that the three on horseback were grinning at him. He cast his eyes sidelong at his hand. Yes, it was there all right, right next to his ear. Yet there had been no sudden gunshot, no gray-uniformed intruder sprawling in the dust with a little blue-black hole in one temple and his eyes popped out from a sudden catastrophic overpressure inside the cranium. Tentatively he wagged his fingers. Still, nothing happened.

Billy McKay offered him a smile. "If you're waiting for your buddy with the deer rifle to lend you a hand," he said cheerily, "forget it. He's indisposed at the moment."

Lewis's hand wilted like a blighted fern. "Um," he said.

"Perhaps you're still thinking of having your friends take us prisoner when they arrive," Sam Sloan remarked. "I see you have a little notebook, there, in your left breast pocket. Would you do me a favor? Take it out, hold it between thumb and forefinger up in the air away from your body. *Well* away from your body."

In stunned silence, Monitor Lewis obeyed. When his arm was at full extension and the notebook aways above his head, McKay said one word. "Casey."

A sudden *crack!* split the air. Impact almost tore the little notebook from Lewis's fingertips. He brought his arm down, and stared in dawning horror at the neat little hole, a third of an inch across, that had been punched through it from front to back. His paramilitary playacting had taught him enough to know that what he'd heard was the supersonic crack of a bullet's passage. He'd never heard the report of the weapon itself. That meant that, in addition to taking out the Valley's hidden sniper, these two intruders in gray uniforms had brought along one of their own. One possessed of a superbly accurate rifle, with a suppressor to kill the sound of the muzzle blast. Monitor Lewis felt very, very sick.

Sam Sloan sat up straight in the saddle and grinned immensely. "Take us to your leader," he said.

CHAPTER
EIGHT ——————————————

After a hurried consultation with the Big House via walkie-talkie, a nervous Monitor Lewis led the three up the valley to meet with the General himself. Lewis walked, the others rode. According to the plan that had materialized when Ari Lavotsky confirmed that the sniper was stationed on the ridge between the two valleys, Tom Rogers had taken the marksman out and radioed the all-clear to Sloan and McKay before they even approached the gate to Edwards's Valley. Leaving George securely trussed, Rogers had nipped off back to New Eden to collect Mobile One. Casey continued to watch from the ridge and keep in touch with the two Guardians. If anything went amiss he'd relay word back to the ex-Green Beret, then do what he could to keep the General's boys occupied while the V-450 rumbled to the rescue.

Susan Spinelli had given them a capsule version of the Valley's history. The valley along Elk Creek was much larger than that occupied by New Eden, six klicks long, widening up to a klick at midpoint. Prior to the war, it had been occupied by three reasonably large ranches, a handful of smaller holdings, and the General's domain at the very head of the valley.

Even as thermonuclear destruction was raining down on the
state and the country, General Edwards had moved to consoli-
date his hold on the valley. He had hurriedly concluded an
agreement with one of the major landholders, dispatched
squads of his militia to deal with the other two. There had
been a certain amount of shooting, and when the smoke
cleared, Edwards was master of the Valley.

The small landowners and their families found themselves
reduced to little more than serfs. Gangs of them, under the
guns of the General's men, or goons who worked for his
"allies" the Donner family, had erected the barbed-wire fence
that sealed off the Valley. Meanwhile, the General and the
Donners had set guards down by the old steel bridge at the
foot of the major valley, and begun denying access to outsiders—without, of course, consulting the other residents of
the Maldita watershed. With a couple hundred generally
rebellious souls to keep in line, Edwards's people hadn't
bothered New Eden—yet. "But we figure it's only a matter of
time," Susan Spinelli had concluded, tight-lipped.

Judging from what the Guardians saw on the ride up to Edwards's house, she was right. The small landholders were now
being graciously allowed to work in their "own" fields, but to
McKay's city dweller's eye the cultivated areas looked sorely
neglected. The work parties they passed seemed dispirited,
doing as little as they could without invoking the wrath of the
rifle and shotgun-toting overseers who accompanied them.

As the land sloped gently up, they passed a number of new-
looking sheds, built by two-by-fours, tar paper, and black
plastic. "Workers' dormitories," Monitor Lewis explained,
becoming voluble as his nervousness slacked off a bit. "Right
after the war, we opened our arms to qualified applicants for
entry. We wanted to secure a nucleus of skilled personnel to
help us with our task of reconstruction."

"In a word, slaves," Sam Sloan said. Lewis's face clamped
shut. Unspeaking, he led them up to the sprawling whitewashed adobe ranch houses with the red pitched roofs that
constituted General Edwards's castle.

"Please be seated, gentlemen—Ms. Spinelli." Major General Manton V. Edwards, USAF (Ret.) gestured toward sev-

eral leather-covered chairs set before the bookcases that lined the walls of his study. "Please excuse me if I don't stand. It's because I can't. Paralyzed from the waist down. Riding accident."

McKay and Sloan exchanged glances. "We're inside," McKay subvocalized. The tiny mike taped almost invisibly to his larynx picked up the words without the need to speak them aloud. "They've brought us in to see the big man himself."

"Roger, Billy." Casey Wilson's voice came through the bone conduction phone behind his ear. "Tom's already back at Mobile One. You need a pickup, like, just holler."

After the little demonstration the Guardians had arranged for his benefit, Monitor Lewis had proven quite cooperative. He'd called the Big House on his walkie-talkie, informed the General that he was bringing the visitors up—and that no armed escort would be necessary. Rather to his surprise, the General hadn't demurred.

Of course, the canny General Edwards knew instantly from the tone of the gate guard's voice that something was seriously amiss. No doubt the security arrangements his aide Fred Halpern had put together had finally broken down. Well, nothing was shaken. No security system was invulnerable. The thing to do now was to play along with the outsiders, try to find out just how they'd finessed the valley's security arrangements.

The three moved to the chairs. McKay and Sloan stood by until Susan Spinelli seated herself in the chair to the right. McKay took the center chair, and Sloan took the one on the left. The General leaned thick forearms on his broad oak desk and regarded his visitors. He had a massive square head, with prominent wide cheekbones, Roman nose, a pointed, curiously foxy chin. His eyes were dark and intense, his hair dark brown and cut short, streaked with white on the sides. He wore the full dress uniform of an Air Force General. His left breast was a colorful blaze of campaign ribbons and decorations. Had he stood, the Guardians had the impression he would have been somewhat above medium height. But, as he had said, he couldn't. They knew from the advance briefing they'd got from Lavotsky and Spinelli back in New Eden that he'd been paralyzed for several years as the result of a horseback riding incident. It had, in fact, probably been the only thing that prevented his launching into a career in politics after his outspoken view led to his premature retirement from the USAF. His disability lay solely in his legs, however; it did not weaken the grip of iron with which he controlled his valley.

"Let me congratulate you gentlemen on the way you buffaloed your way in here. System's been foolproof so far. But no defense is perfect. Isn't that right, Fred?"

The sleek, middle-sized man who stood behind the General's left shoulder nodded quickly. "Yes, General, that's perfectly correct." His voice had the easy sinuousness of a seal sliding through water, and that was what he resembled—an immaculately groomed seal, with slicked-back brown hair and liquid brown eyes, tricked out in a chambray work shirt, blue jeans, and hiking boots, whose immaculate appearance made it abundantly clear that their owner never actually had to stoop to manual labor. McKay wondered how seriously the General had had to threaten him to get him out of a three-piece suit; he just looked the type.

The General waved a square hand at the seal. "Fred here set the system up in the first place. Got it out of some sort of sci-fi novel. By the way, this is Fred Halpern. He handles intelligence and internal security for us. And over here"—he gestured to the man who stood at his right—"we have Captain Mick Waller. He handles security of a more concrete nature."

"Captain" Waller was a tall, well-muscled man who looked to be in his late twenties. He wore black-and-green cammie pants tucked into black jungle boots, and a cammie blouse in the same pattern. It was unbuttoned to the navel, revealing a green T-shirt with white lettering surrounding a Special Forces shield underneath. McKay couldn't see all the lettering, but enough to recognize the slogan, "Kill 'em all—let God sort 'em out." McKay guessed he'd gotten the T-shirt from *Soldier of Fortune* magazine. The rank of captain he'd probably come up with himself.

Waller stood with his hands behind his back, glowering at the Guardians from beneath a black beret. Like the General, he wore a mustache, though his was considerably shaggier than Edwards's. At his hip rode a .45 in an issue web gear holster.

"Pleased to meet you, gentlemen," Sam Sloan murmured. McKay grunted. He was content to let Sloan do the talking; he was an Annapolis man, and well able to handle that sort of thing. Billy McKay was the ideal man to head the Guardians, but one thing was for sure: He was no damned diplomat. "As we told the gentleman at the gate, General, we're a special team on a mission direct from President MacGregor himself. We—"

"MacGregor?" the General barked.

Sloan nodded. "Have you been monitoring radio broadcasts, General? The President has made a number of broadcasts in the weeks since the war."

Edwards nodded abruptly. "Sure have. But what happened to Lowell?"

"His plane was lost during the Soviet attack, General. Just the way the President tells it on the radio." Sam Sloan's voice had taken on just a hint of folksy exasperation. "We'd like to assure ourselves of your cooperation—"

"Cooperation!" General Edwards's hands slammed down on his desk. "Jeff MacGregor is little better than a communist sympathizer! He's got no backbone. It's time for a strong man to take control in America, to set it back on the right course. Not some jellyfish like MacGregor."

"That's the Commander-in-Chief you're talking about," McKay said, low and ominous.

"Not *my* Commander-in-Chief," General Edwards replied. He leaned forward. "And he shouldn't be yours either."

"According to the line of succession established in the Constitution of the United States of America, Jeffrey MacGregor is President of the United States and Commander-in-Chief of its armed forces." Sam Sloan spoke in tones of frosted steel. "Lieutenant McKay and I personally witnessed his swearing-in."

Edwards dismissed his words with a wave of his hand. "Formalities. The situation demands action. The civilians have dropped the ball. It's time for the military to step in and repair the mess they've made."

He looked from Sloan to McKay, eyes bright. "You're military men. You know what these lard-ass civilians are like.

Join us. From this headquarters''—he waved a hand about the room— "I control a network of top flight cadre, all over the richest state in the Union. With the help of men such as yourselves, we can remake America—hell, we can make America into the glory that God intended her to be."

Diplomacy forgotten, Sam Sloan was grimacing openly at the melodrama. McKay lowered his head and glowered. "Sounds a lot like treason, General." Even Billy McKay was aware that was a B-movie line, but it seemed the only thing to fit the situation.

Mick Waller slapped a hand to his pistol butt. His wrist bore a blue tattoo of a screaming eagle—the symbol of the 101st Airborne Division, popularly known as the "One-O-Worst" to the rest of the armed services. "You can't talk to the General like that!" he shouted, turning red behind his mustache.

McKay leaned back in his chair, crossing his arms across his chest. "Ease off, Jack."

"You gentlemen seem to be forgetting something," Fred Halpern put in with an oily smile. "Haven't you put yourselves rather at our mercy?"

Billy McKay unfolded himself deliberately from his chair. He spread his feet wide, so that he loomed over everybody else in the room like the Jolly Green Giant about to squash a few rebellious elves. "Ain't *you* forgettin' something? We've busted through your defenses twice already today as if they was tissue paper. And we been lettin' you off easy. But if you want to learn what kicking ass really means, just keep talkin' the way you've been."

Fred Halpern's composure dropped away from behind his slick plastic smile like a building collapsing and leaving its façade intact. The General's features where stressed almost to the bursting point, brows knotted, muscles around the slash of mouth standing out in bold relief. Waller, his hand still on the butt of his .45, was leaning forward, ready to move. They knew just the one armored car had driven in past their sentries at the steel bridge—but they had no way of knowing who or what had been contained within the car. There might have been a whole squad lurking along the ridges that separated the

Valley from New Eden, instead of the two men who were really there. McKay decided to crank up the dial on their anxiety another notch or two. "Just think what that armored car could do to this precious valley of yours. You really *sure* you want to hassle with us?"

From what the two Guardians had seen on their ride from the gate at the foot of the valley, a rampage by Mobile One might have been a general improvement. But the General's face had now turned so red it was almost purple, and with a sinking feeling McKay realized he'd pushed the man too far. The damned crippled crackpot was about to call his bluff.

Susan Spinelli leapt to her feet. "Stop!" she yelled. "Hasn't there been enough destruction? Have you forgotten we're all that's left of humanity? Isn't there—isn't there some way we could work *together*, instead of throwing everything away?"

Startled by her vehemence, McKay drew back. Waller looked as if he longed for the order to go for her throat, but the deadly anger was seeping rapidly away from General Edward's face. The Guardians had seen too much horror already in the weeks since the One-Day War to be much swayed by the blond New Edenite's peace-love-everybody-working-together rap, and the General and his boys were just too plain crazy. But her outburst had broken the mood of confrontation that had been building in the office.

"You're . . . right, of course," the General said, forcing the words out like toothpaste from a tube. "Ms. Spinelli, my apologies for our unseemly behavior. Both your—friends— and ourselves are committed to the task of rebuilding America before it's too late. In our passion, we got rather carried away." He settled back in his motorized wheelchair and folded his hands on the desktop before him. "So. Your Ms. Spinelli is right, gentlemen. Let's forget our, ah, tactical differences, and discuss how we might work together."

McKay felt the tension unwind inside him. He knew better than to trust this crazy General anywhere near as far as he could throw him—and in his present mood, he'd gladly undertake to chuck the loony little bastard clear down to the Maldita, wheelchair and all, like an athlete putting the shot —but at least they were talking, rather than barking threats at one another. He nodded and forced a smile. "Well, General," he said, easing himself back into his chair. "We're on a reconnaissance across the country, to try and find the best ways to rebuild America—"

Suppressing a sigh, Sloan eased his hand away from the grips of the Colt Python in his shoulder holster. As Susan Spinelli turned to come back to her chair, she caught his eye and flashed him a wink and a quick grin. It was all he could do to keep his surprise off his face. *She may have believed every word she was saying*, he thought, *but she purely staged that little demonstration, just to keep things from getting out of hand*. He felt a temptation to reach over and pat her thigh in appreciation, stifled it. That would be a patronizing masculine gesture—McKay's style, definitely not his. He settled for giving her a slow grin and a nod in return, then turned back to the negotiations.

"Gentlemen," Fred Halpern said as he settled into the black-leather-and-chrome secretary's chair that he'd wheeled in behind the General's broad desk, "since we'll be working together, and to display our good faith, I think we can provide you with a little information that might serve you on your quest." He crossed his hands on the blotter and smiled moistly at them, as if feeling the mantle of leadership of the Valley descending on his round shoulders. Sam Sloan had the fleeting sensation that the former P.R. man was indulging himself in a foretaste of what he felt the future had in store for him.

From outside came the sound of hammering, as a work gang put together a greenhouse next to the Big House. "We're all ears," murmured Sam Sloan.

Halpern's fingers stabbed a button on the elaborate phone unit. "Baxter? Come into the General's office, now." In a moment a door opened behind his left shoulder. It apparently led back into the depths of the sprawling ranch house; a couple of minutes before, pleading exhaustion, the General had excused himself and had the high-strung ex-sergeant with the One-O-Worst tattoo on his forearm wheel him off to rest.

Now an unbelievably shabby man entered. He had a rat's pointed face, large mobile nose, a weird stubble of whiskers like short white wires jutting out any which way from his deeply grimed face. He wore what had once been a set of white mechanic's overalls, which long exposure to dirt, sweat, foliage, and human grease had turned into a very serviceable *ad hoc* camouflage pattern of green, brown, yellow, gray, and black smudges. Despite the heat of the late afternoon outside, he wore something that had apparently started its existence as a knit woolen or synthetic stocking cap, and that now seemed to have grease as its main component. A few strands of lanky, silver-gray hair draggled down from beneath the cap. Despite the grayness of his hair and the whiteness of his beard, the deeply tanned little man didn't appear particularly old. He might have been anywhere from a horribly decrepit twenty-six to a disreputable sixty-five.

Fred Halpern waved a well-manicured hand; no work gangs for *him*. "In my capacity as the General's aide, I've had what amounted to a fairly sophisticated intelligence network spread out across the state for several years. It's served me in particularly good stead in these troubled times. This gentleman is one of my most valuable informants."

The man shuffled forward, small dark eyes moving from side to side. They lit on a chair next to a display case filled with the General's medals, and a picture of him gesturing triumphantly from the cockpit of a prototype fighter he'd just test flown. The man shambled forward, to be brought up by a sharp, "Don't sit there, man! You can say your piece standing." It seemed a rough way to treat one's star operative, but McKay sympathized. Once this specimen had plumped his behind down in a chair, the only thing left would be to burn it.

"Mr. Baxter has been all over the state in the guise of a refugee. He can give you an excellent picture of what conditions are like out there."

McKay looked at Sloan and Spinelli, both of whom shrugged. *What the hey*, McKay thought. *We can use all the information we can get. Some of what this geek has to say might even be true.*

In a high-pitched, nasal voice, Baxter began to recite details of his journeying to the far corners of California. After a moment, Halpern snapped, "Never mind that, man. Just tell them what it's *like*." Baxter's eyes blinked rapidly. He drew an unbelievably filthy rag from his back pocket, dabbed at his huge nose, stuck the handkerchief away, and resumed his narrative.

It seemed that survivors had fallen into two main classes in California. One was the mass of refugees, disorganized, homeless, and for the most part without hope. The epidemics that had stalked the land in the wake of the One-Day War had claimed a heavy toll of these, huddled together in desperate camps with little food and barely a pretense at sanitation. The pattern of the rest of the country was repeated here: At least as many died after the war, of disease, privation, or random violence, as had died during the attack itself.

The other class of survivors had fared markedly better. In fact, New Eden and Edwards's Valley were shining examples. Before the war people had tended more and more to band together in affinity groups: clubs, factions, religious and political groups. Even though the policy of both federal and state governments was to discourage survivalism and retreating, many of these groups moved off into the mountains or small towns to establish their own communities. Those that hadn't still offered their members a cohesiveness, a safety in numbers and in common purpose beyond raw survival that was unavailable to the masses of the displaced.

The new California that was arising from the ashes of the old seemed to consist of a hodgepodge of special-interest communities, structured around politics, religion, or even diet.

"You wouldn't believe the sorta setups people got," Baxter said. "You got the Hare Krishnas, the knucklebusters scavenging down on the outskirts of L.A., the Duchy of New Carolina, the Coasters up north of Big Sur, four or five communities fulla them Church of the New Dispensation types"—the two Guardians repressed a shudder at that—"shitload of greaseball squatters down in the San Joaquin Valley, the Free Love folks at Ojai—any kind of weird folks you wanna name, they got their own little patch of ground where they're trying to make a go of it." He gave a grim chuckle. "Already a lot of 'em have got to beatin' on their neighbors. Why, just a couple of weeks ago I watched a little shootin' scrape between a bunch of them New Atlanteans and this group callin' themselves the Sons of the Frontiersmen, left half a dozen dead.''

He shook his head in amusement. "And to think that there's some crazy guy wandering around trying to get all these loonies to cooperate in some kind of network—''

Suddenly Sloan and McKay were leaning forward in their chairs, eyeing the filthy little man intently. "Tell us more about this 'crazy man,' '' Sam Sloan said.

CHAPTER
NINE ──────────────────────

The next two days were busy ones for the Guardians. With the help of electronics expert Sam Sloan, New Eden's technicians were able to modify their communications gear to exchange computer-scrambled communications with Heartland itself. Battle-hardened though they were, the Guardians shared a common sense of excitement. With the discovery of New Eden, a major chunk of the Blueprint for Renewal had fallen into place.

With Ari Lavotsky along, the Guardians made a sortie in Mobile One to the lowlands the day after their arrival in New Eden. In the Sierra Nevada foothills, near the new ghost town of Aruba, they found a level stretch of highway with open fields giving a good half kilometer's field of fire in every direction. It was ideal for a C130S Super Hercules dispatched from Heartland to put down, to take on a load of vital super seeds, trucked down from New Eden.

They had rolled on a few klicks west of Aruba when Casey, who was driving with his hatch open, said, "Hey, Billy, look up ahead." McKay pushed himself off the fold-down, where he was straphanging across from Lavotsky, and moved forward to hunch down and peer over Sam Sloan's shoulder through the ESO's vision slit. There was a giant truck stop half a klick away, imaginatively identified by a huge plastic sign: GIANT T UCK STO . Several big-rig trailers were parked along this side of the lot, next to the restaurant. "There're a couple of trailers with tractors hooked up. You think, like, one of them'll still run?"

McKay shrugged. "We'll find out." He glanced sideways as Lavotsky moved up beside him.

"Looks like there's been trouble in Dodge," Sam Sloan remarked, ducking his head back inside. He was in a folksy mood today. "Couple of bodies up there on the tarmac."

The young Israeli had gone tense. "*Been* trouble, my friend?" he said. "One of those bodies is moving."

A figure broke from the front of the restaurant, running with pumping elbows for the truck parked beyond the covered pump island, parallel to 99. He got halfway, twitched, and went down hard, rolling with the water-loose joints of a deader. A moment later the *crump* of a distant shot pushed in through the open hatches.

"Aw, shit," McKay said. "Not our fuckin' truck!"

Casey braked to a halt, and the big eight-cylinder diesel settled down to a subdued grunting. Somebody ran from the restaurant and knelt beside the man who'd been shot. Hot morning sunlight glinted off black leather pants, the spikes set into belts crossing his naked and sweat-sheened chest like bandoliers, the skull shaven but for a spiked for-and-aft crest of orange hair.

"Road gypsies," Sloan said. The sound of Mobile One's engine obviously hadn't penetrated the firefight ringing in the Mohawker's ears. He knelt by the man, knife in hand, then moved on to the man who was still moving. He lifted his head by the forelock, began sawing. Screams drifted downwind to the armored car.

"Hey, now, no atrocities!" McKay exclaimed in irritation.

Sam glanced at him. "Fire 'em up?"

McKay rolled his eyes. *You can always tell a Navy man*, he thought, *but you can't tell him much*. "Negative. Even if there ain't nothing in the tanks but fumes, we punch a .50-round through one of those pumps, our chances of scavenging a truck could get hairy. And I don't even wanna think about what a Willie Peter grenade'd do.''

"We might find other places with intact trucks," Lavotsky suggested.

"We're supposed ta be rebuildin' America," McKay rumbled, "and greasin' road gypsies definitely comes under that headin'. We take 'em."

Casey grinned down over his shoulder at McKay. "Cowboy 'em, Billy?"

McKay stuck his thumb in the air. "Fuckin' A." He glanced at Lavotsky as Case and Sam dogged their hatches. "Your dance card filled?" The Israeli was already checking the chamber of a spare MP-5.

If a ten-ton armored car could've popped a wheelie like a dragster blasting into its run, that's what Casey would have made Mobile One do. As it was, it shot forward with a squealing of huge tires, and Lavotsky would've gone ass-over-head backwards if he hadn't had the reflexes of a stalking leopard and caught the back of Casey's seat in time. Hanging on to the ESO chair, McKay grinned at him, then made a long arm back to unclip his Maremont chopped M-60 from its brackets in the hull beneath the passenger-side firing slit, forward of the hatch.

The truck stop had been poured into a depression in the generally flat landscape, falling fairly steeply for at least two meters before bottoming. Casey swerved the car across the eastbound lane and off the highway in a squealing-scrunching tempest of gravel, then munched the curb and sailed straight into space. "Hope the suspension'll take it," he remarked, as Sam and Ari both cried out in alarm.

The suspension did—barely—but asphalt buckled beneath the deep-cleated tires as the AFV landed. The Mohawker looked up and his face opened up into an ugly blossom of horror. He let his victim's head and severed scalp both fall and took off like a jackrabbit. If he'd dodged back toward the island, he might have made it. Instead he let instinct guide him, and ran straight away from the roaring behemoth.

Mobile One's sharp-angled snout caught him in the middle of the back. Sloan winced as they heard his skull pop between the right and left view slits. "That's what you get for working off the left hemisphere of your brain at the wrong moment,'' Casey remarked, his words disappearing as the heavy-metal thunder of Rogers's turret guns filled the car, firing high for sheer noise value. The .50 and the M-19 were pretty heavy-duty artillery; the very sound of them should suffice to send the faint-hearted scattering.

He braked abruptly and threw the wheel hard right. The car skidded, heeled way, way over, recovered, and squirted out the ramp at the western end of the lot onto 99 like a water-melon seed from a peckerwood's mouth. He cranked the bucking monster around another right and goosed it back toward the eastern ramp.

Ari Lavotsky was back hanging to a strap to portside and looking at the world through very wild eyes. Not even *Israelis* drove like this in action. McKay, miraculously, was still stuck to the back of Sam's chair, though his knuckles were white under their freckles and wiry hair. ''We're bailin' out this pass,'' he told the *Sabra*. Sloan had unclipped his Galil-203 from beneath his console and started out of his seat. ''We'll be goin' right, onto the island, then into the restaurant while Tom gives covering fire.''

''Right? *Onto the island?*'' His normally dark face had turned the shade of typing paper. McKay nodded his close-cropped head as Casey turned the V-450 back into the lot with deceptive gentleness.

He gunned it. ''You know,'' Sam remarked conversation-ally, ''there's a car parked in the aisle.''

''Yeah.''

Casey shot past an ancient broken-down red-and-silver Peterbilt, then cut left into the aisle between the pump stand and the café. Brakes howled and the car rocked forward. Ari winced as the nose of Mobile One came to a halt five centi-meters from the rear bumper of a beige Korean-made station wagon. He noted the sticker in the rear window that read ONE NUCLEAR BOMB CAN RUIN YOUR WHOLE DAY with the awful clarity of the condemned, and then McKay was out of the star-board hatch, and Sloan, and then it was his turn, and he took a deep breath and jumped—

The V-450 banged into the rear of the station wagon. With a fingernails-on-blackboard screeching it rode up slightly on the lesser vehicle, then pushed it ahead for several meters. It slewed away left and rolled to the right, over and over in slow motion as the armored car shouldered past.

The professional soldier in Ari Lavotsky had taken over the instant the crepe soles of his desert boots touched blacktop. He dodged behind a pump, the silenced H&K held ready, a cool weight in his hands, familiar yet unfamilar. *It's been a long time*, he thought, *but you don't forget*.

Sloan was crouched behind the gasohol pump to Lavotsky's left. McKay stood with his legs spread and the Maremont hanging from his neck by his Israeli-style sling, right out in the open. It seemed to go right past bravery into sheer stupidity until Ari saw McKay snap something in through the busted-out window of the diner and then drop his right hand to the rear pistol grip of the MG. Instantly there was a flash and a bang that went into Ari's ears like an icepick, and McKay was blazing off a long burst, side-to-side at waist level.

Sam left cover to lean his mouth close to Ari's left ear. "I go first, high right. Follow me low and left." The Israeli bobbed assent and the former Navy officer was gone, sprinting in the open door of the café.

A foul smell hit Lavotsky in the face like a towel soaked in sewage as he burst in the door. Ignoring it, he instantly dove left into the broken glass that littered the red cracked-vinyl booths and the floor beside them. Bright shards clawed his shoulder and back through his black-and-red striped soccer shirt. Disregarding them, he rolled onto his belly, submachine gun ready as Sloan began to pump single shots from behind the cashier's counter.

There had been five road gypsies inside the restaurant when McKay's stun bomb went off. One of them had had a potbellied man on a stool by the lunch counter that ran along the far wall, punching his face in with a pair of brass knucks. He and his victim were both sprawled in a lake of blood at the base of the bar, caught in the firestorm of 7.62 mm slugs. So had another gypsy been, to judge by the holes punched in the milk machine, the red splotch down the front of it, and the green-tufted bulge of cranium just visible over the bullet-gouged bar.

Another Mohawker was still standing, gaping through the

red slits in a pair of green plastic bugeye shades. Sloan shot him through the throat, and he went down, dropping a little black CAR-15 assault rifle. A nanosecond later he ducked beneath a shotgun blast that showered him with plastic pieces of the register. Down in the glass on linoleum stained by countless spilled Cokes, Ari sighted on a head that sported three black crests running parallel, front to back, as its owner levered himself up for another shot with his Remington pump. The Israeli squeezed off and knocked a triangular chunk of skull and some clots of brains from between the right and center 'hawks.

Sloan popped up and ripped out a burst. Behind the bar at his end a gypsy screamed and fell back, tossing a lever-action rifle into the air. It came down with a clatter that rang loud in sudden silence.

Waiting in the stillness, Lavotsky became aware with a start that someone was sitting in a booth right over his left shoulder.

He found himself staring into the giddy grin of a dessicated corpse. *Dead a long while*, he thought, then instantly knew he was wrong. The eyes were still there, glaring at him through shrunken lids. He knew what the smell was now. *Cholera. The poor devil shit himself to death*. The tissue dehydration that had shrunk-fit skin to skeleton had mostly occurred before the death of which it was a major cause.

From the service bays through the door to his right came the boom of a magnum pistol, echoing and reechoing, followed by a thunderstorm of gunfire that could only come from the M-60. The wall-shaking echoes had scarcely died when McKay's voice said, "Don't shoot," and the burly ex-Marine stepped into the café, holding the Maremont in the patrol position before his hips, by both pistol grips as though the nine-kilogram weapon were an SMG.

Holding the machine gun in his right hand, he picked a cigar out of its box in the broken-open counter, tore the wrapper open with his teeth, sniffed at it. He nodded in satisfaction, stripped off the rest of the plastic the same way, stuck the cigar in his grin, and fished a lighter out of the breast pocket of his cammies. "Couple of scumbags in there, thought they could hide behind a car," he said in a cloud of smoke, and held up the M-60. It would shoot through a car from one end to the other, and never mind side-to-side. "All clear now."

"Casey," Sam Sloan said. "What's the situation outside? Anything moving?"

"Negative, Sam." Unable to hear that end of the conversation, Ari raised his head cautiously and peered out the window. Mobile One had taken station at the eastern ramp again, where its guns could rake the entire front of the truck stop. "Uh, Billy, looks like the cab on the truck parked out front here's burned out. Don't think it's going to run anymore."

"Roger that. I'll check out the Pete parked next to the building, then. Be watchin' me 'n' shit, Big Brother."

"Will do, Billy," Rogers said quietly.

McKay started out the door. He paused, looked at Ari a little quizzically. "You wanna cover me?" he asked, jerking his chin toward the windows on the east. The polarized glass in them was still intact, cooling the dazzle of sunlight on the metal of the tractor's cab and nose.

"He didn't hear you, McKay," Sloan said. "He doesn't have a communicator."

"Fuck," McKay said, and explained what he was going to do. "What happened to your friend there?"

"Cholera, I think."

"Great. Maybe we did the gyps a favor, if they been too exposed to that shit." He shook his head in disgust. "Rogers is gonna make us take many, many shots." He went out into the shade of the covered pump island.

Ari moved past the cholera victim and slid onto a torn chair. Sloan had stationed himself in the door that led into the service bay, just in case any smart lads were hiding out in there or in the kitchen. Lavotsky saw McKay pause at the corner of the building, take his cigar out of his mouth to eject a fragment of tobacco, spit it onto the tacky asphalt, and trot forward.

But from his hiding place on the oblong trailer a road gypsy rose to one knee, holding a Russian-made AKM assault rifle on the center of Billy McKay's broad chest.

Swiveling his head left and right on his bull neck, McKay didn't see him. Lavotsky snapped the MP-5 up, knowing he was too late, that the big ex-Marine was dead.

There was a crack like one of the world's hinges giving way.

It was a sound heard once and never forgotten, and in his bones Lavotsky knew the M-2HB in Mobile One's turret had fired a single .50 caliber round.

It caught the road gypsy just above the brass dish of his belt buckle. He just rose up in the air, a big cloud of blood and organic stuff billowing out behind him, up and up and turning over once before dropping away out of sight behind the silvery trailer.

Watching him go, McKay took the cigar out of his mouth again. "Hell of a way to make a living," he said.

CHAPTER
TEN ───────────────────────

The old tractor-trailer rig proved to be in movable condition, if you didn't mind the bloodstains on the box. Scrounging around, the Guardians liberated sufficient diesel fuel to get it up to New Eden and back. They stayed the night there, and headed back early the next morning. McKay drove the big rig, with his Maremont LWMG stuck between the seats at his side. Riding shotgun with him was Lavotsky, cradling his MP-5 between his knees.

They delivered the Peterbilt to New Eden, where some of Mahalaby's elves, displaying yet another set of unlooked-for talents, swarmed over it making sure it would be serviceable for the run back down. The Guardians took advantage of an afternoon more or less free to maintain Mobile One and their weapons. That done, Sam Sloan wandered off to the communications room, ostensibly to see how his scrambler rig was holding up. Since he had the exquisite Susan Spinelli in tow, McKay wondered just what kind of communications he was going to be dealing with.

On the other hand, McKay had begun to strike up an acquaintance with Anna Yoshimitsu, the lady he'd first seen weeding the beanfield in a rust-red jumpsuit. She turned out to be Mahalaby's master mechanic, of all things, and while Billy McKay was old-fashioned enough to feel uncomfortable with women doing men's jobs . . . well, what the hell. Civilization had collapsed, and you had to make do with what you could.

The Guardians' surmise, supported by Major Crenna back in Heartland, was that the odds were very good the mystery man the rat-faced Baxter had referred to was the same as the unknown Blueprint participant. At the very least, what he seemed to be doing—attempting to organize survivors of the holocaust into a trade network—was wholly consonant with the aims and designs of the Blueprint for Renewal. Baxter's testimony was as yet the only thing even resembling a clue as to the possible identity, or at least whereabouts, of the unknown human key to the puzzle of the Blueprint. While the occupants of New Eden loaded their life-giving supplies into the semi the Guardians and Lavotsky had brought back, the Guardians would make a flying tour of the state of California, hunting for the mystery man.

And even if he *wasn't* the man they were looking for, at the very least he could prove quite valuable if his aid could be enlisted.

That evening Fred Halpern rode over in a late-model Ford Bronco with a heavyset, surly young man with a sunburned neck and a Caterpillar Tractor cap, who proved to be a descendant of the Donner family. They were there to discuss arrangements tentatively made with Spinelli the day before, by which New Eden would share some of its surplus foodstuffs with the Valley in exchange for building materials. It was a handout, pure and simple—New Eden didn't need any more construction supplies. Yet it was painfully obvious that Edwards's Valley needed all the food it could get. There was no way its lackluster slave laborers were going to be able to support themselves. After they had taken their leave of the General's boys, both Sloan and McKay had argued energetically with Spinelli against sending the food. It smacked of appeasement, they said. But Susan insisted it was part of New Eden's mission to help its neighbors. Underneath that lovely, fragile-seeming exterior and occasionally spacy manner, Susan Spinelli possessed a core of tungsten carbide. The two Guardians got nowhere with her.

Buddy Donner just sat with his arms folded and glowered during the confab with Mahalaby and his assistants. McKay had a good idea of why; he could swear he'd seen that stocky form gesturing madly at them from the steel truss bridge when they'd driven in a couple of days before. Halpern, however, was the soul of congeniality, and the arrangements were quickly concluded.

That done, the Guardians drifted off to spend their free evening in their various ways. Sam Sloan went off for a walk with Susan Spinelli, to sample the delights of nature or whatever. Casey Wilson took off to go sit on a rock and meditate under the stars. McKay cadged a bottle of homemade organic brandy, which packed a punch like Muhammad Ali, and went in search of his new friend Anna. Tom Rogers retired to Mobile One, and the solitude he preferred.

The next morning, the Guardians set forth in a pink-and-gray dawn on their reconnaissance of the wonderland that was post-holocaust California.

It was another vest-pocket valley in the mountains, tucked into the low jagged Diablo Range, across the San Joaquin Valley from the Sierras. Back in Edwards's Valley, Baxter had mentioned it as one of the nearest places where any sort of organization still existed. The so-called Dutchy of Cew Carolina wasn't much more than a hundred klicks from New Eden, but it had taken Mobile One half a day to work its way across the San Joaquin Valley, much of the time crossing neglected fields to avoid the congested highways. It was a good thing Baxter had given them really specific directions. Otherwise they would never have known that one of the little dirt turnoffs up into the scrubby hills led to anything but a state camping site, or possibly a deserted ranch.

In the days since the One-Day War the Diablo Range, like most of the North American continent, had received a good deal more rain than it was accustomed to. Normally, by high summer, the hills would have been covered by vegetation a little lighter in color than your average shopping bag. Now they were furred with dense green growth. Still, McKay was a little surprised when they swung around the hip of a mountain and found themselves looking out over cultivated fields. To his inexperienced eye it looked as if they covered a couple of hundred hectares. He wondered how much of a population they'd support.

The road led down into the shallow valley. Mobile One rolled along in the heat of the day with the hatches popped and the Guardians' heads stuck out in the hot dry breeze. "Make you homesick, Sloan?" McKay asked, waving a hand at the nearby field where a man was plowing with the aid of a mule. The man stood in place as if his hands were welded to the handles of the plow, gaping at them in openmouthed horror.

Sloan gave him a reassuring nod and a wave. "Jesus, McKay, they haven't used mules where I come from since back in the days of the Great Depression." The man continued to stare at them as they trundled past with a great chugging of the engines and farting of diesel stink.

Ahead of them rose a mounded hummock. At its top sat a house of substantial size, with curious flat slablike walls pierced by thin slits of windows. Scaffolding had been erected at one corner, and workmen toiled in the sun as if adding something to the structure. They looked up as Mobile One approached, and then scattered in all directions, flinging tools as they ran. To the left and right of the dirt track a scatter of tents, trailers, and jerrybuilt lean-tos were sucking up a number of people whom Mobile One's approach had frightened out of the fields.

"Like, they don't seem to think we're friendly," Casey Wilson commented as he braked the massive beast to a stop in front of the main house. "Whatever happened to old-fashioned country hospitality, Sam?"

"It kind of suffered in the war, like everything else," Sam Sloan said. "I imagine that since then, any kind of strangers might mean bad news—especially ones armed as heavily as we are. I think these people are probably like New Eden and Edwards's Valley. If they weren't fairly hidden away, they'd have been overrun by refugees in the first weeks after the war."

The white-painted double doors of the house opened, and a

young boy came hesitantly down the broad steps, blinking at Mobile One in wonder through the dazzling sunshine. He was wearing a medieval-style tabard, a sheathlike, sleeveless garment that came clear down to his grubby young knees. It was brown, and the front of it was emblazoned with a yellow shield with a red lion on it surrounded by a double border of red lines with funny little projections bumping out from them at intervals. McKay guessed it was something heraldic, although he had no idea in hell what it might have been supposed to signify. He opened the side hatch and stepped out as the boy approached.

"Gee—I mean, good day, sir," the boy stammered. He looked to be about eleven years old. "His Grace, the Duke of New Carolina, demands to know why you invade his dominions without his let and leave."

McKay blinked.

"We beg the Duke's indulgence for the manner of our coming," said Sloan from the passenger-side top hatch. "We're a special team on a mission from the United States Government, and beg that he permit us an audience."

"What he said," grunted McKay.

The boy gave a last, doubtful look at the towering ex-Marine, then turned and sprinted back up the stairs and into the house. "Jesus," McKay said. Baxter had warned them it would be like this, but still it was kind of hard to take. He crossed his arms over his chest, leaned back against the hot flank of Mobile One, and waited.

McKay was not normally a patient man, and the broiling afternoon sun did nothing to improve his patience. He was just about to order Casey to stand off twenty or thirty meters, and have Rogers do a little remodeling of the turret thingy they were building at the corner of the house with the M-19, when the front doors swung open again and a squad of armed men came trooping out. Grunting a curse, he dropped his hand to the butt of his .45. With a whine of servos, Tom Rogers brought the turret weapons to bear on the front of the house.

The squad split into two groups and formed into lines flanking the doorway, strung out along the front of the house. They were as unlikely-looking a group as McKay ever expected to see. They wore *kilts*, for God's sake, with tartan sashes over their shoulders and bonnets on their heads. They carried a motley assortment of long arms: a big black H&K 91, a couple of Mini 14s, a British Lee-Enfield Mark V Jungle Carbine, a pair of Remington riot guns, and assorted bolt-action sporting arms. They looked straight ahead, eyes staring glassily, as if they were trying desperately not to see the armored leviathan parked right before their noses. Adam's apples rode up and down like exposed elevators.

A moment later the boy in the tabard reappeared. He trotted down to the foot of the steps, stood to one side, and bellowed "His Excellency, Duke Charles, by the grace of God, Lord and Protector of the Duchy of New Carolina!" McKay took his hand off his pistol butt and stood to attention. *What the hell, it's only polite.*

An eyeblink later, His Grace himself emerged from the gloom inside the great house. He looked like Henry VIII got up as a Scot. Waddling down the steps toward McKay, he appeared to be a hair under six feet in height, and must have weighed upward of three hundred pounds. The vast rounded oblong of his face was fringed with a reddish chin beard, and curly chestnut hair wisped from beneath the rim of his fancy feathered bonnet. From behind the swell of one hip jutted the basket hilt of one of those straight broadswords that, McKay knew from reading somewhere, were called claymores, even though they weren't. He came to a halt a few meters away from McKay and waited expectantly. McKay snapped a brisk salute.

"I'm William McKay," he said crisply. "I'm commanding a team on a special mission from the President of the United States." He was getting sick of that speech. "We've come looking for information."

The Duke eyed him coolly. For all his silly getup and this ridiculous panoply, McKay had to give him credit for sheer balls. Against the armored bulk of Mobile One, this squad of sad-sack bodyguards would have had as much chance as medieval villagers beset by a dragon, with no Saint George in sight. "I see," the Duke said. His voice was oddly high-pitched to be emerging from such a mound of flesh. "May I see your bona fides?" McKay held out a manila envelope sealed with red wax to make it look official. The boy in the tabard scuttled forward, took it from McKay, and carried it back to his duke. With thick fingers, His Grace broke the seal, and began to sort through the to-whom-it-may-concern authentications provided by President McGregor.

Both Sam Sloan and Casey Wilson had, it turned out, already heard of the self-styled Duke of New Carolina. They seemed to have all the answers already, and McKay wondered if he and Rogers shouldn't just have stayed back at Heartland and sent them out to conquer California on their own. Charles Stuart Chadwick had, in the days before the One-Day War, been a fairly popular science fiction writer. He was primarily known for his best-selling series of stories and books concerning the adventures of the Highland Guard, a band of Scottish space mercenaries in the far future, who are commanded by no less a personage than a direct descendant of Bonnie Prince Charlie Stuart, Pretender to the throne of Scotland and England. "Bonnie Prince Charlie," Sam Sloan had told them, over a dinner of stir-fried vegetables in New Eden's commissary after the return from Edwards's Valley, "was possibly history's greatest counterargument to the divine right of kings. He was a nitwit, an utter incompetent, and he betrayed his followers repeatedly. But Charles Chadwick's always been obsessed with him. He's a monarchist, honest to God, and for him Bonnie Prince Charlie somehow personifies all the virtues of the monarchic system." He forked a piece of broccoli into his mouth and chewed thoughtfully. "He may have a point, there, at that."

He'd declared his little hideaway the Duchy of New Carolina, with himself as Duke. The anachronist revelers had joined Chadwick's hired hands, and the coterie of hangers-on who generally surrounded him like flies buzzing a honey pot, as his subjects. The "Highland Guard" had acquired the task of guarding his monumental person for real.

Casey Wilson, his head and shoulders sticking out of the driver's hatch, suddenly stiffened and looked closely at one of the Guardsmen to the Duke's left. "Barry! Barry Corso—how's it going, man," Casey Wilson exclaimed. The Guard with the Enfield, a gangling man who looked to be about Casey's own age, with sallow skin, dark hair, and a fleshy nose, swallowed visibly, but didn't take his eyes off the middle distance. "Hey, Billy, I know this guy. He was an old friend of mine. Hey, Barry, man, don't you remember me? It's me, Casey."

"Let him be, Case," McKay said.

The Duke looked up from the papers McKay had given him. He turned around and bellowed at the house front, "Seneschal! It's all right. Get those clowns back to work." Arms akimbo, he stood until a sheep-faced work gang appeared from behind the house and began policing up their tools from around the base of the new construction. Nodding in satisfaction, he turned back toward his visitors. "Welcome to the Duchy of New Carolina, gentlemen. What may we do for you?"

McKay explained that they were looking for a man of unknown description, who was traveling through California trying to organize a network of survivors. "We heard he might've come through here," he concluded.

"Yes, a man such as that did visit us," the portly Duke acknowledged. In the hot sun, sweat began to cascade down his forehead. "Rather elderly chap, with thinning hair and a little goatee. He wore a brown striped robe of some sort, and Ho Chi Minh slippers. He wanted to know if we had some manner of surplus which we could trade to other communities of survivors in exchange for things we needed." The massive shoulders rose in a shrug. "Of course, we have no wish to sully our hands with trade. Yet it is true that our little haven is not entirely self-sufficient. We grow most of our own food, and can salvage equipment and materials from the towns below— though that's a very dangerous proposition. We told him that, in the interest of our subjects' well-being, we would be willing to participate in his scheme. Of course, we'd insist on sending emissaries to any community with which we dealt, to offer our protection and enlightened rule to them. These troubled times demand a return to feudalism—the only system in which each man knows, and is secure in, his place. We have no doubt but that our offer will be most generously accepted anywhere."

Is this fuckin' guy for real? McKay wondered. "When was this man last through here?"

The Duke frowned thoughtfully. "Not that long after the

war. Five, perhaps six weeks ago. We haven't seen him since.''

McKay's heart sank. He wasn't exactly a woodsman, but he knew that a trail five weeks old was cold indeed. "Which direction did he head?"

"South, I believe."

McKay thanked the Duke for the information, and apologized once more for intruding on his little valley. "Oh, but you must stay the night, and regale us with news of the outside world," Duke Charles said.

"I'm sorry, sir."

The Duke's broad face tightened. He obviously wasn't used to being refused.

McKay faced him down. "We got a job to do. And it won't wait."

"Perhaps another time, if you'll be so gracious as to extend your offer of hospitality," put in Sam Sloan, ever the diplomat. "I'm sure we'd all very much enjoy hearing about the society you've built up here in the Duchy. But now, I fear, duty calls."

Duke Charles brightened visibly. "Duty. Of course, I understand." He nodded, and gave the sheaf of papers back to the herald, who trotted them over to McKay. "Perhaps, when your mission is done, you might consider seeking mercenary employment. We can offer most generous terms, I assure you."

It was all McKay could do not to laugh out loud, but Major Crenna had warned him against pissing off the indigs. "Yeah," he said. "We'll think about it." He clambered back into Mobile One and shut the side hatch. "OK, Casey, let's roll—and no jackrabbit starts. We don't want to give His Holiness a face full of dust."

Casey put the armored car in gear and rolled away, slowly gathering momentum. "Barry Corso. After all these years, and he wouldn't even talk to me." Casey shrugged. "He always was a nerd, anyway."

It had once been very colorful: a genuine Buckminster Fuller–style geodesic dome, covered with triangular panels of mylarized plastic, all different colors. Now the reds and blues and greens and yellows and whites had faded to lifeless pastel

in the sun. The wind and the rain had torn rents in the plastic;
some of these had been repaired indifferently with tape or ir-
regular stitching, some not at all. A battered tin pipe with a
little triangular Chinese hat-like covering on top jutted out
from the rear, dribbling a thin acrid brown smut of wood
smoke into the washed-out afternoon sky. "No, man," the
painfully thin blond young man with the beard said,
"Nobody's been around here asking us to trade anything."

The wind belled the plastic sides of the habitation out and
then whomped them in again. A woman in a faded, dirty cot-
ton dress stood nursing an infant at one shrunken breast in
front of the dome, watching the strangers with their ominous
vehicle through wind-blown strands of mouse-colored hair.
The young man—farmer, McKay guessed you could call him
—dressed in a black vest over a skinny bare chest, blue jeans,
and tennis shoes, had stood protectively by the woman as
Mobile One rumbled up the dirt track toward their dwelling.
Another man, bigger framed but with his ragged clothes hanging on him like a scarecrow, stood in the little bean patch with
his hands crossed over the handle of his hoe, the way he had
since Mobile One had come into view. His head was a mass of
black curls and beard. The only distinguishable features were
a large nose and a pair of wire-rimmed spectacles, which were
missing the right lens, giving the man's face an appearance
that might have been clownish under other circumstances.

A yellow shepherd dog emerged from beneath the ancient
Ford pickup rotting on blocks next to the dome. He trotted
forward at a lazy pace and stopped to sniff McKay's ankles.
With a city boy's inbred distrust of animals, McKay reflexively dropped his hand to his gun butt. Sam Sloan, who had
climbed out of Mobile One along with McKay to stretch his
long legs, laughed, knelt by the dog and scratched its ruff.
"Good boy," he said, allowing the dog to sniff and then lick
his hand.

A little girl with unwashed blond hair in pigtails tied with
bits of orange yarn and a drab torn frock had come out to
stand beside her mother, holding onto her skirt. The pinch-
faced man nodded at the dog. "That's Spirulina. My daughter
Carrie named him. Always used to slip him her tablets of the
stuff, back when he was a pup. Silly damned name for a dog."

He rubbed at his nose and blinked up at the sun. A few clouds rolled by, high and fluffy and lazy, not giving a fuck for the travails of those bound to the earth below. "Used to have a bunch of dogs, shit, four or five. Had to kill them all and eat them. So many of them, with not enough to go around, they were turning vicious anyway. And Tracy with the kid and all —needs more protein than she's been getting—Spirulina, here, he keeps the rats and rabbits out of our garden. Otherwise we'd shoot him too, though I'd sure hate to do it. Carrie'd be heartbroken; he's her favorite."

McKay scratched the back of his neck where the hot sun was making it sting. "Case?" he asked.

Casey's head popped out the driver's hatch. "Right here, Billy," he replied.

"You know those pressed protein bars we got? Those emergency rats we hate so much?" *Rats* meant *rations*. In the case of the experimental emergency nutrient bars the Guardians had been saddled with, McKay suspected it referred to the contents as well. *Still, if I was starvin'. . .*

"I'll get them, McKay," Sam Sloan said. He turned and clambered back into the dimness of Mobile One.

The emaciated farmer watched in silence as Sam Sloan came out and laid a crate of the ration bars at his feed. "Ah, thanks." He tried to smile through his tangled beard, but it was a feeble effort. The ration bars would help for a while, but once they were gone . . .

"We know some people might be able to help you," McKay told them. "At a place up north called New Eden. They might be able to spare you some food too, but mostly they got these fancy seeds, you can grow a lot more crops on a lot less land, with a lot less effort. They'll be happy to send you some."

The farmer smiled again, more strongly this time. His teeth were brown and starting to tumble in his shrunken gums. "Thanks. I sure wish I could help you with this other thing. But nobody's come around asking us to trade anything." He gestured around at the wretched little homestead with a bony hand.

"We don't have anything much *to* trade."

CHAPTER

ELEVEN ───────────────────

Late afternoon in the southwestern reaches of the San Joaquin Valley. "Smoke ahead," Tom Rogers said from behind the wheel.

"I got it," Billy McKay said from the turret. He squinted into the hot wind of Mobile One's passage. A thin spire of dirty white smoke trailed off into the sky from what looked like several klicks ahead to their right.

"Shall we go check it out, Billy?" Casey Wilson asked from the Electronic Systems Operator's seat.

Sam Sloan said, "Might be trouble." It was his turn off watch, and he'd been drawing sack time on the air mattress abaft the turret root.

"No doubt." McKay knew there might be a thousand innocent explanations for the smoke. But these days it was always safest to assume the worst.

"Where there's smoke, there's people," Tom Rogers said in his soft drawl. "We're lookin' for contacts."

"Yeah," McKay said. "Let's go for it."

Here the land was comparatively flat. As usual Mobile One was cruising an out-of-the-way country road, to avoid the derelict cars that choked most major highways. Rogers parked them out of sight of the road in a small stand of cottonwood trees about a klick away from the smoke. It seemed to come from an old round-backed trailer, as far as McKay could tell from his field glasses. "Sloan, deass the vehicle and go check it out," he said. He didn't believe in leading with his chin in an AFV; you couldn't hide 'em, and they acted as irresistible magnets for any heavy ordnance that happened to be lying around.

"Ah, right, McKay. I'll get right on it." Sloan's voice sounded dubious. Unlike McKay, who was always uneasy in the confines of the car, Sloan was used to going into combat in a cozy armored womb. Traipsing around the landscape with his fanny hanging out went against everything he'd learned back in his Navy days. That was one reason McKay picked him; a little simple snooping and pooping would be good drill for him. And for all that McKay and Sloan sometimes had their differences, Sloan was a good troop. Like it or not, he'd do the job, and do it well. Sloan opened the rear topside hatch, boosted himself out with his M-203–mounted Galil slung over his shoulder. He gave McKay a quick wry grin, dropped to the dark earth, and set off at a trot across the field.

In a few minutes his voice came crackling back in McKay's earphone. "You people can come on up. It's all clear. Uh, better have Tom break out the medkit."

It had been just what it looked like: an ancient humpbacked silver trailer standing up on a little rise, with a big rusty water tank on a stand out back, and a couple of oil drums next to it. A couple of acres around it had been planted to beans and corn. The green stalks leaned languidly with the humid breeze. The trailer had mostly burned itself out by now. The heat of the blaze had turned the sides plastic and made them bulge out; most of the roof had melted and caved in. Though no flames were visible, the air was thick with the stink of burned furniture, plastic—and flesh.

In the bare dirt yard out in front of the ruined trailer lay several bodies. Sam Sloan knelt next to one of them, his Galil slung over his back. Bad practice, slinging the piece like that, but McKay decided to let it slide. He sat alert, thumbs on the firing buttons of the two turret weapons, scanning the surroundings as Rogers turned the driver's seat over to Casey Wilson and bailed out.

The survivor was an unconscious young girl, thirteen perhaps, a lovely child with her hair caught into braids at the side of her head and twisted into coils. She was naked except for a bloodsoaked T-shirt, the unstained areas of which were salmon pink. "She's been shot at point-blank range with a small caliber, high velocity projectile, probably a 5.56 mm round," Tom Rogers said, examining her. "Bullet passed cleanly through her biceps, didn't damage the bone. She's lucky." He began to debride the wound with a tool from his medic's bag. "From the tearing of tissues in the genital area, I reckon she's been raped several times."

"What kind of animals would do that?" Sloan asked, sickened.

Tom shrugged. "Two-legged ones."

"There's a whole family of them," Sam said grimly. "Three other kids, middle-aged couple I gather are their parents, an older man. All shot." He jerked his chin at the hollowed-out trailer. "Have the impression there was somebody in there too. Haven't been up to checking it out."

"No point," McKay said. Tom Rogers spoke up then, asking Sloan to fetch some fluorocarbon blood-replacement fluid from the vehicle. Looking glad to have something to do, Sam Sloan complied.

After brief debate, they decided to take the girl with them. There actually had never been a chance that they wouldn't. By now, every man of the Guardians had seen enough of the aftermath of the One-Day War that they knew they couldn't save *everybody*. But the thousands and millions of huddled survivors of the catastrophe were one thing—statistics, overwhelming, ultimately impersonal. A single survivor, an injured, frightened teenaged girl at that, was something else entirely.

Using the tiedown rings inset in the deck of Mobile One, they secured her on the air mattress so she wouldn't be jounced off. With Tom Rogers hovering over her like a mother chicken, they set off again. In a little while, when the transfusion of artificial blood and massive doses of nutrients began to have their effect, she became fully awake and began screaming. Tom Rogers spoke to her softly in the Spanish he'd picked up with the Special Forces in Latin America, and eventually she calmed down.

The nighttime desert air was cool and still. Mobile One was parked on a low hilltop, surrounded by a swastika of claymore mines. They were set to sweep four sides of an oblong perimeter on command of an electronic detonator called a *clacker*, which was hung on its wires inside the open turret hatch to be quickly accessible to Casey, who was on lookout. The Guardians broke out the evening's freeze-dried dinners, heated them in the V-450's microwave, and settled in to eat.

The ever-informative Baxter had told the Guardians that Tejon Pass, which led through the Tehachapis where the Sierra Nevada and the great Coastal Range converged at the southern extent of the San Joaquin Valley, was hopelessly blocked. *So far that little rat-faced bastard's been right on,* McKay thought. *Still, I don't feel right about trusting him too far.* Following Baxter's advice they'd cut southeast after passing Bakersfield, crossing Tehachapi Pass into the fringes of the Mojave Desert. Tomorrow they would check the fringes of the great charnel house that was Los Angeles.

Their search for the mystery man had gotten frustrating. Some had seen him, others just claimed to have. He gave the impression of a will-o'-the-wisp, elusive, always just ahead of his pursuers.

As they finished their meal the girl regained consciousness. Rogers gave her a drink, and the Guardians gathered around to hear her story, except for Casey, who listened in over the intercom. She spoke in good English, which lapsed into Spanish at the painful turns.

There were too many painful turns.

Her name was Amparo Dieguez. Her family had moved north from Zacatecas, Mexico, a decade before to become migrant workers. It had been a tough life, but better than anything that was offered in the slums or deserts of northern Mexico. Her father, Ramón, had eventually put by enough money to buy a small plot of land and an ancient clapped-out trailer; they were no squatters. The war had come, but its passing had left little mark on the family. They were well away from the stricken cities, and far enough away from the major arteries that they weren't inundated with refugees. Many of the Anglos who lived nearby panicked and fled. The Dieguez family, like most of the other immigrants in the area, stayed where they were. Life in post-holocaust America was no worse than what they'd been accustomed to back home.

Until that morning, when a fancy black Jeep and a gray pickup truck with California state markings had driven up to the Dieguez trailer. In the Jeep rode a stocky, sunglassed Chicano named Rivera. The pickup carried half a dozen enforcers for the Farm Workers' Collective, an ultraradical offshoot of the UFW. Rivera had demanded that Ramón Dieguez turn over a portion of his food stocks to them. The California Liberation Front had been proclaimed, and it was the duty of all good peasants and workers to contribute all they could to *la causa*.

Dieguez refused. He had scarcely enough for his own family. Rivera ordered a couple of his goons to tie his arms, and they began beating him with the butts of their rifles. The old man, Eladio Olguin, uncle to Amparo's mother, burst out of the trailer with a shotgun. He fired at Rivera, missed, and was chopped down in a panicked spray of automatic fire. The marauders had then hosed down the trailer with bullets. The thin-gauge metal of its side offered little protection against the copper-jacketed slugs. Mr. Dieguez' seventy-year-old mother had been killed instantly. His wife and four children, miraculously unhurt, had been prodded out into the dawn light.

A couple of Rivera's men held Dieguez while the others took turns raping first his wife, then his eldest child, Amparo. That done, they systematically gunned the family down. Lying on the ground, her stomach ablaze with pain, her mind reeling with horror, Amparo had been shot once through the arm. The man who shot her wanted to finish her off, but Rivera wouldn't permit it. "A lesson's no good if there ain't somebody left to pass it on," he remarked. "Let her be." They'd looted the trailer of what pitiful possessions and stockpiles it had, set it afire, and driven off.

The story mostly came out in English, which Amparo spoke

quite well, but she lapsed into Spanish at moments of stress.
"Nice people," Sam Sloan commented when the story was
done.

"I guess they were trying to elevate the consciousness of the
proletariat," Casey Wilson said. Holding down the ESO seat
while Casey drove, Sam Sloan looked abruptly around. Sarcasm wasn't normally the ex-fighter jock's style.

Tom Rogers gave the girl an injection to help her sleep.
McKay and Sloan went outside, feeling a strong craving for
fresh air. When Amparo went under, Rogers came out to join
them. His square face looked troubled. "Billy? You think
there's anything in this California Liberation Front business?"

"No," McKay said, wondering, *Is that all that's eatin' him,
or is he upset about the kid, even a little?* Maybe there was
such a thing as being *too* hard-core. He couldn't tell. He'd
known Rogers for two years, and he still just couldn't read
him. "Just a bunch of bandit assholes dressing up like revolutionaries."

"Billy," Casey said in an urgent whisper. "I think there's
something moving out there."

McKay froze. His eyes searched the darkness. His ears fil-
tered the night sounds, the sighing of wind among the mesas,
the chirping of crickets. He sensed nothing, and seasoned
campaigner that he was, he could usually tell if something was
out there or not. On the other hand, Casey Wilson had the
eyes of an osprey. McKay couldn't discount what he said he
saw. *Still*, he told himself, *Casey ain't experienced on patrol.
He probably just saw—*

From inside Mobile One blared a series of raucous buzzing
blats—the alarm indicating that the fancy sensors with which
they'd surrounded the perimeter of their little camp had detected movement.

Hot yellow muzzle flashes split the night wide open.

CHAPTER
TWELVE

They're coming over the wire! Cursing the fancy *Star Wars* gimmickry they'd been saddled with, Billy McKay threw himself toward his Maremont lightweight M-60, propped against a rock with an Australian half-moon ammo box clipped to its receiver. The movement saved his life. He felt something brush his left side, heard the loud splang of bullet impacts against the steel skin of Mobile One.

To his left, fire bloomed. Less seasoned an infantryman than McKay or Rogers, Sam Sloan had allowed himself to get out of arm's reach of his rifle-grenade launcher combination. He'd ripped his big shiny Colt Python out of its shoulder holster and was blazing away at the dark forms rushing out of the darkness. McKay heard one cry out in pain, then his big hand closed around the pistol grip of his machine gun.

And the hilltop exploded in flame and noise.

For one instant, Mobile One was encased in a box of flame. Casey had tripped off all four claymores at once. The attackers barely had time to scream before wave fronts of pellets and hot gas blew them away, like the dynamic overpressure of a hydrogren bomb blast punching tract homes to kindling.

Deafened and dazzled by the multiple blasts, Billy McKay

threw down the bipod at the front of his machine gun, snugged the butt against his shoulder, and cut loose. From the quick stutter of orange light that flared from the door of the vehicle behind his left shoulder, throwing his hunchbacked outline into relief on the ground, McKay knew that Rogers, who'd been inside tending to Amparo, the Mexican girl, had opened up from the doorway with his Galil. A moment later he felt the ground vibrate beneath him, and the night lit up again like daylight as Casey brought the turret guns into play. They were loud enough to penetrate even the ringing in McKay's ears, the M-19 thumping away like a big bass drum. Forty mm grenades began to chew up the landscape a hundred meters from the vehicle.

But they were just busting caps, trying to make sure that any survivors of the assault wave were headed in the right direction —away—and stayed that way.

McKay fired off fifty rounds from the ammo box, slipped another out of the Rhodesian pouch slung across his chest, popped open the feed tray, and inserted the end of the new belt. The others had quit firing, Casey having burned the better part of a belt of .50-caliber ammunition in his three-hundred-sixty-degree sweep of the countryside. McKay felt rather than heard his feed-tray cover snick home.

In the darkness, nothing moved, except the pale yellow-and-blue dance of little fires in the brush ignited by the claymores' detonation. The night air was thick with the smell of burned powder, blood, spilled intestines, and Composition C-4. "Cover me, Billy." If the bone-conduction earphone hadn't been taped to the mastoid bone behind his ear, McKay never would have heard Rogers.

"Got you. Go for it."

"Shall I fire a flare?" Sam Sloan asked.

"Negative." Hell, they could even have set out trip-wire flares. But old-time covert-ops hand McKay always hated to pinpoint his position so flagrantly. Booms and flashes in the night were one thing; if an enemy didn't have them in line of sight, he couldn't learn too much from them. Having a flaming sword hanging just above your head was another matter entirely.

Crouched low, rifle at the ready, Tom Rogers moved forward. McKay could hear groaning now. The claymores had left a couple of wounded, apparently. *Good thing most of the bastards were in the kill zone when Casey hit the clackers*, he thought.

"Thank God for the sensors," Sam Sloan said, staying prone with his rifle at the ready. "They gave us just the margin of warning that we needed."

"*Fuck* the sensors!" McKay snarled back. "That *Star Wars* shit almost got us killed. It tipped off the intruders that we knew they were out there. If we'd been able to cut loose on them before they were ready—didn't you learn *anything* in training?" His returning hearing caught Sam Sloan drawing a ragged breath.

"Billy." It was Casey's voice, pitched low. "Ease off, man."

Yeah, so I'm being an asshole. Mentally, McKay shrugged. They'd been caught flat-footed—them, the ee-lite Guardians. He didn't like to think anything like that could happen.

In a minute, Tom Rogers came back, dragging a limp body by a collar. "This one's got a few minutes left, I think," he said, depositing the man next to Mobile One. "Maybe we can get some information out of him."

McKay put Sam Sloan on top of the vehicle to keep watch with Casey, and knelt down with Rogers beside the prisoner. The explosion of the claymores and subsequent muzzle flashes had shot his night vision pretty much to hell, but enough was coming back that he was able to make a few details out by starlight. The captive was a man of indeterminate age, about middle height, and lean to the point of emaciation. His dark hair and beard were a wild crow's nest, but it didn't seem to be a deliberate effect, as it had been for the cannibals in South Dakota. He was in a bad way. The blast had chewed off his right leg around the knee, and the right side of his filthy shirt was sodden with blood, and looked mushy.

McKay leaned close. "Can you hear me?"

The man moaned, stirred. Half-closed eyelids opened. His eyes glinted like marbles in the starlight. The bearded lips writhed a moment, then: "Yeah . . . I hear ya talkin'."

"Why'd you attack our camp? You must've known you didn't stand a chance."

The shattered chest began to shudder. McKay glanced up in alarm. *Are we gonna lose the son of a bitch?* he was on the verge of asking, when suddenly the truth hit him.

The puke was laughing.

"Bullshit. We . . . almost had your asses, that time. Earth—Earth-star commune . . . been living out in the desert. . . . Away from the pigs." He struggled, as if to rise, got his right arm under him, grimaced, fell back. McKay realized that most of the flesh had been shredded from the man's right forearm, baring the radius and ulna. "Shit. Hadn't been for your . . . mines, would . . . *had* you. Had that fancy . . . armored car. We had it, we'd off some pigs . . . *for true.*"

The man stank horribly, and McKay was unsure whether it was from voiding his bowels or long usage. McKay bent close. Suddenly the man's left hand shot out and grabbed him by the collar of his fatigue blouse. "You fucked us, man. But van Damm . . . he's gettin' it together. He's gonna . . . fu-f-f-fuck *you.*"

The man croaked laughter, spraying McKay's face with spittle and blood. McKay jerked away as the laughter turned to a coughing spasm, a hideous jagged sound as if the man's lungs were tearing themselves apart inside him. He rolled onto his left side, hacking, black froth gushing from his mouth and nose. His fingers scrabbled at the dirt; his left leg kicked aimlessly, at the air, at the ground. He gave one final heave and lay still.

Slowly McKay straightened. "Who the hell is van Damm?"

"Van Damm?" Casey said from the turret. "He used to be the Lieutenant Governor, man. Real lefto, real movie-star type."

"What's he got to do with a gang of crazies running across the desert like lizards?" Sam Sloan asked, pleased at the chance to paraphrase Hunter Thompson, one of his favorite authors.

McKay shrugged. "Guess we'll find out." He looked around. Night vision had returned enough that he could see the twisted forms lying all about the vehicle in the darkness. He'd never read Dante, but he'd heard enough about the man to figure this scene was a lot like something he'd cook up. "Let's shift base the hell away from here. It smells like shit."

Bright and early the next morning, Mobile One was working its way south. The Guardians were preparing for the plunge into the wreckage of L.A. when from the turret Tom Rogers called, "Something moving up ahead."

McKay sat in the rear on a fold-down seat, keeping an eye on the Mexican girl, Amparo. She was awake, regarding him solemnly from big brown eyes. Since telling her story last night she'd said nothing.

McKay bounded forward to stand with one hand on the back of Sloan's ESO seat. "What about it, Billy?" Casey asked. "Should I pull us off into cover?"

"Negative. Just stop right here." They were driving a back road, but even it was strung, like some kind of charm bracelet, with stalled cars gleaming like dirty glass beads in the early sunlight. "Tom? Can you make out what it is?"

The car shuddered to a stop. "Looks like a panel truck of some sort—wait, it's stopped now. Range, 'bout twelve hundred meters." McKay popped the escape hatch aft of the two front seats and poked his head out. He raised a pair of heavy field glasses to his eyes and scanned the distant vehicle. It was stopped on the soft shoulder, squeezed between a tractor-trailer rig and the side of a ten-meter cut. It looked innocent enough—just a truck, white cab, silvery box. The passenger side door opened, and he caught a new glint of sunlight reflecting off glass. He frowned, then suddenly grinned.

"Son of a bitch. I'm looking at them, and they're looking back at *me*." He lowered the binoculars. "Sloan? I bet they have a CB. Why don't you get on the horn and see if you can raise their freek."

The occupants of the truck turned out to be a skinny white dude in khaki shorts and red-and-black soccer shirt, who called himself Lancelot, and a stocky, shaven-headed black dude with wraparound shades, who answered to the unlikely name of Idaho. They came forward to shake hands with McKay and Sloan when Mobile One had stopped ten meters away. "Good to meet you boys," Idaho boomed, pumping their hands. "You say you on some kind of special mission for the President?"

"Man, you almost scared the shit out of us when we saw that big armored car coming toward us," Lancelot said excitedly.

Idaho waved a hand at him. "Don't pay him no mind. He's the nervous type. But he just happens to be the best mechanic still on his hind legs in Southern California. Me, I'm the executive type." Lancelot murmured something about the blind leading the blind. Idaho just grinned more broadly.

"What are you gentlemen doing, anyway?" Sam Sloan asked. "We haven't exactly seen a whole lot of traffic since we came to California."

Idaho gestured at the truck. "Haulin' a load of salvage to this place we heard of up the coast. Pumps, generators, some industrial-grade solvent, load of little donkey engines. Little two-stroke things, real useful. Folks we're taking them to gonna bore em out so they'll run off alcohol. They're gonna give us fuel, a shitload of dried food, and a whole entire engine for a 'dozer. One of ours burned out its bearings."

"You're trading with them?" Sam Sloan asked.

"Like, it's all Balin's idea, man," Lancelot said, flapping his hands in agitation. "Like, I just know we're gonna get ripped off, I just *know* it."

Idaho frowned at his partner. "We turn up anymore vitamins, I gonna hide 'em from you. Make you too hyper. Yeah, we're tradin'. Dude who come through a couple of weeks ago turned us onto it. Man, they people all over this damned state, like, gettin' their acts together, raising up a few crops, scratchin' in the ruins like we're doing. Alone, maybe some of 'em have kind of a hard time makin' it. Now us, we do pretty well. But there's still, you know, stuff we got too much of, and stuff we have a hard time scraping up enough to get by on. So we're gonna go with this deal."

"Capitalism, man, that's all it is. Bummer." Lancelot made a mouth and shook his head.

"I don't care what you call it, man. They got stuff we want, we got stuff they want. That's all. Look to me like the best chance we got to get back to livin' decent."

Lancelot looked ready to continue the debate, but both McKay and Sloan broke in simultaneously. "This dude—" McKay said, and Sloan said, "You say a man—"

They stopped, looked at each other. McKay gave a little nod. "You said a man came through your, ah, place a few weeks ago? Who'd set this whole trade deal up?"

Idaho nodded his shiny head. "Did he say where he was going?" Sam Sloan asked.

Idaho glanced sidelong at Lancelot, who shrugged. "Don't

know, man," Lancelot said. "Have to, like, ask Balin."

"Balin? Who's Balin?" McKay asked.

"Balin the dwarf, man. Owner and operator of Balin's Forge. The main man of our little salvage operation. You thinkin' of lookin' him up?"

"Yeah," Billy McKay said slowly. "We might just do that."

The truckers had confirmed that Tejon Pass was blocked; the coastal roads, at least as far as the heavily bombed Vandenberg Air Force Base, were even worse. The truckers were bound for some sort of colony on Estero Bay, just north of San Luis Obispo. They figured their best route lay up through the Mojave to Tehachapi Pass, through the Sierra Nevada and across the San Joaquin Valley, and then finally across the Diablos to the coast. A roundabout route, but much quicker than trying to fight through the masses of stalled cars north of L.A. "We been tryin' to clear streets some in just our own area," Idaho told them. "To get them coast roads clear— man, that gonna take *years*."

In their turn, the Guardians were backtracking Idaho and Lancelot from where they'd encountered them, just north of the point where the desert met the San Gabriel Mountains. They crossed Soledad Pass, which was bad but not impossible, and cut off into a little back road paralleling State Road 14, through the San Gabriels to what had been the northern reaches of Los Angeles.

Los Angeles was . . . bad. An expert had once theorized that it would have taken about forty megaton-range warheads to destroy L.A. According to what the technicians at Heartland said, based on radio reports, satellite observations, and even a few scattered returns from seismographic stations, the L.A. area had taken well over half that many hits. Why that had happened was hard to say. A fair concentration of military targets existed in the vicinity: the Pacific Missile Test Center, near Port Hueneme; March Air Force Base, near Riverside; and, farther down the coast, the Marine training base at Camp Pendleton; as well as a substantial number of airports, which the Soviets generally considered legitimate military targets. But a handful of warheads would have canceled those targets. Primarily, the Soviets had targeted their missiles on installations that threatened them directly, such as launching-silo farms, MX "racetracks," and SAC bases. For the most part they had not allowed themselves the luxury of terror-bombing the civilian population. Yet from San Diego, with its big naval station, up to Vandenberg AFB, the California coast had been well saturated with thermonuclear warheads. The main reason, as far as McKay could tell, was pure meanness.

Having raised Balin's people on the radio and told them they were on their way, the Guardians reached the ragged interface between the little suburb of Simi Valley and the desert as the day went to orange and amber and the sun began its kamikaze dive into the hidden Pacific. Shortly, they saw the sign, crudely hand-drawn in Gothic letters: BALIN'S FORGE. It sat atop a low whitewashed cinderblock building, with a green-painted flat roof on it, that had once been the front office for a construction yard. A raised-planking porch with an awning over it had been added, and a number of house trailers pulled up out back. The yard itself, in which several men and women worked, was surrounded by a two-meter chain-link fence with barbed-wire strands running along the top. On the front porch, an old woman in a faded dress sat in a rocking chair and rocked determinedly, not taking note of the diesel-blatting armored car pulling to a stop barely ten meters from her.

As Tom Rogers stopped the car, the screen door banged open and out stepped a man who could only be Balin himself. For once, it seemed, McKay didn't need the inevitable Sloan and Casey Wilson to interpret for him. As it happened, he'd actually read J. R. R. Tolkien's *Lord of the Rings*, and knew that Balin was the name of a member of the race of beings called *dwarves* in the books. Boosting himself out through the turret hatch to go meet the man, McKay could see why this Balin was called that.

It wasn't that he was actually a real-world dwarf, with the usual small body, outsized head, and stubby limbs. He was, in fact, of fairly normal proportions—if you were a powerlifter. He was maybe five-three, nearly a yard across the shoulders and belly, and bandy-legged. He had on a blue work shirt that was stretched out in the front like a square-rigger's sail in a stiff breeze, blue jeans, and scuffed-toe work boots. His face was round and red, his eyes cheerful little crescents above apple cheeks. His nose bore a passing resemblance to a crab-apple. He wore a fringe of black curly beard, and his hair was gathered into a little queue at the back of what neck he possessed. He wore a baseball-style cap with a red dragon on it, surrounded by the inscription, DRAGONRIDERS DO IT IN MIDAIR which made no sense to McKay.

McKay dropped to the gravel and walked forward. "Hello! Welcome to Balin's Forge!" the man boomed. "You must be McKay. I'm Balin. Pleased to meet you."

McKay wanted to ask him if that was the name that was on his birth certificate. But he guessed these days it didn't matter —and, this being California, it *might* have been. "That's right." He reached out a hand; Balin took it. For a moment the two men squeezed, each testing the other's strength. Then they grinned at each other and let go. McKay had the impression the little man could have made pulp of his hand if he'd wanted to. *Jesus*, he thought. *I'm built like a linebacker, but I can't weigh more than a few kilos more than the little fuck.* Balin, in fact, looked like nothing McKay had ever seen, nothing at all except . . . one of Tolkien's dwarves.

"And is this your mother?" McKay asked, nodding toward the woman rocking on the porch.

Balin laughed. "No, that's Granma. We found her wandering in the rubble, and kind of adopted her." He reached up to clap McKay on the shoulder. "Tell your boys to come on in. You're just in time for supper."

The front door popped open again and a small woman in her mid-thirties, with short, straight blond hair and glasses, bustled out. She wore a T-shirt with a picture faded past intelligibility. She was good-looking in a stocky sort of way, at least to McKay's eye. "Where's the poor injured child you told us about?"

"In the car, resting, ma'am."

"Bring her in at once. We've got a bedroom prepared for her, in back across the hall from ours."

The Guardians stashed Mobile One in a wooden shed with a tin roof in the compound just behind the main building. A screened-in wooden porch had been built out from the rear of the cinderblock office, and this served as a combination kitchen and dining area. The salvagers had turned up one of those wood-burning ranges that had gotten popular in the late eighties, before wood burning was outlawed, and set it up next to the wall of the building on some fire bricks.

Dinner was served on a couple of scrounged redwood picnic tables, by the light of kerosene lanterns. "We got generators for electricity," Balin explained, "but we don't like to use them unless it's necessary." The meal itself was a pungent stew, some kind of stringy, unidentified meat swimming with carrots, celery, and potatoes, heavily seasoned with oregano and a number of spices including—if McKay's nose didn't mislead him—marijuana. It was ladled into an assortment of bowls by the camp cook, Shep, a tall, skinny, saturine man.

The Guardians set to eating with a will, sopping up the stew with chunks of buttered cornbread. It was one of the more pleasant ways McKay could think of to get to know Balin's crew. Which was quite a varied lot.

The forge seemed to be home to about forty souls, of various sizes, shapes, and ages, from a child nursing at the breast of a thin blond woman named Marcie, to old Granma, who wouldn't be budged from her rocking chair on the front porch until it was time for bed. Perhaps a dozen were crowded onto the back porch for dinner; the rest were off busy at various chores, maintaining equipment, cleaning salvaged goods, or off rooting in the ruins.

"We're lucky, here," Lonny Chin said as he spooned himself a second helping of stew. He was a tall, lanky young man with Chinese eyes, whose Baltimore Orioles baseball cap didn't quite conceal the fact that his hair had turned gray and was falling out in patches. The skin of his face was slightly mottled, discolored, but obviously clearing up. The depilation and discoloration were a transient effect of exposure to radiation—Sam Sloan, who'd been exposed to a hefty dose in the crater at Colorado Springs, was showing some of the same signs still. "We didn't get too much fallout this way. And it's mostly died out all over the place, except around the craters where some of the things actually hit. Only problem is when you stir up buried dust. Some of the stuff under the surface is still pretty virulent."

"How'd you people get together, anyway?" Casey Wilson asked. He directed the question at Balin, but his eyes were on a woman who sat across the table from him. Her name was

Rhoda. She was a tall, buxom redhead in her early twenties, with a nose that turned up at the tip and eyes that turned down at the outer corners, especially when she grinned, as she was doing now. She wore overalls with a tank top underneath, and on the whole looked good enough to eat. From Casey's expression, McKay judged that was about what he had in mind.

Balin shrugged. "Oh, you know, we just kind of fell together." The woman sitting at his left gave him a hearty elbow in the ribs.

"That wasn't very informative, Balin," she said. She grinned across the table at the four Guardians. Jeannie was the businesslike lady who had met them out in front of the office and taken charge of Amparo with the solicitude of a mother hen. She was Balin's wife.

"Balin used to be president of the San Bernardino chapter of the Hell's Angels. But unlike most of his buddies, he saved his money. Eventually he grew up enough to quit that whole mess, so he bought this place and settled down."

Balin looked pained. "For God's sake, honey, I'm grown up."

"The only way you've grown since you were twelve is *out*."

Balin said, "Aw," and reached out a trash compactor of a hand to tousle her hair.

"Anyway," she went on, "some of his old biker buddies, like Shep there, or like Marcie's husband, Frank, gave it up too and came to work for him here. Some of them just moved into the trailers we had on the place. Other folks were people we knew, who came by here when things blew up. Or like Lonny, there, just wandered in one day and offered to work his keep if we'd give him a place to stay."

"What about Lancelot and Idaho, we met out on the road?" Casey Wilson asked.

Rhoda twinkled at him. "Lancelot was a mechanic, just down the street. Idaho . . ." She giggled. "I don't know if I should tell you."

Balin's face turned the color of boiled beets. "*I* will," Jeannie said. "He used to be Balin's parole officer."

Sam Sloan finished the last of his stew and sat back with a contented sigh. "You don't know what a relief it is, to get some good home cooking after days of freeze-dried rations. I didn't recognize the meat, though—it had an interesting flavor, kind of tangy. What was it?"

From the corner of his eye, McKay saw Tom Rogers grin. Since Rogers grinned about as frequently as the seated statue in the Lincoln Memorial, McKay wondered just what in hell was going on. Jeannie looked at Sloan in wonder. "Oh, didn't you know? It was wild dog. Shep's got a great recipe for . . ."

Her voice trailed away. Sloan and Casey Wilson were looking at one another, their faces gone yellow-gray in the amber lantern light. As one, they clamped hands over their mouths and bolted out the screen door. "Oh dear," Jeannie said. "Have I said something wrong?"

Tom watched the departure of his comrades with mild eyes. "Ever try making *nuoc mam* sauce?"

Later, when Sam and Casey had recovered their composure, the Guardians drank coffee and asked Balin about the mystery man. "Yeah, he was through here about a month or so back. He set this trading scheme up with the folks up to Estero Bay. It works out, there's all sorts of people we can trade with. Maybe get some more fresh food—that's something we need most." Casey and Sam traded queasy glances.

"Did he say where he was going?" McKay asked.

Balin shrugged. "North. Said we'd see him when we saw him. Offered to let him take a vehicle, but he said he'd never get it out of the congestion north of here."

Business out of the way, Balin brought out a guitar and played with skill while Jeannie sang in a high clear soprano. They talked a while longer, then went to bed, Tom Rogers to bunk down in Mobile One in its shed, Sloan and McKay to share a room in the main building, and Casey . . . McKay didn't inquire too closely. But he thought, *Lucky son of a bitch*. The last thing he heard before sleep was the far-off yapping of a pack of wild dogs, and he drifted off with a smile on his face.

CHAPTER
THIRTEEN ────────────

Casey Wilson woke with Rhoda's arm across his chest and alarms going off in his mind.

He and the redhead had found themselves in the next-to-the-last bedroom at the north end of the cinderblock building, on the east side. It apparently had been a bedroom even before the war; Balin had evidently set it up to serve as both living quarters for himself and some of his friends, as well as to provide office space when he bought it. Now an ugly cement-colored light was filtering in past the edges of the cracked, yellowed pull-down shade, and from outside he heard a truck engine idling. And voices.

He sat up. The day's heat had already started to thicken around them. Rhoda stirred sleepily, said something muzzily inquisitive. "Shh, honey. Don't make a sound." Her eyes came open. They were huge and amber, but he didn't have time to appreciate their beauty just now. He put a finger to his lips. She frowned, nodded.

He got off the bed—box springs and a salvaged mattress set on four cinderblocks, like a derelict car in a hillbilly's yard—and moved to the window, his bare feet making no sound on the linoleum floor. Trying to remember if his Guardian training in Arizona had covered a situation like this, he sidled up to the window, laid the side of his head to the cinderblock wall, and tried to see out without actually moving the shade. Couldn't quite do it—with one fingertip he edged the blind ever so carefully back away from the open window.

There was a truck parked out front, one of those flatbed things with wooden sides on the bed, used to haul cabbages and whatnot. In the early dawn, men were jumping out the back of the truck and fanning out to both sides of the main building. Men with guns—Casey felt a thrill of apprehension as he recognized the stubby assault rifles with gas cylinders above the barrel and banana-shaped magazines. AK's. Soviet-made.

Balin stood out in front of the building, barefoot in jeans and with his shirttail out. He was talking to a neat, compact man in a bush jacket who had a sandy beard and some kind of automatic strapped to his hip. Balin didn't look too happy. Behind him on the porch Granma sat and rocked, oblivious to the confrontation shaping up before her.

The men deploying around the building seemed to be about evenly divided between black guys wearing Army surplus jackets and white guys dressed in haphazard combinations of civvies and military drag. A couple of the blacks passed Casey's window, and he shrank back. On the right breast pockets of their jackets he saw cream-colored circular patches, sporting crudely embroidered black serpents with flaring hoods, rearing up as if to strike. He recognized it as the emblem of a radical black group calling themselves the Black Mambas—dramatic, but a little silly, since mambas didn't have hoods, and were in fact more closely related to rattlers than cobras.

He catfooted back to the bed, sat down, and began pulling on his trousers with one hand. With his other he picked up his personal communicator from the cable spool table set next to the bed. "Billy?" he said quietly. "Tom, Sam—anybody. This is Casey, please come in."

He got the pants on. Cold sweat started all over his body as he heard shouts from outside and then the clanging rattle of somebody shaking the chain-link fence at the north end of the building, probably frustrated to find there was no gate. He was just about to repeat the message, when a gruff and familiar voice growled, "McKay. Sloan's with me. What the fuck, over?"

Trying to fasten his web belt one-handed, Casey said, "Trouble, Billy. Truck out front, ten or fifteen intruders spilling out. Armed with AKMs, looks like. Leader's out front talking to Balin. They're spreading out to secure the place."

"Tom? You copy?" McKay asked.

"I copy." Casey felt relief at hearing Tom Rogers's voice. If they'd caught him, unsuspecting, in Mobile One—

"Casey, you stay put. Tom, you too. Stick with Mobile One; make them find you. Sam'll try to make his way to the south end of the building."

Casey stuck his personal communicator back in its little holster on his belt, and fastened the mike over his larynx with its adhesive pad. "What about you, Billy?"

"I'm coming across the corridor to the front of the building. We're in the last room at the north end. You across from from us?"

"One down." Casey ran an eye over his gear. McKay insisted, come what may, that the Guardians keep their personal weapons near to hand at all times. Fortunately, Rhoda found all this hardware kind of sexy.

The shoulder holster with his long-barreled .44 Magnum Smith & Wesson was hung over the back of a green-painted wooden chair, which looked as if it belonged in a cheap Mexican restaurant. His elaborate M-40X sniper's rifle with the ultrasophisticated electronic scope was propped against one wall. He barely glanced at it; it was a long-range weapon, and under fifty meters useful mainful as an unwieldly club. That being the case, Casey liked to carry an extra weapon for close combat.

He picked it up off the table. An Ingram M-10, a true machine pistol, in itself not much bulkier or heavier than a Colt .45. Good thing he'd screwed the foot-long Sionics noise suppressor onto the stubby muzzle the night before, to show Rhoda how it worked. Without its counterbalancing weight, the gun was virtually impossible to control. With a rate of fire of almost a thousand rounds a minute, it wasn't much use for targets beyond ten meters anyway. But for targets *inside* that range—

Rhoda tugged his arm. He turned around. She was leaning half out of the bed, and Casey reflected that while he'd never liked big breasts particularly, she'd done a lot to turn his head around. She mouthed the words, "There's somebody in the foyer."

He nodded acknowledgment and passed the information subvocally on to McKay and the rest. "Roger that." McKay said. "Sam—you take him."

"What about Balin's people?" Sam asked.

"We hope they have the sense to keep their heads down."

Casey eyed his fatigues, draped over a low dresser. At the top of the heap lay his Kevlar bulletproof vest. He looked at it longingly, but there was no time for to struggle into it now.

He started toward the window. And two shots cracked the dawn wide open.

Using a key on the ring Commander Steel's guards had taken off the fat man when they frisked him, Marcus and Phil opened the padlock that held the big gates south of the main building shut. "Hey, watch it," said Phil, the shorter, curly-haired one with the brown mustache. "Might have some kind of mean dog in here."

Taller, darker-haired, and heavy-faced, his buddy jerked to a halt just inside the gate. No dog appeared. "Shit," he said to Marcus in disgust, and pushed on through.

It looked like your basic junkyard. Near the fence were stocks of construction materials, lumber stacked under traps, bags of cement, piles of bricks and cinderblock. The yard itself was crowded with rusty machinery, plunder of foraging expeditions in the ruined city. Parked in the clump behind the office were a couple of pickups, a tow truck, and a chartreuse bulldozer. Beyond, at the north end of the lot, sat several house trailers. Phil pointed to them. "Want to go check them out?"

Marcus jutted his sharp foxlike chin at the wooden shed directly behind the cinderblock house. "Check that first."

They moved forward, keeping a watchful eye in all directions, especially on the main building. A couple of seasoned grunts from the Cienfuegos Brigade of the People's Republic of the Bear, they knew the firepower of their automatic weapons gave them quite an edge. But sometimes the pigs just didn't know when they were beat. You had to be careful.

"Hey, look. It's open," Marcus said as they approached the double wooden doors. He hesitated, frowning. "That's strange. The pigs are usually more paranoid about their precious private property."

"Shit," Phil said again. He strode impatiently up to the doors, with Marcus reluctantly at his heels. He grabbed the metal handles with either hand, took a step back, and threw the heavy doors open with a heave of his thick shoulders.

Marcus had a brief impression of something squat and huge and glinting metallic, poised in the gloom of the shed like something from a horror movie. Then flame flashed from the dimness, and Phil doubled up with a grunt and went sailing backwards as though he'd been punched in the gut by a giant fist.

Marcus just had time to gape at his friend rolling in the yellow dust, trying to stuff his intestines back into place. Then a second charge of number 4 buckshot caught him at the base of the throat, and that was all she wrote.

In a single bound, Casey was at the window, Ingram in hand. "Keep down," he hissed to Rhoda. He twitched the blind back a hair and peered out.

The yard was full of armed men staring at Balin and the sandy-bearded man, who were rolling around in the dust in a tangle of flailing limbs. The leader's two bodyguards danced frantically around with their AK's pointed downward, trying to get a clear shot at the infuriated Balin.

That icy combat calm settled over Casey Wilson. He snapped back the little wire folding stock, brought it to his shoulder and fired twice, scarcely bothering to aim. The guards went down.

The noise suppressor ate most of the sound made by the rounds going off, and the .45-caliber slugs moved too slowly to produce a supersonic crack. Nonetheless, at these close quarters there was no way the intruders wouldn't spot him. His best chance was to grab fire superiority *now*. He thumbed the weapon to full automatic and held the trigger down.

At the sound of the gunshots, Sam Sloan pulled the pin on the stun grenade in his left hand. Holding the lever down with thumb and forefinger, his Galil in his right hand, he moved to the door. His every nerve cried out for sudden, violent action, but the arduous Guardian training kept faith with him. With the last two fingers of his left hand he turned the knob of the door, slowly, slowly.

The door opened inward. He pulled it far enough that he could stick his head out and peer cautiously past the jamb. Seven meters away, down the corridor, a bearded man stood, an AKM held negligently in his hands, but ready at any time to snap up and spray bullets into the helpless form of Jeannie, who stood before him in a faded robe. Right now, he was frowning past her toward the back porch, in the direction from which the shots had come.

Left-handed, Sloan lobbed the grenade down the hall. The bearded man's peripheral vision was good; Sloan saw his head snapping around before he himself ducked back into the doorway.

The grenade went off with an ear-splitting crack. Sloan heel-kicked the door open and sidestepped into the hall, bringing the Galil to his shoulder for maximum control. The guerilla was looking right at him, his eyes blinking rapidly in the manner of one flash-blinded. But the AK's muzzle was swinging up.

Following standard anti-terrorist doctrine, Sloan fired a single aimed shot. The needlelike 5.56 slug punched through the man's right eye and the brain behind, making a neat little exit wound in the rear of the skull. The man's limbs flailed once, and he collapsed on the floor.

Sloan was already in motion down the hall. He heard a woman screaming, judged it was Jeannie freaking out from the grenade's explosion, hoped he was right. He burst into the foyer. The door was jammed as at least three revolutionaries tried to cram through at once.

Most rounds for the M-203 grenade launcher slung under

the Galil's barrel refused to arm themselves inside of ten meters' free flight, as a safety measure to protect the shooter. The one exception was the one he had up in the spout now—a multiple-projectile round, which turned the grenade launcher into an outsize shotgun. He pivoted left and fired from the hip. The roar was enormous in the confines of the foyer. The giant charge of buckshot simply shredded the trio in the doorway.

Overriding a lifetime of Missouri gallantry, Sam Sloan stiff-armed Jeannie in passing, knocking her into a weeping huddle at the foot of the wall. He hoped to Christ she'd stay there—it was all he could do for her. Jacking open the receiver of the single-shot grenade launcher, he pelted into the southern corridor.

As soon as Sam Sloan was out the door, McKay was right after him, lunging for the closed door directly across the corridor. He hoped like hell it wasn't hardwood; if it was it would be the flip of the coin whether the hinges or his shoulder gave way. It turned out to be plywood sheets on a pine frame, and McKay went *through* the door in a blast of splinters.

He had a quick flash of a bedroom in use as a storeroom, a table upside-down on top of a bed, stacks of chairs and assorted clutter. That was all he got, because the venetian blind on the front window was pulled down with the slats horizontal, enabling him to see outside. A pair of Black Mambas, having figured that there was no way through the fence to the north of the building except to climb over the barbed wire, stood frozen two meters outside the window, trying to look in all directions at once and see what the hell was going *on*. Holding the front and rear pistol grips of the machine gun, McKay fired two quick bursts from the hip as if the M-60 were an outsized submachine gun—and he had the strength and mass to pull it off. The two Mambas spun away in a welter of blood.

McKay moved forward toward the window. Not *to* the window; only in the movies do soldiers poke guns out windows and blaze away, or when, as with Casey, reality leaves them no choice. In real life, whenever possible they keep back a ways to do their firing, lessening their chances of being spotted and picked off by the opposition. Ideally, McKay would have moved the stripped-wood desk to a position about a meter inside the window, dropped the bipod, and set the machine gun up on top of it. No time for that now—he just braced his legs, snugged the gun butt against his shoulder, and sent a long burst ripping into the truck outside.

Tom Rogers laid aside the Remington 1100 autoloading shotgun. For surprising anybody rash enough to poke into the shed, he'd reckoned it would be ideal—and it had been. Now a serious firefight was shaping up, and he wanted his Galil short assault rifle. He picked it up from where he'd laid it on the deck of Mobile One, then moved back and around the rear of the vehicle, so he could cover the gate from the protection of Mobile One's angular snout. He braced his elbow on the front glacis, just behind the welded tubular cage protecting the left headlight, and waited, peering over the Galil's battle sights into the gathering daylight.

When the four Anglos in their big armored car found her and tended to her injuries, Amparo had thought she was safe. But safety was a dream, and now the nightmare had begun again.

She didn't know what woke her. Probably the sound of angry voices in the front yard. She had been given a bedroom at the southern end of the house in back, across the hall from the one that Balin and his wife shared. She sat upright in bed in the pink nightdress, scavenged from a department store, that Jeannie had lent her. She propped herself on her left arm, since her right was immobilized and strapped across her chest. She knew something was horribly wrong.

Where the first shots came from, she couldn't be sure. She backed up against the wall with her knees drawn up, and whimpered. *No, not again, I can't take it again.*

Shattering noise erupted right outside her door. An explosion, shots, screaming. In a frenzy of terror, she jumped off the bed, lunged for the window. It was unscreened and open against the heat. *I won't let them get me again. I've got to get away.*

The door to her room burst open. The sound galvanized her. With a leap she was through the window, stumbling, recovering, running frantically across the yard. "Amparo, *no!*" Sam Sloan yelled at her back. But she never heard him.

"Casey, cover the foyer," Casey Wilson heard through his earphone, as the M-60 began rocking 'n' rolling from the next room. Casey blew off the rest of the clip and backed away from the window, changing magazines as he went. He caught a glimpse of Rhoda's well-rounded rear end between the bed and the wall where she'd flattened herself. *Smart lady,* he thought, and went out the door.

It was a reckless thing to do. Two guerrillas stood in the foyer. As they started to turn, Casey triggered off a quick burst and dove for the floor.

One of the two yelled hoarsely and fell back against the fake oak paneling of the wall, bloody blossoms on the front of his khaki shirt. The other blasted a long burst from the hip, right over Casey's head, filling that end of the corridor with the dust of shattered cinderblock. Casey fired back from the floor. Two bullets caught the man in the chest and knocked him backwards over a low table, scattering magazines and clipboards.

McKay's machine gun had fallen silent, having run out of targets. "Casey? You all right?" his voice asked in Casey's ear.

"Oh, yeah," Casey said. "No problem."

Four of the guerrillas came through the open gate at a run, heading for the cover of the vehicles parked behind the main building. Rogers, firing from the shed beyond the vehicles, knocked one down with a burst of 5.56. The other three dove to their left, behind a white dumpster sitting in the southeast corner of the yard, diagonal to the two sides of the fence. From its cover they returned Roger's fire.

The ex-Green Beret ducked as a burst knocked splinters from the frame of the shed's door. He saw Amparo clamber through her window in her nightgown, one arm pinned across her chest like a crippled bird's wing. She raced heedlessly into the yard.

She'd gone perhaps ten meters when bullets struck her in the shoulder, left side, and hip. She screamed, fell, started crawling on one arm and one leg. A second burst knocked her down, and she lay still.

Casey crouched in the doorway where the corridor gave way to the foyer, covering the front door with his Ingram. From outside came the groans of wounded men, and pinging clanks as the metal of the truck cab, indented by machine-gun bullets, relaxed back to a semblance of its original position. Across the foyer and down the other corridor, he heard the stuttering of Sloan's Galil, the 5.56 rounds sounding oddly like an amplified air gun as they went off.

A dark shape loomed in the front door, filling it, blocking the spill of milky morning light. Casey's finger tightened on the trigger.

The figure sagged against the doorframe, and at the last possible instant before the breakpoint when the sear would release the firing pin and send a stream of slugs tearing into the figure, Casey's fighter-pilot's eye registered the stocky form of Balin. He shuddered. *God, I almost shot him!*

The bearded man held up his huge hands, staring at them as if he'd never seen them before. "I . . . killed him," he muttered. "With my hands. I broke his neck, and he died . . . just like that."

Nothing moved in the front yard, and the intruders' truck, leaking gas and radiator fluid from a score of 7.62 holes, wasn't going anywhere any time soon. "Casey, keep an eye out the front door," McKay ordered, and moved south to where the noise indicated a firefight was still on.

He found Sloan in what had been Amparo's bedroom. The bed was rumpled, and there was no sign of the girl. The ex-Navy officer was hunkered down beside a south-facing window, slamming the breech of his M-203 shut. "They killed her," he said in a harsh voice. His face was pale and taut in a way McKay had never seen it before. "She panicked—climbed out the window and ran out in the yard. And they just shot her down."

McKay sidled to the window and poked his crew-cut head past the bullet-gouged frame for a three-second look. The Mexican girl lay in a pathetic heap in the dust, the bloodied nightgown up around her hips. "Who?" he asked.

"Three of the bastards. Hiding behind that dumpster." There was a loud rattle of fire from behind the shed, and the white side of the dumpster flexed as a burst from Rogers's rifle slammed into it. "Our bullets don't seem to reach through."

McKay nodded. Maybe the thin steel walls of the dumpster weren't defeating the two Guardians' rounds—perhaps the trash heaped inside the container was deflecting the light bullets. But their fire wasn't having any effect.

McKay heard the stutter of an AK, slower and deeper than a Galil. He held up his machine-gun in his right hand. "Want me to take care of them? *This* baby'll punch right through that shit."

"In a minute." Sloan raised his combination weapon to his shoulder and pulled the trigger of the M-203 with his left hand. It roared. There was a bright white flash, and the dumpster exploded.

Sloan had put an HEDP round into the thing—a grenade that added concussion and fragmentation effects to a shaped-charge warhead. The projectile had sent a lance of incandescent gas stabbing through the thin metal, through the rubbish inside, and out the other side. A scream pealed shrill and mindless as a fountain of blazing trash erupted from the dumpster.

Two burning figures appeared from behind the dumpster, weaponless and running flat-out for the gate. They never made it.

So total had the revolutionaries' arrogance been, in waltzing boldly in to browbeat what they took to be just another nest of poorly armed scavengers, that the only survivors of the Guardians' impromptu ambush were two injured men, a Black Mamba and one of the People's Republic types. Both refused to talk to their captors until McKay drew his sidearm and put a .45 slug through the Mamba's head. After that his companion, a skinny young white man with shaggy brown hair, was only too glad to talk to them.

Geoff van Damm, former Lieutenant Governor of the State of California, had a plan, it seemed. Uniting the remnants of the old radical-left network with the rising generation of violent crazies in a California Liberation Front, he was going to

assert control over the entire state. Armed bands were busily
whipping scattered survivors into line, in a program orches-
trated, rumor had it, by a right-on dude from Russia itself.
"You fuckers don't have a chance, man," the captive told
them, his courage returning. With Jeannie's help, Tom Rogers
had bound his leg, which had caught one of McKay's
machine-gun bullets through the thigh. "He's organizing the
people, man. Once they realize they've got nothing to lose but
their chains, there'll be no stopping us."

White-lipped with fury, Jeannie glared at him. "But you
were coming here with guns, to kill us!"

The young man shrugged, then winced at the pain the motion sent stabbing through his leg. "Yeah, but like, you people
are capitalists, pigs."

She looked at him in disbelief. "Then who are the people
you're supposed to be *liberating*?"

"You know. The *people*. The working classes."

"Like Amparo and her family," Sam Sloan said grimly.

"Fuckin' A," McKay said.

"Where's this van Damm working from?" The question
came, soft-voiced, from Tom Rogers, who was checking on
Lonny Chin's dressing. The young man, like the rest of Balin's
people, had had the sense to stay inside when the shit hit the
fan. A spent AK round had punched through the wall of his
trailer and lodged in his calf, causing a painful but basically
superficial wound. Aside from Amparo, and a few assorted
gashes and contusions on Balin's lumpy person, he was the
only casualty. On the porch out front, Granma still rocked in
her dim print dress.

The guerrilla clamped his mouth shut. His eyes made a
quick circuit of the room, lingering beseechingly on the faces
of Jeannie and Rhoda—and with a shock like a bullet's impact, he realized that no one, not even the women, showed the
slightest sign of mercy.

It had been grand to be an armed insurrectionary, back in
the days before the One-Day War. The straights were like
sheep, man. The least little bit of armed propaganda had them
shitting their pants—and if you got caught, they'd just line up
in droves to sign petitions demanding your release.

Now, he realized, it was a whole new ball game. These

strange men, these Guardians with their gray uniforms and steely eyes, could by Christ pull him to pieces, and none of these straight citizens would object. They might leave the room—but they wouldn't stop these pigs from doing anything to him that they pleased. He felt sweat starting on his forehead.

"San Simeon, man. He's got his headquarters in Hearst's old castle." And threw back his head and laughed at the astonished looks on their faces.

They buried Amparo early that afternoon, inside the fence of the compound so the wild dogs wouldn't get at her. Sam Sloan raised New Eden on Mobile One's communications gear, and learned that the semi was loaded, the miracle seeds ready to be flown out by a transport from Heartland. Mobile One was needed to escort the truck to the landing zone. It was time to go.

Early next afternoon found them back in the Sierra Nevadas. The guard at the truss bridge waved them through with markedly poor grace. Susan Spinelli came to meet them riding her palomino mare. She shouted, "Hurry up! We've got a surprise for you," then turned the mare's head and sent her racing back toward the commune at a full gallop. Sam Sloan had the wheel, and since the Maldita valley bottom was still marshy, the blond horsewoman beat him, to his chagrin and MacKay's heavy sarcasm.

A crowd of excited New Edenites welcomed the Guardians with happy cries and waves. Leaving Mobile One cooling slowly in the yard, they walked into the semisubterranean dimness of the Main Habitat, Susan Spinelli leading Sam Sloan by the hand, barely able to contain her excitement.

Dr. Mahalaby sat in the commissary, sipping a mug of his unspeakable herbal tea. Seated across the table from him was another man. A spare, graying, weather-beaten man in a black-and-brown striped robe.

"Gentlemen," boomed Mahalaby, rising to his feet, "allow me to introduce my very good friend, Dr. Jacob Morgenstern —the mystery participant in the Blueprint for Renewal!"

The wind rustled through the branches of imported trees,

making little wavelets on the surface of the swimming pool. Pulling his attention away from the images of the stars overhead in the California night, breaking apart and reforming on the pool's surface, Ivan Vesensky looked up and said, "You're sure? The Guardians are here, in California?"

"I'm sure," said the small, shabby man. His eyes kept straying to the Roman marble statue of a nude woman, beside which he stood. "I saw them myself, at General Edwards's place." He shook his head. "Man, they had that crusty old fart buffaloed like nothing you've ever seen."

Vesensky's aristocratic features hardened into grim planes. *The Guardians! They can knock down everything I've built up here.* Such an elite team, well trained, well disciplined, and well equipped, could cut apart the confederacy he was welding together by means of van Damm like a bayonet through butter. Sketchily trained, with doubtful communications, little or no popular support, and cohesiveness that seldom lasted longer than it took any two components to discover the sort of hairsplitting doctrinal differences for which they seemed constantly alert, van Damm's merry men were hardly the ideal tools to build an empire with. They were simply all Vesensky had on hand.

Van Damm interrupted Vesensky's gloomy reverie with an abrupt laugh. The two men and their informant, with the ever-present Marlon silent in the background, stood next to the outdoor pool. It was a marble extravaganza bracketed by crescent arcades and shielded by a high, statue-topped wall from sight of the road that wound around the rise in which the pool was sunk. From the nearest house, one of the lesser palaces, came the sounds of loud merrymaking; most of van Damm's people seemed to think that the revolution was meant to be a permanent party.

No sound at all came from the cordon of California Liberation Front stalwarts and JRA wolves, invisibly ringing the pool in the darkness. Their presence was not indicative of paranoia; since Van Damm had arrived a week before there had been two separate attempts on his life. Not by counter-revolutionary zealots, but by dissident elements of his own organization.

"Thank you, Baxter," the former Lieutenant Governor

said. "Your intelligence, as always, was very valuable. Is there anything in particular you'd like before you set out again?"

The little man squeezed the statue's marble hip, leaving smudged fingerprints. "Well, ah—it's been, you know, well, a long time since I've been with a woman—"

Van Damm cut the man's whining off with a raised hand. "Say no more, comrade." He gestured with his chin toward the palace from which the frat-house sounds of laughter and loud talk were issuing. Loud seventies-revival rock blasted from unseen speakers. "Go on up to that house and tell Commander Sálazar I sent you. He'll let you take your pick of his female recruits." Baxter bared foul teeth to the starlight and hurried away.

Van Damm turned to Vesensky to see the Russian's eyebrow raised. "You disapprove, Ian? Surely you, of all people, know that sacrifices must be made for the Cause." Vesensky shrugged and turned away. Van Damm came forward, laid a hand on his shoulder. "You're concerned about these, these Guardians, aren't you, comrade?"

Vesensky watched the dark reflections of the nymphs on the wall undulate across the pool's surface. This assignment was nerve-grating, even for such an experienced cadreman as he. "Yes."

Van Damm laughed again. The hand patted Vesensky's shoulder familiarly. "Well, don't be. When the people from the Murieta Brigade get here, there won't be one damned thing those imperialist bastards can do to stop us. Nothing anybody can do. You'll see."

From somewhere higher on the hill, someone let loose a shuddering blast of gunfire at the half-moon. Vesensky winced at the pool. "You've been acting coy ever since you got that message from the Joaquin Murieta Brigade," he complained. "What in bloody hell is going on?"

Van Damm only smiled.

CHAPTER
FOURTEEN ─────────

Billy McKay sat on the dock and watched the gypsy fleet bobbing against the setting sun. With the sun this low, reflection off the dancing water no longer sent eye-hurting spears of bright white light dazzling off toward the shore. It had been a hectic ten days since Mobile One had returned to New Eden, and McKay was grateful for the chance to rest his weary bones on the deck chair.

Dr. Jacob Morgenstern was, in fact, the missing key to the Blueprint for Renewal whose existence had been postulated by the computers at Heartland. He'd been born in Israel in the early thirties, had been jailed for the first time at the age of thirteen, protesting against the British occupation of Palestine. Despite his youth, he'd seen service with the Palmach during the 1948 war. In 1956 he jumped as a captain of paratroops with the First Battalion of Colonel Ariel Sharon's 202nd Parachute Brigade at the eastern end of Mitla Pass. After the Sinai War, he'd resigned from active service in the military to pursue his interest in economics. In 1967 he was a major in the Reserves, and Arab resistance collapsed so rapidly that his unit never saw action. In 1973, as a full colonel, he commanded a tank brigade of his own, in a counter-attack against the Syrians on the Golan Heights.

After the Yom Kippur War, Morgenstern had remained in Israel only a few more years before leaving, dissatisfied both with his country's socialist economic structure and the expansionist policies of Prime Minister Menachem Begin. He'd emigrated to the United States, where he'd become involved with the so-called Chicago School of economics, whose guru was Milton Friedman. The School espoused decreased government influence in the marketplace, an idea he found tremendously attractive. Disenchanted in turn with Friedman's monetarist policies, he'd broken with the Chicago boys to champion his own free market, minimal government views. And from industry he won acclaim as nothing less than a genius, with a much publicized contract from the Japanese to attempt to help them out of an economic stagnation into which they'd increasingly slipped in the later eighties.

It had also won him a much less well publicized offer to participate in a top secret United States Government project code-named *Blueprint*.

By that time Morgenstern believed more than ever that the best thing the government could do for the economy was to keep its hands off, but if the government was putting together a massive contingency plan for rebuilding the country in the event of nuclear war, he was only too happy to have his ideas be a part of it. He had, in fact, become one of the main architects of the plan, specifying fields of expertise which would be at a premium in the event of a nuclear war, and in many cases suggesting participants themselves. By the time his association with the project ended, two years before the outbreak of the One-Day War, he carried more information about the Blueprint for Renewal in his head than was compiled anywhere else, except in the special databanks carried on the presidential NEACP. His return to the fold—for which McKay wished the Guardians could actually claim credit—brought as much as a third of the entire Blueprint within reach.

That fact sparked the first contest of wills between Major Crenna and the cantankerous economist. Crenna wanted Morgenstern to fly back to Heartland with the Super Hercules that was bringing in the load of miracle seeds from New Eden. He

envisioned the economist working around the clock with
Heartland technicians, both to piece together as much as possible of the master list and to begin bringing the still-incom-
plete Blueprint into operation. Morgenstern refused flatly.
Months before the One-Day War, sensing nuclear Armaged-
don was eminent, he'd begun laying the groundwork for a
reconstruction plan of his own in the resource-rich state of
California. Now, in the wake of the war, he was putting that
plan into effect—the establishment of a trade and production
network that would encompass the entire state.

"The Blueprint is still hypothetical," the doctor explained
over the radio to Heartland. "My plan is in operation, benefit-
ing the people of California *now*. I will not leave it at such a
crucial stage."

For what McKay reckoned to be one of the few times in his
career, Majora Crenna found himself stymied. The crusty old
Israeli would not be reasoned with, cajoled, or bullied into
changing his mind. He would be more than happy to dictate
what he knew of the Blueprint for transmission to Heartland
—in the spare time his work on his own project left him. In the
end, Crenna had had to give in. Agreeing that the work Morgenstern was doing in California was important, Crenna
ordered the Guardians to place themselves at the doctor's
disposal.

Crenna could not be convinced to honor one request of
Morgenstern's, however. He refused, as mulishly as Morgenstern, either to ship a helicopter in the Super Hercules
transport or to dispatch the technicians to salvage one.
Morgenstern was to conduct his vital work from New Eden,
and not budge from the secluded valley. The doctor fumed
mightily at this, but in the end he'd given in.

To an extent, Billy McKay felt honored to be operating
under the temporary command of such a distinguished military leader as Morgenstern. On the other hand, in many ways
it was a royal pain in the ass. Morgenstern was a perfectionist
and something of a martinet, and altogether much too inclined
to treat the Guardians as glorified errand boys. It took all of
Sam Sloan's Annapolis-acquired diplomacy to keep the gears
turning, sometimes.

A major area of disagreement concerned the former Lieu-

tenant Governor of the State of California. The Guardians
unanimously favored direct action against van Damm and his
California Liberation Front. Acknowledging the peril posed
by the Front, Morgenstern insisted that if his trade network
prospered, the guerrillas would have no chance of winning the
popular support they needed, and that the best defense was to
provide the various components of the network with the
means of defending themselves. Both Rogers and Sam Sloan
had agreed that might be a workable strategy—as opposed to
McKay and Casey Wilson, both of whom held out for immediate action—but pointed out that, given their limited resources,
it was quite a large order. With several hundred trained
cadremen, perhaps. But the four of them simply couldn't train
enough militia to make much of a *difference*.

McKay radioed Heartland for permission to make a
head-on attack on van Damm's stronghold in Sam Simeon
castle. "Negative," Crenna replied. "The reports you've sent
us indicate he's got the place well garrisoned, and well
equipped with mainly Soviet-made matériel. Maybe most of
them will panic when you cut loose with your heavy weapons
—but all it takes is one cool head with an RPG7, and we're out
one set of Guardians."

"But we could try infiltration—" McKay began.

"*Negative.*" A pause. "Don't forget that Maximov has sent
in one of his heavyweights to raise trouble. Where the hell do
you think he wound up? If he's not tied in with this van
Damm, I'm a Girl Scout troop leader. And you can bet your
ass he'll have things set up so you can't simply waltz in, clap a
pillowcase over van Damm's head, and haul him out the back
door." Boggling at the image of the scarred, one-eyed Major
dressed in a green uniform skirt, McKay ruefully agreed and
signed out.

So they were playing it Morgenstern's way, driving all over
the state, burning up the fuel cached in various underground
locations at a fabulous rate, trying to teach the various communities tied into Morgenstern's net how to defend themselves
against van Damm's terrorists. And meantime bringing ever
more communities into the net.

They were finding, as the doctor had found before them,
that the *ad hoc* communities, such as Balin's Forge, and the

special-interest communities like the Duchy of New Carolina, proved a lot more receptive than those townships where formal authority still held sway. City and county officials meant well—McKay kept telling himself that—but their solutions tended to involve confiscation rather than trade, coercion and conscription instead of cooperation. McKay was inclined to favor the System—but having mayors and chairmen of city councils talk down their noses at him, or sheriffs or police chiefs shake their fists under *his* nose, had begun to wear pretty thin. On two occasions, officials had tried to sequester Mobile One and its occupants. Some municipal property had gotten damaged in the process.

McKay wasn't exactly comfortable with Mobile One gadding about the state like some sort of militant bookmobile while the key to Project Blueprint stayed back in New Eden under the protection of Dr. Mahalaby's shaggy idealists. Jacob Morgenstern was a prize of incredible strategic value, and if Yevgeny Maximov had a man on the ground, sooner or later he'd sniff the doctor out. Fortunately, Morgenstern had hit it off quite well with Ari Lavotsky, a fellow expatriate *Sabra*. Together they were doing what they could to beef up the security of New Eden.

To the Guardians' wonder, the scheme seemed to be working. Van Damm's problems—and those of his gray eminence —were at least as great as those of the Guardians. From intelligence reports garnered by Morgenstern's network, van Damm at any one time could call upon the services of several hundred stalwarts, most of them armed with assault rifles. The CLF's own salvage operations, which mainly took the form of "expropriation" raids against homesteaders and retreaters, had so far managed to supply them with a fair amount of transport. Yet California was a big state to cover.

In the meantime, van Damm's bravos tended to be long on revolutionary swagger, but short on staying power in a real firefight. As much as he might like to pretend otherwise, he wasn't fighting a real guerrilla war. That called for small forces operating with the support of a good portion of the population, against a ponderous, conventional military establishment—preferably one consisting of invaders easily distinguishable from the native population. What he actually had was a flat-out war of terrorism, trying by sheer frightfulness to coerce the scattered populace to obedience.

He was dealing with the survivors of the greatest catastrophe of recorded human history. Some of them, unable to bear the new horrors of terrorist attacks on top of the horrors they'd known before, gave in. Others, though, figured that they hadn't survived the rain of thermonuclear destruction merely to be pushed around by gangs of punks spouting slogans. Those who had agreed to take part in Morgenstern's network were even more adamant. In Idaho's words, they'd seen the hope of a better future, the promise that they—or at least their children—would know a manner of living that wasn't just scraping by. They also knew they were no longer facing a whole hostile world alone; other survivors were out there in the network, to give moral support at least—and sometimes more than that.

Near where Amparo's family had been slaughtered, their neighbors, mostly immigrants from northern Mexico, decided they'd had enough of the Farm Workers' Collective, which —among other things—was dominated by Chicanos, who tended to have nothing but disdain for their cousins from across the border. The next time Commisar Rivera came around, with his sunglasses and his swagger, a volley of rifle fire cut down three of his goons. The rest turned tail and fled with the vehicles, leaving him stranded. What followed was highly educational: The man whose organization made liberal use of the name and likeness of Mexican revolutionary Emiliano Zapata learned first-hand about Zapata's harsher methods of dealing with opponents, from the descendants of men who had actually ridden with him.

And so it went. A forage party composed of an uneasy alliance of retainers from the Duchy of New Carolina and the Hare Krishna commune a few kilometers away caught a sabotage team from a radical eco-action group that called itself the Sons of Hayduke, trying to blow up a power station in a small town in the Diablos. The Duchy and the Krishnaites had been trying to get the plant into operation. None of the saboteurs got away.

In a road gypsy–like attack, the San Fernando Liberation Army ratpacked a convoy bound for Balin's Forge, carrying dried fish and, of all things, edible seaweed. They were repulsed soundly, with heavy losses. Just a few klicks from van Damm's redoubt at San Simeon, two truckloads of CLF boys were picking their way along a seven-meter strip between the edge of the jammed highway and the verge of a cliff when a concealed charge of dynamite, obviously command-detonated by unseen observers, blew both vehicles over the edge in an eight-and-a-half gainer into the Pacific, a hundred and fifty meters below.

Van Damm ranted and fumed and threatened in his nightly radio tirades. But he couldn't disguise the fact that his campaign of terror wasn't working out as planned.

Closer to home, Sloan, Mahalaby, and Fred Halpern had worked a deal whereby General Edwards's people pulled security for New Eden in exchange for food. It had the makings of a beautiful arrangement—Mahalaby's people growing the beans, Edwards's people stopping the bullets—but McKay didn't like it. He'd already had to growl at a couple of gun toters from the Valley who were trying to throw their weight around in the commune. Tom Rogers, who'd spent a lot of time with the Green Beanies in remote and unpleasant corners of the world, making alliances with bandit chieftains, summed up the situation: "You're going to have to shoot some people," he said matter-of-factly, "before you convince Edwards to keep his hands off New Eden."

The Guardians had come to rest temporarily in a little sheltered anchorage north of the blasted San Francisco Bay Area metroplex. They were working with the sea gypsies, a group markedly different from the so-called road gypsies who'd terrorized the nation's highways even before the One-Day War, but who bore certain similarities to the ethnic group whose name both factions had appropriated without permission. Like road gypsies, sea gypsies had existed even before the war, and like them they were nomadic in life-style. There the similarity ended.

Just as the biker gangs of earlier times had been engendered by *The Wild One* and subsequent biker flicks of the fifties and sixties, the road gypsies had taken their inspiration from the movies—appropriately enough, a rash of films imitating the

Australian *Mad Max* movies, depicting the post-holocaust swarms of garishly attired thugs cruising the countryside on dune buggies, chopped motorcycles, and scratch-built armored vehicles. Like their celluloid predecessors, the Mohawked road gypsies based their life-style on the internal-combustion engine—and destructive, malicious mischief.

Not so the sea gypsies. They were cruisers, sailors, retreaters on the open ocean, many of whom disdained to so much as allow a "mill"—an engine—within their sleek and frequently hand-built hulls. Most tried to minimize contact with the land; some disdained it completely, relying on the sea for their whole sustenance.

Nonetheless, they formed a vital part of Morgenstern's plan. The sea was traditionally a cost- and energy-efficient medium of transportation. It was especially useful in California, with its hundreds of kilometers of sea coast, innumerable inlets that could be used as anchorages—and its highways clogged to uselessness by the rotting husks of cars. Oceanic transport of trade goods could make all the difference for the survivors in Morgenstern's net, the difference between doing well or just making it—or not making it at all. But the doctor had a problem: getting the sea gypsies to cooperate.

For all their aloofness, though, only a few sea gypsies managed to derive their living entirely from the sea. Like it or not, the majority had to go ashore from time to time, to stock up on fresh water, foodstuffs—especially vegetables and fruits— and medical supplies. Also, the sea gypsies formed a tightly knit confraternity, and liked to have a place where they could gather to swap stories. So they congregated at a number of sheltered anchorages along the coast—natural contact points for Morgenstern's network.

San Agustin Cove was one such place. A tiny anchorage sheltered by great sheer gray cliffs, it had housed a little marina and charter service, with a sway-backed wharf, a few wooden slips, a store, restaurant, and ten-unit motel. The facilities had been trashed and looted by refugees fleeing north from the stricken Bay Area after the war, and then abandoned. With advice from Morgenstern and material help from his network, it had been taken over as a trading post and general gathering spot by a pair of sea gypsies, a lesbian couple named Lori and Donna. The Guardians had come here to pitch the sea gypsies riding at anchor, trying to convince them to become waterborne truckers for the network.

McKay watched sea gulls skimming in low over the beaten-copper waves. He heard soft footfalls on the planking behind him, and when he judged that whoever was approaching was right behind him, said "Shouldn't sneak up on me like that."

He was rewarded with a little gasp. "Oh, I'm sorry, I didn't think." That, and the light high voice, identified the speaker as Donna, the taller, younger member of the pair. Lori, shorter, darker, and gruffer, would have growled something about "typical adolescent male macho games."

McKay still hadn't quite got his head adjusted to dealing with lesbians. On the other hand, he'd worked cheek by jowl with Brits, Israelis, Swedes, fanatical Muslims, Red Chinese, and even Soviet agents, so he figured he could adjust to dykes.

He turned and looked up at the woman. She was a little raw-boned for his taste, with narrow shoulders, and small breasts almost invisible within the bulky folds of her sweatshirt. She had an odd fringe of close-cropped brown hair, and very light blue eyes, which stared startlingly from her deep-sea-tanned face. "The Commodore sent me to fetch you," she said. "It's time for dinner."

McKay grinned and stood up. "The Commodore" was what the sea gypsies had dubbed Sam Sloan. One of the plums the Guardians were offering the sea gypsies, to entice them to participate in Morgenstern's network, was that the hero of Sidra Gulf, Sam Sloan his own self, would instruct them in the tactics and means of defense against one of their prime enemies: pirates. Of course, Sloan's own training and experience dealt almost exclusively with big-gun ships and fast missile boats; what he was teaching owed more to the romantic age of fighting-sail sagas of Alexander Kent than it did to anything he'd picked up at the Academy or in the Mediterranean theater. He cribbed a lot from the Guardians' own training, as well as from articles he'd read on retreating at sea in various survivalist periodicals during that training, but the sea gypsies seemed to think that what he was giving them was good stuff.

McKay stretched, winced, felt his ribs gingerly. "Let's go." He'd been serving as a hand-to-hand combat instructor that afternoon, showing the sea gypsies how to repel boarders with gaff hooks, marlinespikes, axes, and shotguns; and an overenthusiastic pupil—a woman scarcely more than five feet tall, to McKay's mortification—had slipped a lucky one past his guard and zapped him with a broomstick boarding pike.

The former restaurant—diner, actually—had a counter with swiveling plastic stools, and a few booths with high-backed, vinyl-upholstered seats that McKay could have sworn dated from the fifties. The other three Guardians sat at a couple of booths inside, chatting with some of their trainees. A teenaged black girl named Tina, a refugee who'd hired on with Lori and Donna as a helper, served McKay a big bowl of fish-and-potato chowder, with a slab of bread on the side. The bread was fresh-baked, dark brown and delicious, but what McKay liked best was the schooner of beer Tina set down beside his bowl. It was salvage, and a little flat—but, by Jesus, it was *beer*.

"You've got to understand that real boarding actions were uncommon," Sam Sloan was telling his rapt listeners in the next booth. "Most boarding actions took place in adventure novels. On the other hand, those that *did* take place—"

Over in the corner, stocky, black-haired Lori was fiddling with the multiband radio. It was a very powerful sending and receiving unit, salvaged from a foundered yacht. In a world where survivors huddled in little isolated knots, such radios, providing as they did contact with the outside world, were a main source of entertainment. "—shall suffer the Satan's breath of Hell!" a familiar voice thundered from the receiver. Sam Sloan choked off in mid-sentence, and Billy McKay coughed as beer went suddenly down the wrong way.

"Turn that shit off." Even the stolid Tom Rogers was stung into speaking sharply by that voice. The Guardians' encounter with the Church of the New Dispensation had been so traumatic that none of them much cared to listen to the exhortations of its current First Prophet, Nathan Bedford Forrest Smith. Lori flashed a quick grin; she'd tuned in Smith's broadcast deliberately, knowing it would irk the Guardians. Actually, she and her softer-spoken partner welcomed the aid of the Guardians and Morgenstern's network were giving them. On the other hand, it chewed her ass to accept help from a man, especially such a macho set of males as the Guardians. She had a tendency to try to get her own back in small ways, when she could.

"Let's see what Chairman Geoff has to say," suggested a slat-thin, tall sea gypsy captain named Warren. He seemed to have been carved out of mahogany. Lori nodded and turned the dial. The usual pips and squawks and squeals of atmospheric interference—at a much higher level than before the war, due to residual effects of the huge amounts of energy released into the atmosphere—ensued, and then came the strains of rock music. McKay frowned, trying to recognize it.

" 'Caroline.' " Casey Wilson, wearing a Beatles baseball cap, looked smug at having come up with the answer. "Jefferson Starship. Early seventies." That figured. In between propaganda broadcasts, van Damm's pet radio station played a lot of rock from the late sixties and early seventies—which made it the most popular radio show in a lot of survival holdouts inhabited by aging baby-boomers. The selection was heavy on the Jefferson Starship. Van Damm *loved* the Starship. Of course. McKay dug into his chowder again.

The song faded away, to be replaced by a brassy fanfare. Lori frowned. "Tell me that's not the 'Internationale.' "

"Love to oblige you, ma'am," Sam Sloan said—calling her "ma'am" to pay her back for tuning in Forrest Smith. "But it'd be a lie. That's the 'Internationale,' all right."

The grandiose strains ended with a flatulent flourish. The voice of a young black announcer intoned, "Comrades, workers, and citizens of the People's Republic of California. Please stand by for a message from the Chairman." Grinning at each other in the gloom, the listeners sat back to enjoy the show. Van Damm was the funniest thing since "Saturday Night Live" went off the air.

"Good evening, comrades," came van Damm's voice, as rich and round and full and warm as a fresh turd. "I bring you tidings that will raise the hearts of all those locked in the struggle for the People's revolutionary justice. As you know, the former state of California teems with pockets of counter-revolutionary activity. Of late, an effort has been made to draw them together into a web of capitalist exploitation and reactionary terror. Instrumental in this effort is the gang of four supercriminals, running dogs of the former United States of America who call themselves the Guardians—" Applause drowned the next words. McKay and Sloan grinned; Casey stood up and performed a little bow.

"—efforts will come to naught," van Damm was saying. "For the California Liberation Front has come into possession of a weapon against which all their counter-revolutionary scheming will not avail them.

"This afternoon, technicians in the service of the People's Republic informed me that they have restored to working order a one-megaton hydrogen warhead, salvaged from a missile that landed near the outskirts of the imperialists' Vandenberg Air Force Base. We are ready, willing, and able to use this device against any who would attempt to prevent us lifting the yoke of oppression from the necks of all the peoples of California.

"Comrades, rejoice! The hour of liberation is at hand!

"That is all."

Into the stunned silence that filled the little diner to bursting, the young announcer said, "Thank you, Comrade Chairman. In other news, a gang of counter-revolutionary bandits masquerading as freedom fighters has been uncovered and smashed by security forces of the California Liberation Front. The so-called Joaquin Murieta Brigade—" A touch of Lori's fingers cut him off.

She looked around the room, her heavy face dead-pale in the lantern light. "Do they mean that? Can they do that?" Tendrils of incipient hysteria ran through her voice.

McKay shook his head. "No, that's just some bullshit that lunatic cooked up. . . ." The words trailed off. Sam Sloan was looking at McKay, shaking his head. His eyes were very, very large.

"They can do it." It was almost a whisper. "God help us, they could do it."

"We got your answer, McKay," came Major Crenna's rasping voice, relayed via satellite from three thousand klicks away. "It's affirmative. They could conceivably have scavenged a warhead intact enough to be made workable."

"But *how*?" It was as close to yelping as Billy McKay had

come in his life. "I thought those things had safeguards up the ass, stuff to make them useless if you tried to dick with them."

A pause, crackling with atmospherics. "They used to. Not anymore. Radiation from the fissionable materials in the warheads causes pretty rapid decay of circuits exposed to it. Those fail-safes were just too vulnerable to malfunction. Over the last few years, the fusing mechanisms on thermonuclear warheads have been as simple as we—or the Soviets—could make them."

McKay lifted his head and looked at his three comrades. They were crowded together in the red-lit interior of Mobile One, hunkered over the comm set. "Fuck *us*," he said.

But Casey was shaking his head. "No, man, it's not that simple." The others looked at him. "What can they *do* with the damn thing? What are they going to use it on? Some group of forty, fifty survivalists up somewhere in the coastal range? It'd be, like, using a sledgehammer to kill a mosquito, man. They'd have to be crazy to use it—"

"Which they are," Sam Sloan interjected.

Casey nodded briskly. "Yeah. But the point is, there aren't really any targets worth dropping an H-bomb on—and once they set the thing off, that's it. Its like the hostage situations we learned about in training. Terrorists actually start killing off hostages, like, suddenly they don't have any leverage anymore."

McKay relayed Casey's arguments to Crenna. "Very reasonable," the Major replied. "Unfortunately, we're dealing with people who are going to be acting in anything but a reasonable manner. A lot of folks out there are going to be convinced it's their heads van Damm will set his damned bomb off over, if he doesn't get what he wants. Hell, they may be right—this van Damm sounds nutty enough to blow off his ace in the hole just to see the pretty flash. And maybe he *could* find a target he'd think was worth spending a bomb on. What do you think might happen if he touched it off in the same valley with New Eden, say—or even just a couple of klicks upwind?"

The Guardians sat for a moment, staring at each other. Outside, a stiff wind from the sea buffeted the iron car, and in the stiff chop the warped and ancient boards of the wharf groaned

like damned souls. It was McKay who broke the eerie stillness.
"So I guess we know what we've got to do."

"Right." If McKay hadn't known Crenna better, he might
almost have imagined he heard him sigh. *Must be a trick of the
atmospherics.* "Cancel his check. Just what you've wanted to
do all along. Only for Christ's sake, don't let anything happen
to either Morgenstern or New Eden. And try not to get
yourselves killed. Crenna out."

McKay shook his head. "We might as well go for it. Sam,
give New Eden a call, make sure they're up-to-date on the
situation." Sloan turned back to the console, began pressing
buttons. His lips moved, but no sound came out; his throat
mike was picking up his subvocalizations and piping them
through Mobile One's powerful transmitter.

After a moment, he frowned, and poked at the keyboard
again. The Guardians sat and watched with growing alarm.
Finally, he took off his headphones. "Nothing. I can't raise
New Eden."

"Holy shit," Casey said softly.

Hours later, sometime past midnight in the eastern San Joaquin Valley, passing a long file of cars stalled nose-to-tail like
circus elephants—humped forms silvered by moonlight—they
finally raised the commune on the radio. "This is New Eden,"
Anna Yoshimitsu replied, her voice teetering on the edge of
hysteria. "Thank God it's you! We've been attacked. Everybody's dead—and they got Susan Spinelli and Dr. Morgenstern!"

CHAPTER
FIFTEEN ───────────

"Valley's closed," said the man who stood blinking, across the hood of the boulder-laden truck that blocked the end of the truss bridge, into the glare of Mobile One's turret spotlight. McKay recognized the younger son of the Donner family, which shared dominion over Edwards's Valley, a thickset, round-faced, fat-necked youth in a cowboy hat. He seemed to be in charge of the crew on watch at the entry to the valley of the Maldita.

The time was about 0300. Casey, their best driver, had driven from Lori's Landing, and he'd performed like the fighter ace he was. Mobile One had careened along the shoulders of hopelessly blocked highways, roared over embankments, bumped over formerly cultivated fields. Given the darkness and the condition of the roads, he'd done a fantastic job.

Sam Sloan frowned. "Looks like you were right not to trust them, McKay." The guards from Edwards's Valley were supposed to let Mobile One through without question. Yet when the V-450 had started across the bridge, the sentries showed no sign of moving the truck that barred the far end. "Wonder if they do have antitank weapons."

McKay showed him a mirthless smile. "If they do," he said, "we're just about to find it out." He laughed at Sloan's stricken expression. "Don't sweat it. These bastards are dumb enough that if one of them had been hunkered down there, waiting to nail us with a LAW, the spotlight would have picked him right out when we turned it on. And they let us get too close—no antitank weapon is going to arm itself in the distance between the barrier and us." He hunkered over to squint past Sloan's shoulder out the vision lock. "Patch me over the loudspeaker."

Sloan nodded. McKay said, "Donner, you got two choices. Either you move that fucking truck or we're gonna move it for you." As a courtesy, Tom Rogers had kept the muzzles of the turret guns averted from the barrier. Now, to emphasize McKay's words, he swung them directly to bear on the pudgy kid.

Donner blanched. "Awright. Move the truck." He scampered out of the hot blue-white beam of the million-candlepower spot. A moment later, the truck backed off the causeway with a groan of tortured suspension, and Mobile One rolled on past.

On the right, Edwards's Valley was lit up at the far end, where the houses were. "I wonder if they got hit, too?" Sam Sloan said. Since the one frantic communication from New Eden, Mobile One had been unable to reach either of the two communities.

McKay had ordered the spotlight turned out when they passed the bridge. Casey had the headlights to run by; that wasn't why McKay had ordered it switched on. A sudden dose of illumination often revealed that lurking bad guys weren't quite as well hidden as they'd fondly believed, and played merry hell with their night vision. It was an old Russian trick from the Second World War that McKay'd read about some place, and he'd used it to good effect earlier in his career.

The lights were out at New Eden when they trundled up the road. They pulled to a halt on the plaza in front of the Main Habitat. The glassed-in expanse was dark, blank but for the reflected images of a thousand stars. What appeared to be human bodies lay under tarps by the greenhouse to the left. Otherwise there was no sign of anybody.

"I don't like it," McKay said. "Don't like it at all. Tom, you stay up in the turret and be ready to rock and roll. Sloan, you come with me." He picked up his Maremont, popped the rear hatch, boosted himself out into the darkness. The air was cool, crisp, but tainted with the stink of the corpses under the tarps.

McKay dropped to the ground and scanned the darkened buildings while Sloan clambered out. "Might they have evacuated?" the former Navy man asked.

"Doubt it. Let's go take a look." Holding the machine gun SMG style, McKay started for the front door.

A woman's voice screamed, "It's a trap!"

"Down!" McKay shouted. He was already in a long flat dive to the dirt, bringing up his machine gun as fire flashed from the doorway ahead of him. Behind him, he heard Sam Sloan grunt and fall heavily to the ground.

Blinding light flooded the plaza as Tom Rogers punched on the searchlight. The instinctive action saved his life and Casey Wilson's, dazzling and throwing off the aim of the man leveling an M-72 light antitank weapon at the armored car from the corner of a quonset-style lab on the left side of the Main Habitat. Buzzing like a giant wasp, the rocket etched a line of sparks over Mobile One's rear deck and blew up a tractor parked at the far side of the plaza. Rogers traversed the turret quickly left. A hail of .50-caliber rounds punched through the corrugated metal walls of the lab and knocked the blinded rocket man sprawling in a broken heap.

McKay hosed bullets toward the doorway, heard a scream. Fire was coming in from above, too, from the little balcony overlooking the entrance. He knew Sam Sloan lay injured at his back, but he had no time for him now. Shouting, "Pull back and cover me, Casey!" he gathered his powerful legs under him and launched himself off the ground toward the door.

Though the muzzle flashes from the assault rifle firing from above almost singed his eyebrows, he made it to the safety of the building's front. Holding the MG one-handed, he pulled a round concussion grenade from his belt and yanked the ring with his teeth. He tossed the bomb into the open door. When the flash came, he spun inside, leaping over a pair of bodies sprawled in the doorway, and jumped quickly to one side.

Had this been a standard housecleaning operation, he simply would have sprayed the room at waist height. But he couldn't count on any New Edenites who might have been in the building having the sense to lie on the floor, and the bullets from his M-60 could pretty much punch holes from one side of the building to another without slowing down. He was following the highly risky hostage rescue drill he'd learned in Guardian training, taking advantage of the respite that the concussion grenade—with luck—granted from immediate action by any enemies in the room.

And there was an enemy in the room: Mick Waller, pointing his .45 off any which way with his right hand, while his left waved in the air in front of his face, as if to bat away the big blinding globes of light floating before his eyes. In spite of himself, Billy McKay grinned. "You lose," he said, and blew Waller's guts into the wall.

Outside, Casey Wilson slammed the big vehicle into reverse and gunned it, throwing up a wave of dust and gravel. Tom Rogers swung the turret farther to the left, raking the trees on the ridge above the buildings with .50-caliber fire. Not that he thought any bad guys were necessarily up there; mainly he was firing the big fifty just to be firing it. The hideous roar of the Browning M-2, and the Volkswagen-sized muzzle flashes, were potent psychological weapons in and of themselves. And, even more than Billy McKay, he was unwilling to rake the Main Habitat with random machine-gun fire. The .50 caliber would damn near tear it down.

Gravel rained down on Sam Sloan, who lay on his side curled around the worst agony he'd ever known, which burned like a poker driven into the pit of his stomach. *I'm killed, I'm killed, I'm killed!* yammered a voice in his head. He fought for self-control. He'd been shot at point-blank range; yet maybe, just maybe, the Kevlar and steel vest he, like the other Guardians, wore under his uniform blouse would have stopped the bullet. Even if it hadn't . . . he was still alive and he still had a job to do.

Impacts kicked up spurts of dust all around him. As he wrestled awareness out of the haze of pain that enveloped him, he realized they were bullets, fired from somewhere above. *How can he keep missing me?* he wondered blearily. But he already knew the answer. In training they'd been told again and again that troops, especially inexperienced ones, who had automatic weapons tended to use them just one way: to hold the trigger down until they quit making noise. In his own first face-to-face firefight, with the National Guard on a side road near Luxor, Iowa, he'd immediately blazed away the whole magazine in his Galil without thinking. It made a very impressive sound-and-light display, and did put a comforting amount of lead into the air—but muzzle jump made it a piss-poor way to actually *hit* anything. So the man on the balcony, less than fifteen meters away, was inundating the helpless Sloan with gunfire and still managing to miss.

When the shots from the doorway had hit him, he'd dropped his Galil-203. Now, blindly, he groped for the weapon. His left hand closed on the fat muzzle of the grenade launcher slung under the muzzle of the rifle. There was a pause in the firing as he pulled the weapon to him. The man up above had run out of ammunition. He knew the respite wouldn't last.

Electric agony shot from his belly to the top of his skull as he pulled himself to a sitting position. His vision blurred out, and he swayed. *Gotta . . . hold on. He can't keep missing me . . . forever.* Slowly, he raised the Galil.

The man on the balcony opened up again. The orange flares seemed to blossom almost in Sam Sloan's face. Without conscious intent, the forefinger of his left hand clenched on the trigger of the M-203. An HEDP grenade boomed out of the stubby muzzle and struck the lip of the cement balcony directly at the feet of the rifleman. The blast took off both his legs below the knees and launched him shrieking out into the night on a column of flame. His body landed near Sam Sloan with a dull, squishy thump, and lay still.

The battle for New Eden was over.

• • •

They found the New Edenites huddled together in the commissary of the Main Habitat. Two of Waller's commandos had been left to guard them; when McKay burst in, they were cowering under a table with their arms over their heads, sniveling for mercy. Both had served as draftees in the Army, but neither had combat experience. The awesome, ear-shattering sound of the firepower arrayed against them had just plain freaked them out. Likewise the rest of the dozen-member ambush party; when the LAW missed, and Mobile One cut loose with its big guns, they'd simply faded back into the hills.

With the help of some of the released hostages, McKay brought Sloan into the commissary, and laid him out on a dining table. A 5.56 round had caught him about three centimeters to the left of his belly button. The vest had, indeed, stopped the projectile, but it had driven the fabric into Sloan's belly like a fist in a boxing glove, leaving an immense technicolor bruise and causing an involuntary voiding of the bowels. Awareness of this fact having penetrated Sloan's awareness as the pain in his gut ebbed, the former Navy officer apologized over and over for his indiscretion, until McKay growled, "If you don't shut the fuck up about having shit your goddamn pants, I'm gonna coldcock you." Sloan quit babbling.

Later, while Rogers tended to Sloan's injury and brought him a fresh pair of skivvies, Billy McKay learned what had happened that evening. Van Damm's proclamation had caused a lot of consternation. Most of the inhabitants of New Eden had, in fact, been gathered in the commissary, discussing the horrifying turn of events, when suddenly armed men had burst in and begun shooting at everything in sight. New Eden's security force consisted of Ari Lavotsky, a man and a woman who had agreed to bear arms, and four men from the Valley.

They'd fought bravely, if inexpertly—Edwards's people along with communards. The attackers fought without skill, but they displayed the ferocity of rabid badgers. Lavotsky nailed three of them with a Galil flown in from Heartland before being shot in the neck and chest. Dr. Morgenstern had killed two with a shotgun before being clubbed down—the intruders obviously had orders to take him alive. Rushing to his aid, Susan Spinelli had been seized as well. The intruders then withdrew, leaving eight of their number dead or wounded. Of New Eden's tiny security complement, only two survived: a young black New Edenite man and a twenty-year-old kid from Edwards's Valley, both wounded. Three other New Edenites had been killed, and five wounded. Dr. Mahalaby had spent the fight roaring like a bear, trying to interpose his huge body between the invaders' guns and his people. Miraculously, he'd escaped unscathed.

Now he sat in the corner of the commissary, his face buried in his hands, sobbing disconsolately while Anna sat beside him and tried to soothe him. "I tried to spare them this—this horror," he choked. "My people . . . those poor, poor people."

McKay turned to Sloan, who was sitting up now, with his legs dangling over the edge of the table. "How are you doing?"

Sloan managed a weak grin. "A mule kicked me in the belly once, back when I was a kid." Gingerly he touched the left side of his stomach, then winced. "This sort of makes me nostalgic."

"We're going to have to drive on," McKay said. "You can stay behind if you need to."

Sloan stared at him for a long moment. He was still in great pain, and shaken to the very core of himself, as only a man who has just been saved from death by a few thicknesses of special cloth can be. But he shook his head and grinned that slow shitkicker grin of his. "And let a jarhead Marine go busting into trouble without a good Navy man on hand to tell him what to do? Not a chance."

McKay nodded and turned to Anna, who seemed to be New Eden's leader until Mahalaby pulled himself together. "We've got to go after those bastards. You've got medical supplies as good as or better than anything we've got. As for defense . . ." He shrugged. "I don't think the terrorists will be hassling you again for a while. They got what they came for."

"But General Edwards—" somebody began.

McKay silenced him with a glare from beneath invisibly pale eyebrows. "Leave that," he growled, "to me."

The barbed-wire-topped perimeter strung around Edwards's Valley was meant to keep out people on foot. Mobile One went through it without even slowing down. The half dozen men on gate duty dove for cover, too stunned—or too prudent—to open fire.

Mobile One rolled straight up to the Big House, McKay riding half out of the turret hatch, bracing himself with one hand, his Maremont in the other, a pair of hundred-and-five-round linked-ammunition belts crossed over his brawny chest. Mobile One bulled right through the low adobe wall around the courtyard and came to a halt a few meters from the front porch. "Come out here, General Edwards," Billy McKay's voice boomed, amplified over the armored car's loudspeaker. "Got something to say to you."

Startled faces appeared at the ranch house's windows, blinking against the glare of the spotlight. The other dwellings stayed shut up tight. No one wanted to chance calling the iron monster's attention to himself.

In a few moments, the front door opened, and Fred Halpern stood there, barefoot with his shirttail out. "There must be some mistake."

"In one minute," Billy McKay said, overriding him, "we're going to back out of this garden of yours and pound your God-damned house into hell. *Unless* you shag-ass out here and talk to us, General."

Halpern's moist lips trembled. "Now, surely we can be reasonable about this—"

McKay checked his wristwatch ostentatiously. "Fifty-five seconds." Halpern disappeared like a rabbit down a hole.

The count had eight seconds left to run when he reappeared, wheeling General Edwards in his chair. The General had on a maroon robe, with a blue blanket across his knees. His face was white. "I demand to know the meaning of this intrusion!" he thundered. Behind him, Fred Halpern swallowed as if he were trying to choke down an entire baby.

"Can the indignation rap, general. Or we flatten this dump. Just what the hell made you think you'd get away with sendin' that psycho Waller to take over New Eden, anyway?"

With an obvious effort, the General composed himself. "I don't understand. McKay. I sent Captain Waller to the assistance of our neighbors. They'd just been attacked, and certainly needed our help."

"Yeah. Waller and his goons, they assisted 'em all into the dining hall at gunpoint, then tried to bushwhack us. I figure the survivors'll be sneaking down from the hills with their tails between their legs for the next few days."

"Captain Waller has obviously exceeded his orders. I'll have to speak with him."

"You do that thing. In fact, here he is." He drew his Kabar as Rogers traversed the turret ninety degrees right. With a left-handed slash of the knife he severed the rope looped around the turret. The bundle it had secured to the turret's rear dropped into the violated flowerbed. Yellow light spilling from the Big House gleamed on the upturned features of Mick Waller. "Only, he's gonna have one hell of a time speaking in his own defense."

The General's eyes bulged. Fred Halpern gagged and disappeared into the house again. "We warned you before, General. Now we've got business to attend to, so we're letting you off easy—this time. But I promise you this: Fuck with New Eden again, or any of its people, and we'll plow this valley under and pave it for a runway. Do you read me, General?"

Slowly, speechlessly, the General nodded.

CHAPTER
SIXTEEN —————————

"Billy," Tom Rogers's voice said in McKay's ear. "There's nobody here."

Billy McKay looked at the other two Guardians. The sun was halfway up the morning sky and already blazing hot. They were holed up in a brushy *barranca* a few klicks away from San Simeon castle. Tom Rogers, the best man in the group at snooping and pooping, had been sent on ahead to do a daylight reconnaissance of the castle.

They'd parked Mobile One in a draw out of sight of the Pacific Coast Highway, and hiked overland to the castle. In preparation for the hike, each man had stripped himself to the bare minimum gear required: weapons, ammunition, communicators, and medical supplies; several liters of water; and a couple of protein bars apiece: There wasn't going to be much time for eating on this mission. Despite the fact that its firepower could prove decisive just in terms of morale alone, as the fight at New Eden the night before had proved, Mobile One was left behind. There was no practical way to conceal the approach up the single road to the castle of a gigantic, noisy armored car. Besides, its sudden appearance might panic van

Damm into setting off the bomb, taking Dr. Morgenstern and
Susan along with him and his followers.

Of course, once they made their move he might opt for thermonuclear suicide anyway. So they were going to infiltrate on
foot, as close to the castle as they could. When they made their
move, it had to be lightning-quick and decisive. That was their
only hope—and it was a slim one. According to the intelligence they'd received, San Simeon Castle swarmed with at
least a hundred armed guerrillas. Even discounting the hydrogen warhead, even accounting for the Guardians' advantages
of morale, training, and surprise, those were long odds indeed.

So emotionally prepared for a death or glory charge on San
Simeon Castle were the Guardians, that at first they had
trouble assimilating just what Tom Rogers had said. "Say
again, Tom?" Billy McKay said.

"I'm south of the castle. I've been watching for fifteen
minutes, and I haven't seen anything moving."

"No vehicles or *anything?*" Sam Sloan asked.

"Nothing." A pause while the wind whistled down the
gully. "Looks like there's been some kind of battle here. Windows blasted out, bodies laying around."

"Stay where you are, Tom," McKay said. "We're on our
way."

Leaving Casey Wilson with his sniper's rifle on a knoll
about three hundred meters south of the castle, the Guardians
slipped forward, using the cover of the broken chapparal as
they approached the Enchanted Hill. Above them, nothing
moved but the wind.

They went up the hill in short rushes through the transplanted trees. In moments they stood among the terraces and
gardens of the castle grounds. "Tom, you check to the left.
Sloan and I'll look over the main building."

Using the cover of hedges and low walls, McKay and Sloan
worked their way forward from the trees toward the huge
house. They passed bodies sprawled in various attitudes of
violent death, men and a few women, many of them dressed in
army jackets sporting radical regalia: Black Mamba patches,
clenched fists, scowling Zapatas with rifle and crossed ban-

doliers, the Bear and Red Star patch of the People's Republic
of the Bear.

They approached the Casa Grande at a point where a huge
window had been broken out. A dead guerrilla lay slumped
over the sill, half-in and half-out of the house. "I'll go in
here," McKay said quietly. "Move on around to the right and
find another way in." Sloan nodded and moved away.

McKay hunkered behind a much grown-out ornamental
shrub and watched and waited. Nothing. He crossed the flag-
stones quickly, dropped to one knee outside the window and
poked the barrel of his machine-gun into the room. Still nothing. He clambered quickly over the sill and looked around.

The first thing that struck him was the resemblance this
place bore to the White House a few hours after the bombs
went off. There was no structural damage; if the combatants'd
had any weapons bigger than small arms, they hadn't used
them here. But the effect of gilded rubble, of exquisite—or at
least expensive—ornaments shattered and strewn about, was
the same as in, say, the Blue Room.

The room he was in was filled with broken-up furniture that
looked antique. Fragments of a small marble statue lay by one
wall. There was a murky oil painting of an old guy in a black
hat and a white ruff, with a mustache and a liberal spattering
of bullet holes; nearby a tapestry hung in shreds, as if slashed
by a knife. *There was some kind of fight here,* McKay thought,
*but that's not all that went down. Somebody trashed this place
on purpose.*

He moved off through the palace, cautiously, but with the
growing conviction that there was no point. There was nobody
here, unless you counted the occasional corpse. And everywhere was the same, the random debris of battle intermingled
with what looked like deliberate vandalism.

He paused in some kind of a study, gazing down at the torn-
out pages of ancient books that covered the floor like the
broad faded leaves of dying trees. "McKay? Sloan here.
Where are you?" McKay told him as best he could. "Don't
shoot me. I'm coming to find you—and I'm not alone." A
couple of minutes later McKay heard footfalls. He looked up
from the scatter of ancient sheets he'd been perusing—pencil
studies of nude women by Rembrandt or da Vinci or some-

body like that—to see the familiar shabby form of the man named Baxter prodded into the room at the end of Sam Sloan's Galil.

"Look who I found skulking around the kitchen."

McKay stood, swinging up his machine gun. "Why, you two-timing little son of a bitch. You rat bastard. You've been playing off both sides."

Unabashed, Baxter shrugged. "Sure. Why not?" His nose twitched, and he probed it with a grimy forefinger. "A guy's gotta get by, don't he?"

"Yeah. And maybe you've got as far as you're going to. Maybe we oughta just blow your brains out." The tension of the last two hours welled out in a wave of hatred for the informer.

As if in reply, Baxter stuck one hand in the hip pocket of his foul coveralls. McKay's finger tightened on the trigger of the Maremont—and the black-nailed hand came out with a moldy hard roll, which Baxter proceeded to stuff into his face. "Jesus!" Sam Sloan burst out. "You're pretty fucking nonchalant about this, aren't you?"

"What's the difference?" A chunk of bread threatened to escape from the corner of his mouth; he prodded it back in where it belonged with his finger. "Lost my family in the big blowup—wife, two little girls. Lost my garage and everything I had. Seen more people die, since then, than I ever knew to talk to in my whole God-damned life. Right now, you're gonna kill me or you ain't. Don't make me no never mind; nothing I can do 'bout it, either way."

"Billy? Rogers here. There's nobody here. Couple of bodies floating in this fancy outdoor pool, but nobody alive. What's your situation?"

McKay scowled. "We're up in the big house. Nobody here either. You might as well join up with us."

Baxter nodded and chewed, apparently unruffled by the statement that "nobody" was there. McKay glowered at him, wanting to kill the bastard right there. "What the hell happened here anyway?" he asked, fighting the impulse.

"Oh. Van Damm's little bubble burst. Had to happen—you know how these pinko types are. Always ragging each other about this doctrine or that. Shit, you halfway expect 'em to start arguing about how many angels can dance on the head of a pin."

"You mean it was some kind of palace revolt?" Sam Sloan asked.

Baxter shrugged, blew his nose with his fingers and wiped them on his butt. "Well, actually, van Damm pretty much started it himself. He's been acting crazy for days—crazier than usual, I mean—purging people left and right, had 'em shot in the back of the neck for no reason in particular.

"Then these Murieta Brigade types come in, couple days ago, with this friggin' warhead they found. Thought they really had it made, man. Van Damm never liked them, see, and now he was gonna have to give them a piece of the action." He pushed a high-pitched laugh out through his nose. "He showed them. Ordered a big meal made up—canned fruit, some vegetables screwed out of them greasers in the San Joaquin, even came up with a couple of goats to butcher. He did it up brown. Told the Murieta Brigade people it was in their honor, got them so stuffed with food and hooch that their eyeballs were bugged out. Then his boys walked in with their guns and got the drop on them. Marched them on out to this little place by the highway, give them a bunch of shovels, made them dig a long trench. Then they just sort of lined them up and shot them on down into it.

"That got some of the other folks here kind of riled up. They reckoned, he can do it to them Murieta brigaders, he can do it to *us*. Then he made that announcement of his, and whoo-*ee,* did the calls start coming in! Every squatter who could get his hands on a ham set or CB was radioing in, seemed like it, all ready to pledge their support for van Damm's revolution. *Nobody* wanted him to pop that God-damned thing off over their heads.

"So some of the gang, they figure now's the time to make their move, you know? Pop off that crazy fucker van Damm, and then *they'd* run this state. Set themselves up as a revolutionary council, and then they could live like kings off what they sweat out of the citizens."

He broke off to rummage in the pockets of his coveralls again. "So what *happened?*" Sam Sloan urged.

Baxter pulled out an apple that had been half-eaten, say, a

day and a half ago, sniffed it, and took a bite. Sam Sloan reckoned he must have wanted to savor its bouquet; Sloan could smell it from three meters away. Noticing Sloan's disgusted expression, Baxter held up the apple and said, "They'd had to move out in a couple of days anyway. They was out of food." Sam Sloan shuddered.

"Anyway, some of these groups got together—the Republic of the Bear people, the San Fernando Liberation Army, who the fuck can keep 'em all straight? Anyway, they waited until the Japanese Red Army pulled out on their raid. The Nips are even crazier than van Damm; they'd do anything he'd tell 'em. So the rebels went for him. He and Marlon, that bodyguard of his who never says nothing, and this new guy who showed up a couple of weeks ago, an old friend of van Damm's who acts like he's a Limey only everybody knows he's a Russian spy 'cause van Damm can't leave off bragging on him, they held them off until van Damm's CLF bodyguards could come to the rescue. Then some kind of nigger group moved in to help the rebels, and a bunch of militant fruitbars from up to the Bay Area, and before you know it, everybody's shooting everybody else, there's people running up and down the halls, tearing down paintings and knocking over statues and hollering about decadence. Never saw nothing *like it*."

"I can well imagine," Sam Sloan said.

"Ended up with van Damm and his people holed up in this garage down the hill that the State Parks people built, back when this was a tourist attraction. Warhead was in a truck in there, and he said if people didn't clear out and give him some space he was gonna set it off." He pursed his lips, puffed out his cheeks, and produced a long, low whistle. "You shoulda *seen* 'em clear out. They just scattered to the four winds. Like when you pick up a dandelion that's gone to seed and give it a good puff. They just went everywhere. It wasn't ten minutes before van Damm and his crew had the place all to themselves.

"Well, this place wasn't much use to van Damm no more, all wrecked and all, and only a matter of time before some of his former playmates got brave enough to try to sneak back in, conk him on the head, and take his little toy away. So he waited til the Japs got back, what was left of 'em, with that crazy doctor—the one I told you fellows about, back at

General Edwards's place—and this real gorgeous piece of ass with long yellow hair and no tits to speak of."

Sam Sloan went white, but said nothing.

"Then they all hightailed it south, in convoy," Baxter finished with visible pride in his storytelling.

"*You* seem to know a lot of what went on," McKay said. "What the hell, did they have you doing color commentary?"

Baxter tittered, a sound like rats in the baseboard. It gave McKay a twinge of nostalgia for his inner-city youth. "Naw. I'm just the sort blends in with the furniture, is all. The revolutionaries was so used to having me around, they didn't pay me no mind." That didn't reflect well on the guerrillas' hygiene, Sam Sloan thought. Normally, if Baxter was within hailing distance, your nose let you know about it, in no uncertain terms.

"So," he said, "did van Damm just happen to let slip where he was going?"

Baxter raised his eyebrows. "Why sure. Heck, you boys ought to be able to figure out where they went." He moved one hand in a rotary gesture apparently meant to encompass the Enchanted Hill and everything upon it. "You see the place he picked. From here, there's only one place he *can* go."

"*So where the fuck is he?*" McKay thundered.

Baxter blinked at him, as if marveling at his obtuseness. "Why, he went right where he belonged," he said. "Disney-land."

The clouds had swooped down low to unload everything they had. Rain fell so hard the tarmac was lost in a shimmer of back-scatter mist that came clear up to the hubcaps of the big armored car, and the sea gypsy vessels tossing in the little sheltered anchorage of Lori's Landing were almost invisible through translucent gray curtains.

"No," Lori said flatly. "There's no way you're going to find anyone to take you out in this weather. Especially not for a close-in run down the coast."

The four Guardians huddled in the little diner, drinking steaming tea from earthenware mugs.

"Why not just drive?" Donna asked.

Perched like a carrion crow on a stool a few meters away

from the rest, Baxter rubbed his nose and said, "That's wha
these boys wanted to do, miss. But it won't work. The onl
way into the L.A. basin overland right now is through th
Tehachapis. And old van Damm may be crazy, but he ain'
dumb. He'll have people with radios watching for that big ol
armored car, and if they see it come rolling through th
pass—there go the hostages. And maybe that little bomb of hi
—*boom*." He made an expanding-fireball gesture with hi
grimy hands.

"Like, we couldn't get very far into the greater L.A. area i
a vehicle anyway," Casey Wilson explained. "Too rubble
out, too full of dead cars."

"Insertion by sea's our best bet," McKay said. "We can se
down on a beach within maybe twenty klicks of Disneyland
And van Damm's people won't be expecting us to move i
from the west."

Donna sat down the boxes of dishes she'd been carrying
"But what does it matter? Who cares if he's got this bomb?"

"A lot of people, miss." Baxter inspected her minutely wit
his beady eyes. "Say, ah, miss, maybe you and me could, ah
like—"

"For Christ's sake put a rag in it, Baxter," McKay snarled
"Listen, van Damm's terror network may have kind of falle
apart on him. But he's got a lot of people awful cowed wit
this bomb of his. He could still wind up making himself lor
and master of most of the state."

"Its not just the bomb, either," Sam Sloan said. "There ar
the hostages to think of too. Dr. Morgenstern is vital to th
Blueprint for Renewal, as well as to the futures of a lot o
people here in California. Ms. Spinelli's important to the wor
being done at New Eden."

"Plus he's sweet on her—you can tell that just by looking a
him," Baxter remarked with satisfaction. Sloan winced.

Donna looked at Lori. "But who'd take them? It'd have t
be a motor sailer." She turned to Sloan. "Most of the peopl
that anchor here won't carry mills—and even those that woul
probably wouldn't want to get involved in anything like this
They don't feel that what happens ashore concerns them."

"Then they're about to find out just how wrong they are,"
McKay said sourly.

Lori plunked her forearms on the bar. "I know who can take them." She rubbed her cheeks for a moment. "We can. The *Calamity Jane* has got an engine."

She looked around at the Guardians. "Gentlemen, the *Jane*'s a twenty-eight-foot motor sailer. Ought to be big enough for all of us. And I know this coast pretty well. I, uh, used to be involved in a little, ah, informal import-export."

"How soon can you be ready to move?" McKay asked.

"How about right now?"

"But, Lori! It's dark! And the storm—"

"I know, doll. But think of what we worked so hard to put together here. Van Damm will just take it away." She shrugged. "Anyway, deep down, he's always been one of those macho Che Guevara types who believed that a woman's only position in the Movement was on her back. Be a kick to give him one in the eye."

She turned back toward the rear of the diner and bawled out, "Tina! We're taking the *Jane* out. If we're not back in a week, the joint's yours."

CHAPTER
SEVENTEEN ───────────

They put to sea at about the time the sun would have been setting, had they been able to see it—normally an act of suicidal folly for a small boat in a storm off a lee shore. Of the four Guardians, McKay was perhaps the calmest of all; in Force Recon and SOG, he'd been through some pretty funky small-boat insertions in his time. Of the others, Tom Rogers was uncomfortable because he had the least experience with the sea. Navy man Sloan, and Casey Wilson, who'd done a fair amount of sailing as a boy, knew enough to be scared green by the whole experience. Donna was drawn-faced and pale, but Lori was almost cheerful.

One compensation, at least to McKay's way of thinking, was that a means had finally been found at getting through to Baxter. He turned gray-green under his protective coating of filth and grease the instant he set foot on the *Calamity Jane,* and was wretchedly seasick the whole voyage, even after the storm abated sometime after midnight.

They'd held a spirited debate as to whether to leave the rat-faced informer. Casey and Sam Sloan were against trusting him for an instant. Perversely, Billy McKay, normally moti-

vated by a genuine distrust of anything human, was inclined to
believe the little man.

But it was Tom Rogers, drawing on his experiences in the
Special Forces, who settled the issue. "I've run into his type
before," he explained. "Don't make no secret about being
pretty much a double agent. Operates by trying to make sure
everybody he deals with feels he's more use to them alive than
dead." He shrugged. "You'll notice he ain't lied to us yet.
Nobody asked him if he was passing information to the terrorists, after all."

"Like, where does he *get* this information?" Casey Wilson
demanded peevishly. Like Sam Sloan, he was basically an innocent; irrefutable evidence of human perfidy was one of the
few things that tended to shake his mellow Southern California composure.

Baxter stood nearby, calmly gnawing on his apple core. "I
ought to know. Van Damm bragged about it enough. Said he
had technicians down in L.A., getting Disneyland set up to
use as an alternate command post. He was even more tickled
about that than he was about San Simeon Castle as his HQ."

"Did van Damm always discuss confidential matters in your
presence?" Sam Sloan asked.

Baxter shrugged. "He didn't seem to think it was that all-
fired confidential. And, yeah, they didn't seem to care much
what they said in front of me. Like I told you, I'm just kinda
the sort that fades into the woodwork."

Lori took the boat a ways off coast until the storm backed
off. They made a fairly regular ten knots until the engine
broke down at about 1000 the next morning. Ex-cruiser officer Sloan, Casey Wilson, and Lori all went below and had a
grand time alternately hammering and swearing at the recalci-
trant engine, while Donna, McKay, and Rogers sat up on
deck, keeping an eye out for pirates and watching blazing
patches of sunlight dance on the water. Baxter, of course,
spent the time dry-heaving over the taffrail.

At about 1400 hours they were on their way again. It was a
good thing. About an hour later, Donna caught sight of a big
power boat trying to overtake them from several kilometers
back. "Pirates," Lori said grimly. "Those bastards don't give
us any peace."

The Guardians stood to with their potent assortment of weaponry. McKay's M-60 would punch through most small boat hulls; Casey's sniper rifle would be useful for picking off helmsmen or disabling engines; Sam Sloan's nifty grenade launcher could chunk out HEDP or WP rounds; and Tom Rogers was ready with one of the two tank-busting Armbrust disposable rocket launchers they'd brought along. The hardware turned out to be unnecessary; Lori kept away from them by playing cat and mouse among rain squalls until sunset, and then lost them for good and all in the darkness.

And, by 1030 the next morning, they were bobbing among the trash that coated the waters off Huntington Beach.

It wasn't the nukes that killed L.A.

The thermonuclear bombardment had wounded the vast, sprawling city sorely, it was true. But it hadn't finished it off. Neither had the complete disruption of medical care, or the congestion of the highways that prevented food and supplies from moving into the city. Nor was it the epidemics—cholera typhus, dysentery—that had killed as many people in the three weeks after the war as the missiles themselves.

No, it was water that killed L.A. Or the lack of it. With a population big enough for quite a respectable country, Los Angeles had been plunked down in semidesert chapparal with virtually no natural supplies of fresh water. Water had had to be brought down from the mountains that surrounded the great basin via aqueducts, none of which had survived. The Palos Verdes Seawater Desalinization Facility, an experimental solar-powered extravaganza around the point from the Port of Los Angeles, might have alleviated the problem if it hadn't gotten caught in the overkill of warheads aimed at the twin ports of L.A. and Long Beach. So Los Angeles was a burnt-out case, an all but lifeless ruin whose surviving human inhabitants could be numbered, perhaps, in the hundreds.

So it would remain, until the water flowed again.

Lori ran them in to the beach proper in a power dinghy. For a moment they stood staring on the verge of sand covered with fragments of paper and cloth and less identifiable debris, smudged and reeking with fuel oil leaked from ships foundered offshore. Highway 1, which ran parallel to the beach, was a horror. The warheads had hit L.A. just at that time when the torrent of traffic that rumbled ceaselessly all night along its freeways was beginning to swell with a new day's traffic; the rolling blast wave of a nearby detonation had tumbled cars like toys scattered by the impatient sweep of a giant infant's foot. Not fifteen meters from where the Guardians stood, a ladybug-shaped Ford subcompact lay on its back in the sand. Its occupants remained within, dirty brown bones, unbleached by the sun, but picked bare by crabs and decomposition.

Beyond the freeway stood high-rise hotels and office buildings, their glass blown out, their insides gutted by fire. The walls of hundreds of frame-stucco buildings had been blasted down, leaving studs like broken teeth. Damage was worse on the north sides of structures, and you could tell which way cars had been facing before the dynamic overpressure kicked them spinning by which side had bubbled, blistered paint. A warhead detonating over the Naval Weapons Research Center at Seal Beach a few klicks away had caused this devastation.

In the coastal heat and humidity, much augmented by torrential rains, bodies of those who died in the bombing and even the subsequent plagues had long since rotted away, but the air was still thick with the palpable smell of death. "Jesus," Casey Wilson said in a shaky voice. "It's worse than Denver. It's worse than anything we've seen." His usually laid-back exterior was shaken, vulnerable, as he beheld the desolation that had descended upon his beloved L.A.

"Yeah," McKay grunted. He tossed his cigar into the surf. It died with a hiss. Without another word he started trudging up the dirt embankment toward the freeway.

The march into Anaheim was heavy going. The streets were covered with rubble, plastic, cinderblocks, overturned cars, appliances, and drifts of lighter merchandise from the shattered shops. Though at the moment the sun blazed out hot and forthright from a virtually cloudless sky, L.A. had been drenched again by a storm the night before. In many places the rubble had turned to mudlike muck underfoot.

Their progress wasn't made easier by the fact that each

Guardian was struggling under a double weapons load. For the actual assault upon van Damm and his fantasy fortress, silence was of the utmost value; even a half-minute's warning could mean the death of the two hostages, and no one had any clue as to how long a detonation-initiation sequence van Damm's technicians had jury-rigged for their captive warhead. McKay, Sloan, and Rogers all carried H & K MP-5 submachine guns with integral silencers. They were from a special batch made in .45 caliber especially for American counterterrorist forces under a special off-budge contract. Heckler and Kock made the production MP-5 only in the Europeans' pet caliber, 9 mm. While in general the American armed forces had moved to follow the European mode, adopting a 9 mm automatic pistol as standard sidearm to replace the venerable .45, the elite anti-terrorist units were moving in the opposite direction.

Casey carried his beloved Ingram M-10. In addition, each man carried his considerably noisier—and considerably more powerful—primary weapon, for use in case they ran into trouble before reaching their objective. Add to that a couple of days' rations, medical supplies, communicators, plentiful ammunition for voracious automatic weapons, plus that eternal nuisance, water—bulky, heavy, and utterly indispensable —and each man was thoroughly weighted down. They managed to ease their burden by making Baxter tote ration packs and water, which he did with the uncomplaining good grace of a Virginia City jackass. None of the Guardians was complacent enough to trust him with a weapon, of course.

They staggered on through rubble and blinding heat that seemed to mount and mount. Their eyes began to sting. Unlike many cities, Los Angeles had not been freed from its overcoat of smog by the Third World War. Trapped in its bowl between the mountains and the sea, L.A. required very little to make its air intolerable. When the first Europeans had arrived, a combination of ozone released by the trees in the mountains around the basin, petrochemical vapors rising from the LaBrea tar pits, and the smoke of Indian fires had been enough to produce a nice, eye-watering photochemical haze. Now, the smoke of smoldering fires, some of which had burned since the war, added to fumes from ruptured oil tanks

and the ever-present ozone, conspired to keep the all-too
familar blanket in place.

The sun mounted up to the top of the sky and arched down
the other side. The Guardians slogged on, sweat streaming
into their faces from beneath the bands of their urban warfare
camouflage hats. The sludge seemed to suck their feet in to the
ankles with every step, and they had to be constantly on the
alert for chunks that might turn underfoot and torque an
ankle. Flies and mosquitos, bred in an insect heaven of stagnant pools and millions of festering corpses, surrounded them
in buzzing, biting clouds. The air hung thick with the fetid
swamp odors of scummy water, decay, the ever-present tang
of ash.

As the sun began to dissolve in the red haze that clung to the
western horizon, they crossed Westminister Avenue into
Garden Grove, just south of Interstate 22, the Garden Grove
Freeway. Disneyland lay several klicks almost due north.
McKay called a halt for rest and rations and eagerly stoked up
a fresh cigar. They forted up inside the still largely intact
garage of a Goodyear tire store, gratefully shucked off packs,
and sat down.

"Why do I get the feeling we're on a fool's errand?" Sam
Sloan said bitterly, breaking open a ration bar. They were real
miracles of modern science, chock full of useful proteins and
vitamins, but they had the texture of pressed cardboard and
the general appearance—not to mention flavor—of adobe
bricks, and you didn't even want to *think* what they were
made of. Sloan bit off a tiny corner of a bar; they expanded in
your mouth, to try to fake your stomach into thinking you
were getting a real meal, something intrinsically more satisfy-
ing than trying to eat a foam packing crate. "We've come all
the way down here on nothing more than Baxter's say-so—
and we *know* he's a double crosser. Just what makes us think
that we're going to find anything more at Disneyland than an
abandoned amusement park?"

"Or a trap," Casey muttered darkly.

"That ain't fair!" Baxter sputtered. Crumbs of ration bar
avalanched down his chin. He'd bitten off a good third of his
bar at once, and now was trying to talk around the expanding,

gooey mess. "I been nothin' but straight with you fellows. I risked my own ass leading you down here, and I been totin' your crap around in the hot sun all day, and all you can do is run me down!"

"If there's a trap, the trappers're gonna have a surprise in store for them." Tom Rogers took a swallow of water from his canteen. "Baxter ain't had a chance to communicate with van Damm since we left San Simeon. Even if they're expecting us, they'll be looking for us to come down through Tehachapi Pass—not in from the ocean."

Glumly, McKay eyed his ration bar, wishing he could get visions of fat cheeseburgers with fries out of his head. "Yeah, lay off. Baxter here's too smart to shit us. Ain't that so, Baxter?" The informer bobbed his head and chewed lustily. "He knows if he's fucked us over in any way, shape, or form, nothing in the world is going to stop me from twisting his head off for him. Right, Baxter?"

Baxter choked.

"Any idea where in Disneyland van Damm's got his hideout —if he's really there?" Casey Wilson asked.

Ignoring the sarcasm, Baxter shook his head. "He just said he had people down there, making sure there was water in the tanks, fuel for their emergency generators. I know he wasn't planning on setting up in the hotels—way he was talking, he was set on occupying Disneyland proper." He shook his head and wiped his nose on his sleeve. "Had some notion about setting the place up as administrative headquarters for Southern California. Craziest son of a bitch I ever saw."

"So what's our plan, McKay?" Sam Sloan asked.

McKay shrugged. "Play it mainly by ear. Casey, you'll take the high ground with that magic rifle of yours. Rest of us will sweep through the park trying to find van Damm and the hostages. Shouldn't be that hard. Van Damm ain't gonna feel like he's gotta hide—and that don't seem to be his style much anyway."

"What happens if I have to shoot somebody? Won't the noise panic van Damm?" Casey asked.

"With that sound suppressor on, the shots are going to sound more like firecrackers than gunshots," Tom Rogers said. "And there's probably enough commotion around here at night that even shooting fairly close by isn't necessarily going to touch him off."

"Of course, that depends on just how crazy this van Damm is." Sam Sloan looked glum.

"Yeah," McKay said. "If we get discovered, we're gonna just have to put our heads down and go for it—and hope for the best." He hoped he didn't sound as pessimistic as he felt.

Sam Sloan shook his head. "I—"

Baxter jumped to his feet, waving his arms in the air as if trying to take off. "Look, look!" He grabbed at McKay's sleeve. With feline agility the big man leapt away. Even after slogging through wet ashes, mud, rubble, and falling into a slimy pool with a dead, bloated dog floating in it, McKay still didn't want Baxter touching his fatigues. Paying no attention to McKay's acrobatics, the little man danced around, pointing off to the north.

McKay turned and looked. A yellow glow had sprung up into the indigo evening haze. It could only be artificial light of some sort.

"I'll be darned," Casey Wilson said. "I heard the Disneyland people put in solar power accumulators to run the lights off of at night. Looks like van Damm's got them working."

"See! I was right! I was right!"

McKay took a last, sour look at his ration bar, rewrapped it, and stuck it into the breast pocket of his cammie blouse. He stood up. "Right," he said, hoisting his M-60. "Let's get a move on."

CHAPTER
EIGHTEEN ─────────────

Using suction pads strapped to his hands and knees, Casey Wilson scaled the north wall of Disneyland. At his back the Santa Ana Freeway was a silent static river of cars and moonlight. Ahead, the Matterhorn attraction bulked blue and white, its eastern face blackened and blistered by the thermal flash of a warhead's detonation.

At the top of the wall, Casey slipped the pad off his right hand, drew a pair of wire cutters from his belt. He eyed the barbed-wire strands, artfully concealed by the vegetation. *I hope the heck these wires aren't hooked to live sensors*, he thought. Actually, the odds were very good that there were motion sensors hooked to the wires, as well as alarms that would ring if a break in the circuit indicated a strand had been cut. The Guardians simply figured it was unlikely van Damm would have had the means—or the interest—to get the alarm monitor systems back in operation. Crazy or not, van Damm had severe limitations on his resources, and the probability just wasn't all that great anyone would try to break into Disneyland.

And if they are *wired*, Casey told himself, *I may never even know it.* He raised the cutters and snipped.

Nothing happened. Off in the night, a pack of dogs bayed at the swollen moon hanging like a rotten piece of fruit over the San Gabriels; from somewhere to the north came the sporadic thump of gunfire. But no alarms, no shouts with the drum of running feet. He hastily snipped the other strands and slithered over the top.

From the top of the wall he peered out through dense bushes. A narrow-gauge miniature railroad track passed just beneath him on its circuit of the park's perimeter. Beyond was a terrace from which a cement ramp led down to Tomorrowland on the left, Fantasyland on the right. From this vantage point, it was obvious that what had looked to be a blaze of light against the darkened, ruined skyline of L.A., was in fact patchy illumination, mainly from lamps on tall poles. Off to the right, lights danced on the water surrounding Tom Sawyer Island in Frontierland. In front of him, past Sleeping Beauty's imitation Bavarian castle and the central plaza, there were more lights on around the main entrance to the park. Finally, a glow from somewhere north of him, in Tomorrowland, backlit the silent looming Matterhorn, but the concrete fang hid its source from sight. He heard the stinking wind soughing in the trees, the lapping of water from the submarine ride at the base of the Matterhorn, occasional scraps of voices, disembodied and sourceless. He didn't see anybody moving.

"Billy." In a moment, McKay's voice answered. Casey felt a wave of irrational reassurance. There was something about invading this, the world's definitive amusement park, which he'd visited so often as a kid, that he found terribly unsettling. Hastily, he relayed what he'd seen to the other Guardians, who were in position covering the western side of the complex from across West Street.

"I'm on my way," he said.

"Good luck. McKay out."

Casey checked the hang of his weapons. The sniper's rifle, heavy and unwieldy, was slung across his back. His Ingram, with its noise suppressor attached, had hung around his neck in an Israeli-style sling when he scaled the wall. Now, he stripped off the suction pads and stuffed them into a pocket in the leg of his cammies. Then he picked up the machine pistol and moved.

He crossed the little railroad in a quick rush, vaulted over the neglected flowerbeds along the inside and hunched down behind the wall of the terrace. Nothing moved in his field of vision. Crouched low, he moved down the terrace ramp to ground level, then ran bent-over toward the base of the Matterhorn.

Past the sheds for the motorboat cruise in Fantasyland, and a miniature tangle of kiddie-car freeways, he came to the platform where the Matterhorn bobsled ride was boarded. The little sleds were lined up, silent and obedient on their rail, awaiting holiday-makers who would never be coming back. He vaulted the low fence, climbed up onto the track, and walked softly into the dark interior of the artificial mountain.

Just inside he halted. It would take several minutes for his eyes to adjust to the deeper darkness in here, and even then visibility would be none too good. Overhead, starlight and moonlight spilled in through the openings that honeycombed the mountain, silvering the switchbacked track and the trellises that supported it. He waited, breathing deliberately and quietly with his diaphragm, until his eyes had accustomed themselves enough for him to make out the immediate surroundings. Then, moving carefully to avoid betraying clangs of metal on metal, he snapped the lens caps off the scope and raised his rifle to his shoulder.

The rifle was of a standard design, a bolt-action M-40 built from a civilian Remington 700, which the Marines had been using for years. What was fancy about the weapon was its scope. A state-of-the-art, computerized wonder, it gave variable magnification, see-in-the-dark potential, and instant range finding. Right now, it was the night-vision capability that interested Casey. His wonderful scope offered him two options: It could project a beam of infrared light, invisible to the naked eye, which would light up the scene when viewed through the scope in IR mode; or it could make use of passive light-gathering capability, like what used to be called a starlight scope.

Casey opted to use the starlight scope. If van Damm had

stuck some kind of lookout up in the crest of the Matterhorn, the odds were vanishingly small that he was using some kind of IR goggles. But the chance existed, and if he were, he was going to get awfully suspicious when suddenly his crow's nest lit up around him. On the other hand, there was no way on earth to tell that someone was looking at you through a passive starlight scope. Casey moved the selector switch with his thumb and squinted upward through the scope.

Random glints and gleams above him resolved themselves into a weird geometric web of steel. And there, high above his head, Casey could make out an unmistakable human form, ghostly in the scope's green eye, next to a spill of "bright"—to the scope—outside the light, that indicated an access or observation panel had been removed.

Casey lowered the rifle. The rails blocked a clear shot at the sentry overhead. He gazed around in the gloom, then began to work his way slowly into the mountain. After an endless time of moving as if in slow motion, he stopped by a stanchion and raised the rifle again.

The sentry was there, the unmistakable fore-end of an AKM silhouetted against the night sky. Casey sat with his back against the stanchion and drew a breath deep into his belly. He slipped off the safety with a finger, centered the cross hairs at where he reckoned the lower end of the rib cage would be, so that the bullet would pass upward through the sentry's heart. He emptied his mind in all-encompassing Zen concentration, and without conscious intention his finger tightened on the trigger.

The figure disappeared from his field of view as the muzzle jumped with recoil. The long suppressor screwed onto the rifle's barrel ate the muzzle flash as well as the sound of the shot. Casey's gut clenched at the weird brief rippling crack of the bullet's passage upward among tangled beams. A moment later came the clatter of the falling AK, accompanied by muffled thumps as the sentry's body bounced off the rails on its journey down. Even as he winced at the commotion, Casey felt satisfaction; it had been a clean shot. He was unused to having men in his sights, rather than elaborate machines. Concentrating on the satisfaction of making the shot, at an unlikely angle with all manner of obstructions, helped to distance him from the reality of what he'd done.

In a moment the body landed on cement a few meters away with a sodden thud. Casey laid the big rifle down and waited in a crouch with the Ingram cradled in his hands. He expected at any moment to hear shouts from outside as guerrillas came to investigate the noise—or simply a sudden blinding tidal wave of white enveloping the world. But again, nothing happened.

When a quick glimpse under the Velcro-fastened cover of his wristwatch told him five minutes had passed, he slung both weapons again and straightened. Slowly and cautiously, he began to climb.

From across the western wall of Disneyland floated the raucous strains of modern rock. McKay, Sloan, and Rogers waited in a huddle behind stalled cars for Casey Wilson to get into position. "Billy?" the young ex-fighter pilot's voice said in their ears. McKay acknowledged. "I'm up at the top of the Matterhorn. Got a pretty good view of the layout down below."

"What the hell's going on in there? We keep hearing music."

"Some of the terrorists are having a party on the Mark Twain Riverboat in the big lake in Frontierland. They have a cassette recorder or something."

Rogers grinned briefly. "These people are partying fools," he commented. The ever-helpful Baxter had informed the Guardians that life in van Damm's stronghold at Sam Simeon had been a constant round of partying for most of the guerrillas, before the big breakup. At the moment, Baxter was bound hand and foot and stashed safely behind the counter of a Radio Shack a few blocks away from Disneyland. McKay had to admit he'd played them straight so far—but there was only so far McKay was willing to push his luck.

"What else?" McKay asked.

"Lot of activity down by the main gate and Main Street, USA. Since they computerized a lot of the park's operations back in the late eighties, that's where a lot of the stuff is run from. I bet they're, like, playing with the consoles, trying to get the hang of the controls."

"You think that's where van Damm is?" Sam Sloan asked

"Like, maybe. But there's also something going on over
Tomorrowland. That big new exhibit, the 'Gateway to th
Future' is all lit up, and I can see people moving around i
side. Van Damm may be there."

"Figures."

"You mean he's not holed up in Sleeping Beauty's castle?'
Sam Sloan asked. "Shucks. I'm disappointed."

Tom Rogers went up the wall first using the suction pad
At the top, he snipped through the barbed wire and let down
rope for the other two. In a moment they joined him. To th
left, the railroad track left the perimeter to run through Be
Country into Adventureland; beyond loomed the tree-clad ju
of Tom Sawyer's Island, with the lights of the steamboat spill
ing out from behind. Directly in front of them rose the mod
southern-gothic Haunted Mansion, with its attendant plast
tombstones looking considerably more eerie in the pale, spo
adic light than they ever had when the park was open. To th
right was the covered platform of the New Orleans Squa
depot of the Disneyland railroad.

The three Guardians had cached their long arms not fa
from where they'd cached Baxter—though not, of course, i
the same place. The unfortunate Sam Sloan was still carryir
two weapons; in addition to the silenced MP-5 his two com
panions carried, he had a stubby M-79 as well. It was a brea
open, single-shot grenade launcher, which fired the same 4
mm rounds the M-203 did. In the twenty-four-pouch vest h
wore, he carried his standard mix of HEDP, WP, and mu
tiple-projectile rounds, plus CS—tear gas—grenades, alwa
useful in hostage situations. The Guardians were hoping
avoid making any noise at all if they could, but if the
couldn't, it would be very useful to have the clout of Sa
Sloan's mobile artillery. With McKay in the lead, they bega
moving across the southern side of the park.

And almost immediately met near-disaster.

They moved along the tracks between the perimeter wa
and the roofed platform, then cut east along the paved avenu
with a couple of buildings full of shops and restaurants on th
left, and a line of more shops to the right, which fronted th
"Pirates of the Caribbean" ride. Darting from cover to cove

with McKay in the lead and Rogers bringing up the rear, they worked their toward the boundary of Frontierland. This part of the park was dark. And for some reason, while the rest of the outside world—such as had survived the blasts—had been thoroughly looted, the hordes of frightened refugees swarming in the wake of the attack had obviously refused to violate the sanctity of Disneyland. In some places broken glass lay in bright, treacherous shards on the street, ready to crunch underfoot and betray the Guardians' passage, but it was apparently residue from the blast waves that dumped plate glass shop windows on the street.

They passed some kind of outdoor café with white-painted metal furniture, and then McKay stopped, crouched up against the front of a toy kiosk. "What's the matter?" asked Sam Sloan, coming up behind.

"Listen. Some kind of mechanical noise, a thumping off to our right."

Sloan's brow furrowed. "My God!" His grin was bright in the moonlight. "They've turned on the God-damned 'Pirates of the Caribbean' ride!"

"No lights," Rogers said.

Sloan shrugged. "They're probably just punching buttons at random."

"Jesus." McKay shook his head and moved on.

"Hey! You—what do you think you're doing?" Several shapes were approaching down a narrow alley between buildings to their left. McKay swung around, bringing up his MP-5, but Rogers said softly, "No. Go on—I'll take them." Nodding to Sloan, McKay raced off down the street. The other Guardian followed.

Rogers took a few steps back the way they'd come. "There he goes!" someone yelled. He made out three men, armed with assault rifles, pelting down the alley toward him. He dodged back through the outdoor café, and knocked a chair sprawling with a dull *sproing*ing thump that sounded shockingly loud. It wasn't clumsiness; Tom Rogers could move through dense undergrowth with barely a sound. But he wanted to assure that the terrorists followed him. He vaulted through the busted-out picture window of the restaurant proper and moved swiftly past display counters filled with mummified food to the back, seeking some kind of rear utility door. The shouts of pursuit followed him.

"Jesus *Christ*," the young man with the straggly blond hair said. "This fucking place gives me the creeps, man. Why they got these fucking dummies turned on, anyway?" They were stalking the intruder through the "Pirates of the Caribbean" ride.

The lean, bearded black stalking at his side, AKM held at the ready, sneered at him. "Don't get your bowels in an uproar, man. These dummies won't hurt you. Or are you afriad of ghosts?" The other man glared at him; he laughed softly.

"Who could be fucking around in here, anyway?" the young white man asked, giving his favorite participle another run around the barn. "You don't think it could be one of those super pigs van Damm was always raving about, do you?"

"Naw. Just some scavenger lookin' for petrified chili dogs and shit." The bearded man chuckled again.

A flatboat, running on a rail hidden beneath the shallow water, was passing along the canal when they came up to its simulated stone bank. A low bow wave of scummy water shouldered up and sloshed gently against the banks. The blond man shuddered. "It's fucking weird." He said. Where did the dude *go*, anyway?" A breath of cool air, thick with the rank green stink of stagnant water, wafted out of the mouth of the artificial cave to their right, from which the canal flowed.

"Shit, I don't know. Maybe he's on the other side." They began walking cautiously away from the cave mouth, toward the footbridge that crossed the narrow canal.

"I sure hope this fucking thing'll take our weight," the bearded man said nervously, as another boat passed them, the backwash from the first boat's bow wave slapping its sides.

"Shit, you worry too much—" the black man was saying when Tom Rogers, lying on his back in the bottom of the third boat, shot him once under the right arm. The copper-jacketed bullet punched through his lung, stopping his heart with a single blow. He sighed and toppled into the water just ahead of Rogers's boat.

His partner turned and stared down into the canal, his eyes bugging out of his head. He started to scream. Rogers shot him through his open mouth, and he fell flopping, knocking over a one-eyed pirate who brandished a flintlock pistol. Rogers sat up, clambered over the gunwale, and waded to the bank.

His AKM slung, the third terrorist stood by the entry to the ride, craning his neck and peering into the darkness. He heard footsteps approaching. "Muhammad? Randy? Did you get him?"

His brain just had time to register that the figure stepping out of the blackness into the starlight was shorter, stockier, and less hairy than either of his two companions. Then there was the firefly dance of a burst of automatic fire, and that was the last thing he saw.

McKay and Sam Sloan worked their way cautiously through the trees around the central plaza. There were lights on in the buildings on both sides of Main Street, USA, which ran from the plaza to the main entrance mall at the south end of the park. "Let's go scope it out," McKay said. "I'll go first—you cover me."

Scowling with indignation, Noritachi Isamu swung his binoculars away from the fake riverboat. Its engines were thumping, powering the generators that lit the lights bedecking it like strands on a Christmas tree. Laughing and chattering men and women thronged the foredeck, swigging from looted bottles, a few dancing drunkenly to the strains of music blaring from a cassette tape recorder. A woman wearing nothing but a flak jacket dove over the rail and landed in the water with a loud splash. The others laughed and applauded heartily.

Noritachi shook his head. These Americans had no commitment, no sense of the gravity of their mission. The moment of truth had arrived for the Revolution, and here they were behaving as if they were . . . as if they were, well, at Disneyland.

The enemies of the revolution surround us on every hand, he thought grimly. *It is fortunate that at least one loyal fighter remains alert*. He was up at the top of Thunder Mountain, the big roller coaster in Frontierland, a pair of eight-by-ten night glasses in his hand and his AKS-74 propped against a plastic rock nearby. *He* at least was ready, should the counter-revolutionaries attempt aggression.

Unbuttoning his camouflage trousers, a man jumped up on the rail of the riverboat. He toppled over with an even louder splash. *If only we had these* petit-bourgeois *fools in Japan. Rengo Sekigun would know how to handle them.*

He raised the binoculars to his eyes and traversed them slowly left, across the southern reaches of the park. Just as the lights in the "Gateway to the Universe" pavilion began to hurt his eyes, he halted and swung the massive glasses back a few degrees. There. Past the ridiculous spun-sugar confection that was Sleeping Beauty's Castle, emerging from the trees of the central plaza: a pair of figures, bulky and alien. Alarm bells shrilled in Noritachi's mind. *They've come.*

His heart seemed to pulse in the base of his throat. It had begun. The counter-revolutionaries were on the attack. Carefully, reverentially almost, he laid down the heavy binoculars and picked up his assault rifle. He braced his feet against the artificial cornice in which he nestled, raised the weapon to his shoulders, and braced his elbows on his thighs, peering over the sights. Holding on the larger of the two figures, he drew a breath, let it halfway out, and squeezed the trigger.

CHAPTER
NINETEEN ─────────────

From somewhere above and behind him, a 5.45 mm round hit Billy McKay in the rear of the left arm, a couple of centimeters below the indentation where the big deltoid folded in between the biceps and the short head of the triceps. It was fortunate that his Kevlar vest was in fact a vest, instead of a T-shirt design; had it been, the needle-nosed, jacketed little slug would just have clipped the hem of the sleeve, gone into a tumble, and probably torn away the muscles from the back of his arm. As it was, it simply punched a neat hole through his triceps, gouged a line along his latissimus dorsi, and was gone.

He grunted, staggered, then threw himself on the ground and rolled, yelling, "Get down!" Sam Sloan looked around in bewilderment at the sudden eruption of noise, but only for an instant. Then he was down too, crawling after McKay for the cover of a concrete bench.

Not a moment too soon. From the "Gateway" pavilion forty meters away exploded a hail of small-arms fire. The rest of the fanatical Japanese Red Army team, who had appointed themselves bodyguards to Chairman van Damm, were on watch inside the round, glassed-in structure. As always on a hair trigger, wired on adrenaline and lack of sleep, they instantly blazed away into the night at the sound of gunfire, some firing straight through the plate glass windows, which exploded out into the street in a tinkling, glittering rain.

McKay wriggled up next to Sloan. "Billy, are you all right?" Sloan asked anxiously.

McKay grunted, "Yeah," just as Tom Rogers' voice came into his ear, asking what was going on. "Somebody must've spotted us. We're taking fire from somewhere to the north, and the whole fucking Red Army is blazing away at us from the pavilion. Casey? Take out that goddam sniper."

"Got it." Gone was the lazy, laid-back California drawl; Casey had switched to combat mode.

McKay felt wet warmth cascading down his arm, but there was no time now to bind his wound. He squirmed down to the end of the bench, fired a burst at the pavilion. A storm of fire responded, bullets striking sprays of stinging cement fragments from the bench and tumbling off into the night with mosquito whines, chewing up the overgrown sod. The two Guardians flattened themselves behind the bench and stared at each other. Time was of the essence, now that they'd been discovered—but if they charged directly into that withering fire, neither would make it a dozen steps.

"Fuck this. We're going to have to try another way." Sam Sloan looked relieved. He was still new to this sort of thing, and was afraid McKay would decide to get up and go for it anyway. "Sam, you get ready to put some tear gas into the pavilion with the thump gun. Tom, meet me back at Main Street. I got an idea."

He rolled backwards away from the bench, got to his feet and darted back into the trees around the central plaza. Bullets lashed at the trees and flowerbeds, and spanged off the brass lamp posts. He ducked down Main Street, USA, which led from the entrance of the park to the plaza. Most of the lights were on at the south end of the street. He moved quickly down the left side of the street, hugging the darkened storefronts. His left upper arm was numb, the body's usual immediate reaction to severe trauma, but he knew that all too soon, he'd feel as if he'd been stung by the world's biggest wasp. He seemed to have pretty much unrestricted use of his left hand, if not much strength, but that was all that mattered.

A man holding an assault rifle came out of a building across the street, about twenty meters down the block. McKay shot him from the hip, and ducked back through the trellised entrance of what had been a narrow open-air flower market, between two buildings. The real flowers had long since given up the ghost, but the fake ones beamed at him like idiot faces. "Tom," he panted, "where are you? I don't want us shooting at each other."

"Down at the south end of the street, around by the lost and found."

"See anybody?"

"No."

So none of the terrorists monkeying with the controls felt like sticking their heads out just now. Great.

McKay was feverishly trying to remember what he knew from a few earlier visits to the park. The place was updated incessantly; even if his memory were accurate, it couldn't be relied upon too much. "Tom? Is there a little train type of thing parked down near where you are? Runs on a single track, kind of like the monorail?"

"Uh, affirmative. Six cars, looks like about four passengers each, with bubble canopies."

"That's the one." A wild scheme had taken form in McKay's mind. The Super People Mover regularly made the rounds of the park's major attractions on its single track. "See if you can find the controls to the People Mover, Tom. Don't shoot me—I'm on my way to help."

He scanned the street a moment longer, then darted for cover. Almost immediately, a door opened on the second story to his right and a figure stepped out onto the balcony. He pivoted, let go of the remainder of his clip with a spastic clatter of the bolt, and dove back into the shelter of the alleyway flower market.

Back in cover, he quickly changed magazines and poked his head out cautiously. The figure on the balcony lay toppled against the railing. Not slumped, but straight, as if still standing upright, its right arm upraised in exhortation. McKay gaped as what seemed to be a tall, extremely thin man with a long narrow head, dressed in old-timey clothes with a standup collar, and with round wire-rimmed spectacles askew on the bridge of the narrow nose, moved its jaws in an imitation of speech. "There is such a thing," said the speech synthesizer buried within its chest, "as being too proud to fight."

McKay shook his head in wonder. "Well, I'll be God-damned," he said aloud. "I just shot Woodrow Wilson."

He shook his head and ran rapidly down the street.

Lying on his vestful of grenades was like lying on a bag of coal, Sam Sloan reflected, as he tried to fumble in its pouches and become one with the sod at the same time. Bullets seemed to be coming down like rain from a sudden thundershower, pinging off the bench, plucking at the grass all around him. People were shooting from at least three separate directions —and it seemed every last one of them was shooting at *him*. He pulled out what he hoped was an HEDP round, stuffed it into the M-79, slammed the weapon shut. Bringing it to his shoulder, he fired at the riverboat, from whose decks several guerrillas were blazing merrily away at him.

The round exploded on the side of a hill on Tom Sawyer's Island, throwing chunks of simulated vegetation into the air.

Sam Sloan stared speechlessly. He—an Annapolis graduate, expert in naval warfare, former gunnery officer on a cruiser— had just fired at a ship at a range any ship's gunner worth his salt would consider negligible . . . and *missed*.

Thin-lipped, he pulled out another grenade, almost at random, broke open the grenade launcher, and reloaded. He raised the weapon again and sighted with excruciating care, totally ignoring the bullets that cracked and pinged around him.

He fired. Terrible blue-white light glared from the front of the steamboat's cabin. For a moment the front half of the ship was shrouded by a starfish of dense white smoke. Then, as the smoke began to tendril upward in columns into the starry sky, blazing figures became visible on the deck, blundering into each other, toppling over the rail, mindless with the agony of burning. Sloan's throat contracted. He'd fired a white phos-phorus round instead of an HEDP. He repressed a shudder. He'd meant to kill some people, but not like *this*.

And what if I accidently fired a WP round into the "Gateway to the Universe" instead of tear gas? He thought of

Susan, dusted with flecks of blinding light that clung like leeches and melted steel, and shuddered.

Then he got hold of himself and broke open the M-79 again. He was still a Guardian, and there was still a job to do.

In the central control center, behind the shops of Main Street, USA, a half dozen revolutionaries clustered around consoles full of blinking, brightly colored lights. Bottles of wine were making happy circuits, and marijuana smoke hung thick in the close air. It was the world's biggest gas, pressing the buttons that made the capitalist world's ultimate fantasy trip do its multifarious thing. The various buttons were clearly labeled. All you had to do was punch them, and submarines submerged, merry-go-rounds whirled, the Seven Dwarfs silently sang.

"Say," a thin man in rimless glasses and leather vest said, straightening. "What's that noise?"

One of his buddies cocked his head, listening to the sudden crackling, vaguely audible through soundproof walls. "Maybe we, like, set off the fireworks up at the castle."

"Far out."

The door slammed open. The kid in glasses turned. A figure filled the doorway, bloodstained and horrible. He staggered back, clutching blindly for his assault rifle, propped behind him against a console. He bumped into his pal.

"Hey, watch it, Larry. What the fuck—" As one the others turned.

And stared.

"Have a nice fucking day," Billy McKay said. He swept the MP-5 from left to right, just above the controls. When the screams had died away he stepped forward to the console.

Casey Wilson was worried. An unusually alert sniper perched up on the pseudo-stone spire of Thunder Mountain— which always reminded Casey of Devil's Tower from the movie *Close Encounters of the Third Kind*—had spotted Billy and Sam snooping and pooping toward the "Gateway to the Future" and opened up, blowing surprise for the Guardians and, Casey gathered, wounding McKay in the process. Now he was continuing to snipe, and had Sam Sloan pinned down at the central plaza.

And Casey, whose job it was to deal with just such snipers, couldn't see him.

Not that he didn't know where he was. He could plainly see the muzzle flashes of the man's assault rifle a hundred meters away and a little higher than his own vantage point. But the sniper himself was hidden by a shoulder of the artificial mountain. With his own mobility severely restricted, there was no way Casey could move that would bring him into his field of vision.

Still . . . the mountain was made of plastic-coated plaster upheld by a steel framework, not too unlike the Matterhorn. The full-length 7.62 rounds fired by his sniper's rifle would punch through a cinderblock wall. *Perhaps* . . .

He raised the rifle, peered through the scope, waited. In a moment, the left side of his field of vision dimmed slightly, as the starlight scope filters cut the light of the flickering muzzle flash. Casey's fighter pilot's brain made a lightning calculation. He shifted the rifle's muzzle a few seconds of arc to the right, elevated it a hair, and squeezed. The rifle uttered a hearty *thump*! and slammed back against his shoulder.

He brought the rifle back down to aimpoint. But the muzzle flashes didn't come anymore.

The half dozen Japanese Red Army men inside the "Gateway to the Future" pavilion were burning magazines up as fast as they could change them. The reactionaries were attacking out of the darkness; they had to be repelled at all costs. They knew, of course, that they had no chance of survival. If the fascist swine had gotten this far, there could only be one outcome; the Chairman would use his captive warhead. The certainty soothed them, helped them truly live as men already dead. They could fight with total, single-minded determination.

Unfortunately, it wasn't enough.

A 40 mm grenade sailed in the gaping maw of the window, struck a model of the probe that was even now on its way to land on Saturn's moon Titan, and exploded, filling the room with thick, choking smoke.

From the south a miniature monorail appeared, sliding along a winding track. In spite of the CS gas that clogged their throats and filled their eyes with tears, three of the JRA men opened fire on the Super People Mover, punching neat holes in the thin-gauge metal of the bodies and starring the canopies.

The little robot train swooped down its rail and squealed to a stop next to the "Gateway to the Future." Gagging and weeping, a JRA man staggered out onto the cement loading platform and emptied the clip of his AKM into the first cab. Unfortunately for him, it was empty. Tom Rogers had bailed out the far side of the second car even before the train came to a stop, and from the third car Billy McKay blew the man away with a short burst, then vaulted over the side of the car and ran for the building. Two terrorists fired at him from the swirling gas inside the building. Firing aimed single shots from the prone position on the concrete outside, Tom Rogers knocked one down. Charging straight at the second, McKay shot him from such close range that the front of his shirt was smoldering as he fell.

With the lights on inside this part of the pavilion's outer ring, McKay could see fairly well despite his gas mask. He felt time rushing past like a river in flood. Momentary panic fluttered up in his chest like a caged bird frantic for escape. *Is van Damm's finger tightening on the button right now?*

"Fuck it," he said aloud. He shot the three terrorists floundering helplessly in the smoke and raced for the stairs.

"Grenade!" Dr. Jacob Morgenstern yelled as something heavy thudded down the corridor outside the door of the narrow walk-in storage room in which he and Susan Spinelli had spent the last several days. Huddled against the wall, wrists bound behind her by a nylon restraint, Susan Spinelli flopped onto her belly and pressed her face to the cool concrete floor.

The sound was much duller than she'd expected, and the blast, such as it was, failed to knock the door off its hinges. A moment later, she smelled a peppery odor, and something suddenly pricked the inside of her throat like thorns, making her choke. "Tear gas," Morgenstern commented. "Excellent."

The two were haggard from being given food and water only when their captors remembered it—or felt like it—and filthy. Each bore the marks of abuse: bruises, contusions; Susan sported a split lip. To her surprise, she'd not been raped. Several of van Damm's entourage had made the sug-

gestion, but the odd, harsh Japanese men wouldn't permit it.
they seemed to have a marked puritanical streak, and the
others treated them with a good deal of deference. It was one
of the few things she'd found to be thankful for since that
awful night in New Eden.

Now she let herself hope for the first time in days. A pair of
CLF guards had been keeping watch over the two, with orders
to kill them if anything happened. At the first sound of gunfire, however, they'd run off, slamming the door behind them.
In a few moments, she knew it would open to admit the
Guardians. She'd known they would never give up the search
for Morgenstern and her. *And Sam—*

The door opened. She opened her mouth in a glad cry of
greeting. It turned to a gasp. Standing in the glow of the
fluorescence overhead, seemingly unfazed by the cottony gas
wisping in from the corridor outside, was van Damm's bodyguard, Marlon.

He tipped his smooth face down toward her. The reflection
of the fluorescent lights off the round lenses of his glasses hid
his eyes. He licked his lips. Slipping his heavy Smith & Wesson
revolver from its holster, he stepped forward. With her bound
feet, Susan kicked at him. He fended the blow easily with one
huge hand and slapped her back against the wall. With a
Hebrew curse, Morgenstern rocked up onto his knees. Marlon
kicked him back into the corner. Expert though he was in
aikido, with his hands and ankles bound there was nothing the
doctor could do.

Marlon looked down at Susan and smiled. He pressed the
barrel of the pistol against her mouth. Its muzzle was a ring of
cool hardness against her lips. Wildly, she stared up at him.
He reached down and grabbed her by the jaw, trying to pry
her mouth open, trying to force the pistol inside.

From the door came a strange clacking, like someone tap-
ping a pipe with a claw hammer. Marlon grunted and staggered back, lurching against a table. There was a spreading
dark stain on the right side of his blue-and-yellow soccer shirt,
and a trickle of blood starting from the corner of his mouth.

In the doorway stood an unearthly figure. The size and
shape of a man, it had a hideous insectile face, with huge
glassy eyes and a proboscis like a giant moth. Driven past the
point of endurance by fatigue and hunger and fear, Susan for

one wild instant imagined that an alien from one of the pavilion's exhibits had somehow come to life. Then she realized it was a man in a gas mask—a man wearing the jagged-patterned camouflage fatigues of the Guardians.

Choking, Marlon brought up the .41 Magnum. The man in the doorway fired his stubby gun from the hip. Again the clattering noise sounded, and Marlon screamed as a half dozen bullets ripped through his belly and chest.

Then Sam Sloan was at her side, coughing with his face mask pulled up on top of his head, working to free her from the restraints. She stared at him wordlessly, too drained for tears or even greetings. The familiar form of Billy McKay bolted behind him, filling doorway. He pushed his mask up too. "Where's the Russian?" he asked.

"Gone," Morgenstern said. "Van Damm decided that he'd turned against him this morning, ordered him arrested. He somehow escaped from van Damm's Japanese Red Army thugs, and has not been seen since."

"And van Damm?"

"In the lecture hall under the 3-D theater. Down this corridor, double doors to the right."

"Right." He disappeared. Freeing Susan's wrists, Sam Sloan gave the woman a quick hug and followed.

The lecture hall was where certain privileged tour groups gathered to hear experts speak on the wonders of the universe. It was a small auditorium with descending terraces of seats on one side and a raised speaker's dais at the other. The twin doors were solid, with no panels or windows. With seconds ticking away and no idea what they'd find inside, McKay kicked open the door and the two Guardians plunged in. Staying upright, McKay took a step to the left once inside; following standard procedure, Sloan hit the carpeted floor and rolled right.

In the clear half-moon of floor in front of the dais stood a cylinder of metal covered in dull gray paint, a meter across and two meters high. For a moment, that was all they saw, standing in the puddle of light next to the dais. Then a man stepped out from behind the cylinder. He was a short, extremely handsome blond man, looking outdoorsy as hell in his Pendleton shirt and jeans. In one hand he held a clacker of the sort used to set off claymore mines.

"My technicians rigged up this detonator for me, before they ran away," he said. His voice was mellifluous, his tones as level as if he'd been discussing some new spending proposal. "Gentlemen, it's good to see you. Long live the Revolution!"

The utter strangeness of the scene had momentarily frozen even Billy McKay. Now he acted, swinging up his MP-5 to cut down the former Lieutenant Governor. Acting on some obscure impulse, Sam Sloan threw himself at his partner, rolling against his legs and bringing him down behind the top row of seats.

The room exploded in thunder and light.

In swirling smoke and darkness, Billy McKay raised his head. "I'll be fucked," he said. "We're *alive*!"

"It seems unlikely," Sam Sloan said, stirring beside him, "but I guess I can't very well refute it." They picked themselves up. The only illumination in the auditorium was the light spilling in from the corridor. The explosion had knocked out the interior lights. McKay pulled out a pocket flash, played it around the room.

The big gray cylinder had split open like a baked potato left in the oven too long. "Is that it?" McKay demanded. The light wavered. Reaction was beginning to set in; his hand was shaking. "You mean it was bullshit all along?"

Sloan shook his head. "Van Damm's technicians must have messed up. That blast couldn't have been more than a fraction of the high-explosive initiator charge." Suddenly he looked alarmed, and clutched at McKay's arm. "Christ, we'd better get out of here—that was more than enough of a bang to scatter radioactive junk all over the damned room!"

But McKay hung back. "Just a moment." He played the flashlight beam around the foot of the auditorium. A few meters from the base of the warhead lay Geoff van Damm. His body had been terribly scorched by the blast, and his left arm and leg had been wrenched free. Yet his movie star's face remained miraculously untouched. And on it was permanently fixed the smile of a man who has at last achieved his fusion with Destiny.

EPILOGUE ─────────

A special team of technicians was flown out from Heartland o police up the radioactive debris left by the explosion. In heir bulky white protective suits, some of them combed the uditorium with Geiger counters, searching for the smallest leck of fissionable material, while others dissected the borted warhead.

"The warhead had been made operational, all right," Len Maddocks, the black, mustached head of the Decontam quad reported to the Guardians when he rendezvoused with em at New Eden. "It'd also been tampered with. Somebody ad disconnected the detonators for most of the blocks of the nitiator charge."

"But, like, enough went off to kill van Damm," Casey 'ilson said.

Standing with his arm around Susan Spinelli, Sam Sloan inned. "Maybe that wasn't an accident."

Maddocks grinned back, "It wasn't. Both the neutron urce and the charge to fire it down into the mass of lithium uteride to get the whole thing started had been taken out. nd in their place, we found *this*." He reached into a pocket of his coveralls and pulled out a piece of paper.

Looking puzzled, McKay took it. Spreading it out in front of him on the hardwood table in the commissary of the main habitat, he read aloud, "Dear Guardians: The esteemed Lieutenant Governor van Damm proved too mad to be of use to me. If you're reading this—as I trust you shall—then obviously you've had better luck with him than I did.

"I regret I could not meet you in person. I hope to remedy that lack at some happier time. Until that time, I remain, Colonel Ivan Vissarionovich Vesensky, KGB."

Yevgeny Maximov sat alone in his ornate office with his face buried in his heavy hands. It was late at night; the office was dark except for a spill of yellowish light coming from the lamp on his desk. The stars in the cloudless night sky shone through his huge picture window with a cold, unfriendly light that gave no illumination.

He failed. Maximov could hardly credit it. His golden boy, his right-hand man, whom he trusted above all others, whom he loved almost as a son. Yet not even Ivan Vesensky had been able to win Maximov that which he so desperately needed.

In a wastebasket next to the brass desk lay a sheaf of fan-folded computer printouts. The story they told for the future of Europe was grim indeed. Production of food, fuel, and other necessities declining; the rationing and distribution system breaking down; sedition and discontent on the rise. Without some radical action—soon—the Federated States of Europe would join the nations it supplanted on the ash heap of extinction.

With the Blueprint, I could have ruled the world. Without . . . He sighed and opened an ornate ivory cigarette case, drew from it one of his cigarettes, placed it between his thick lips and picked up a gold-plated lighter.

The gilded telephone rang. Maximov stared at it as if it were an unfamiliar object that had suddenly materialized before his eyes. He lit the cigarette, put down the lighter and deliberately lifted the receiver.

"Excellency," said the depersonalized voice of one of his technicians. "We have a satellite-relayed communication from overseas. It's from Trajan. He wants to talk to you."

A quick flash of anger turned abruptly to a laugh. "Trajan's dead."

Hesitantly, the voice said, "Your pardon, Excellency, but computer analysis of the voice confirms that it is our former agent, who operated under the code name of Trajan. There can be no doubt."

Slowly Maximov leaned back in his chair. "Put him through." He could barely keep his voice from shaking. *Could it be?*

In a moment he heard a thin crackle of static. "Maximov? This is Trajan." There was no denying it; he knew that voice. The polish had been chiseled away, but still it was unmistakable. "I have a bargain to make with you."

Maximov's eyebrows rose. "Bargain? What do you bargain for?"

"My life."

Maximov nodded. Trajan had always been perceptive. He drew in smoke, let it trickle out through his nostrils like a recumbent dragon. "Very well. What is it you offer in exchange?"

"That's just the start, Maximov. You'll pay me dearly for this. Oh, you'll pay. But it will be worth it."

"Really?" Maximov's tone was bored. The man was raving. "Just what is it you offer me at this great, if unspecified, price?"

"The Blueprint for Renewal," came the cracked reply, "and the United States of America."

Maximov leaned forward and stubbed his cigarette out in a crystal ashtray. "Tell me more," he purred. "Tell me more, Trajan, my very good friend."

Watch for

NIGHT OF THE PHOENIX

the fourth exciting novel in
THE GUARDIANS
series from Jove

coming in November!